TARZAN ON THE PRECIPICE

*Lennie pushed him into space and the rough stones below
came rushing up to meet him....* [page 68]

Edgar Rice Burroughs'
TARZAN
On the Precipice

A Wild Adventure Of Tarzan by
Michael A. Sanford
Illustrations by Will Meugniot

EDGAR RICE BURROUGHS, Inc.
Publishers
TARZANA   CALIFORNIA

First Edition

Special thanks to Jim Gerlach, Gary A. Buckingham, Matt Moring and
Will Murray for their valuable assistance in producing this novel.

Library of Congress CIP (Cataloging-in-Publication) Data
ISBN-13: 978-1-945462-02-3

- 9 8 7 6 5 4 3 2 1 -

To Darek and Devon
in whom my story goes on

TABLE OF CONTENTS

FOREWORD

When Michael A. Sanford first wrote about wanting to send me a novel that would fit seamlessly into the flow of Edgar Rice Burroughs' original Tarzan series and remain faithful to his style, my natural inclination was, it can't be done. There is only one Master of Adventure. But when he assured me of a ripping good, fast-paced, action-adventure, full of cliffhangers that won't let you put his book down, I became a little more intrigued. Was that possible, and from someone not previously published? That was the beginning of the process that led Edgar Rice Burroughs, Inc. to not only agree to read this story, but in the end, to also publish it.

At the conclusion of Mr. Burroughs classic *Tarzan of the Apes*, Tarzan is despondent but assured he did what was honorable to enable Jane to leave with his cousin, William Clayton, who believes he is the rightful heir to the Greystoke estate and can appropriately provide for Jane when they marry. But what then? To my knowledge, his activities after his presence in Wisconsin and before his passage on the boat to Africa have never been revealed—until now.

The author has created an adventure filled with thrills and fraught with so many entanglements and complexities that after a few chapters you feel you are reading excerpts from the Master himself. This novel is full of fantasy and imaginative fiction, and yet it grabs your attention and keeps it to the very end. And the author brings to your vision descriptions of Canada that make you feel as if you are there, touching and feeling all that Tarzan does. Thinking time and again that Tarzan's demise is imminent, he escapes only to encounter still more dangers, with each episode building more suspense and anticipation for the next. Tarzan's discovery of a lost Viking civilization and the author's description and explanation of it brings the reader a clear picture of the village life and the gruesome realities of their existence.

While one might think this is a novel of pure fiction, archae-ologists are continuing to discover new Viking sites in North America. A thousand years ago Vikings braved the icy waters from their home in Greenland to travel to the Americas in search of timber and plunder. Just recently, satellite technology has revealed intriguing evidence of a second Norse settlement in North America, further south than ever before known. A new Canadian site was discovered after infrared images from 400 miles in space showed possible man-made impressions under layers of vegetation; later excavation came up with telltale signs of iron-working. And now the reader has the opportu-nity, while joining Tarzan, to unearth and experience a new set of adventures in a land never before imagined.

And of course, *Tarzan on the Precipice* has a double meaning. He is indeed chained, with his life hanging in the balance on the precipice of a volcanic crater, the depth of which cannot be determined. But he is also on the precipice of the rest of his life, not knowing his future, abandoning his right of birth as an English Lord and bereft of the thing in life he cherishes most, Jane. All that is left for him now is Africa, which is at least known to him. Enjoy this tale and join Tarzan on his Canadian adventure as he prepares to return to Africa and a future even he cannot predict. This is a story worthy of your time that will pass quickly as you immerse yourself in it. You will not be disappointed. Instead, you will marvel at how sat-isfying it was to absorb yourself in this fantasy and adventure.

Jim Sullos
President, Edgar Rice Burroughs, Inc.

Prologue

You of modern times will not believe this tale or even admit to a possibility of truth in it, but as I sit here in the dark and the story unfolds before me, it is all true. For years I resisted nightmarish dreams until I finally decided to find their source and collect them into a novel. Judge it not by the great books that precede and follow, because this fantastic tale came in jumbled bits and pieces in the dead of the night, and I am only the Chronicler trying to make sense of it all. Any errors of person, place, or time should fall on me as an inadequate interpreter, but don't let it spoil the story.

When I discovered the dreams started just before the hundredth anniversary of the first publishing of *Tarzan of the Apes,* I realized the nightly transmissions were part of an effort to reach a centennial deadline. Though I was born in Edgar Rice Burroughs' hometown of Chicago within months of his passing, I do not conjecture that this mere coincidence suggests that some sort of transference occurred. God never closes one door without opening another, but I totally reject the possibility of reincarnation because this is the only manuscript I have ever written.

Most probably, I was chosen as a kindred soul because I am well versed in his works. In the Venus series, Carson Napier uses telepathy to send his story to Mr. Burroughs. Being proficient at receiving books in this way, it makes sense that he would be able to transmit a narrative to an equally willing participant. Recent medical advances give plausibility to the

Old Hag Syndrome of dream invasion. Currently called sleep paralysis, the inability to move and vivid dreams of fantastic events are conveyed during the transition from deep sleep to partial awakening and feel like they last for hours. This is similar to my own experiences and is my explanation for how I was his conduit.

With this communication thrust upon me, I guess it makes me a true ghost writer. Feel free to check the facts within and you will come to accept that this did happen, just as it was relayed to me. Believe what you will, but I know with certainty that when the story was all told, the visions stopped coming. Hopefully this novel honors the legacy of Edgar Rice Burroughs, but be forewarned, it is only for the stout of heart—a saga to be read by firelight dancing against an encroaching darkness.

TARZAN ON THE PRECIPICE

Chapter One

LEAVING JANE

I t was earlier in the day than was customary for Tarzan to hunt. Most predators wait until just before darkness when there is still enough light to see, but with lurking shadows for cover. Then they slink to a favorite vantage point affording a view of a trail crossing or a watering hole. From then on, it is a waiting game of silence and patience until the unwary prey shows up. Passing unsuspecting along the path or drawn by thirst to the water, the target falls victim to the sudden furious claws and teeth of a superior stalker. One must die that another may live.

Thus, in the endless struggle to survive does the improvement of each species take place. The injured, sick, and weakest are lost first, sacrificing their lives so that the stronger, faster, and fittest remain to carry on. In this way, the herd constantly improves its ability to elude and escape. So too must the predators also improve to outwit and overtake their selected prey, or their diet and health will degrade and they would also fail in nature's grand scheme of things. The reward of a longer lifespan comes to those who answer the challenge of nature by becoming the best they can be.

As the supreme predator, Tarzan of the Apes need not concern himself with such doctrine. As more beast than man, he lived by the simple law of the jungle that honors the righteous and strong. Unlike their animal counterparts, with a few exceptions, only men can exhibit petty and baser instincts that allow them to sink to lower levels of humanity. The noble savage is too concerned with staying alive and protecting his mate to engage in the subterfuges of civilization.

And only man imposes rules on himself that do not allow the natural order of things to take place. This was troubling Tarzan as he was silently waiting for his prey. By allowing his estate to pass to his cousin, William Cecil Clayton, he had left himself a pauper, dependent upon the generosity of his friend, Paul D'Arnot. Even more onerous were the societal rules that bound the woman he loved to this English imposter. That propriety should tie Jane to the false Lord Greystoke because he asked for her hand in a weak moment leaves no room for the passion of true love. Tarzan was sure Jane loved him, but she was indecisive and fearful of the primal intensity they shared, and so it had come to pass that their happiness became secondary to the principles of class convention. These rules did not allow a primitive man to sweep his mate away by virtue of his own prowess. The ape-man had not pursued his unspoken proposal in order to give her the wealth, status, and entitlement that she was accustomed to with Clayton. Tarzan suffered that she might be happy.

The pain cut deeper than any knife, wounding his soul. Tarzan's love for Jane held him tighter than the claws of Sheeta the leopard, ever could. The distress of lost romantic love was as painful as the loss of his mother's love, when Kala the ape died and he first cried. To some, the loss of love leads to the lack of a will to go on. But there were no tears here because Tarzan knew where there is life, there is hope.

Tarzan silently mouthed the words, "I still live."

Earlier in the day he had left Jane and Clayton at the train station intent on escaping the grief of man in the forest of the beasts. When a primeval man feels the pain of a broken heart, he responds by withdrawing unto himself, seeking peace in solitude. Instead of going back to Chicago and crowds of people on the train, Tarzan hired a driver to take him further north through Wisconsin, around Lake Michigan to Sault Ste. Marie, and then into the Canadian wilderness past Lake Huron. Time had no meaning, and he could eventually get back to New York on this route by crossing over at Niagara Falls.

His touring car was a quiet machine with a powerful engine luxuriously appointed inside, and Tarzan was lounging in the back seat, taking in the endless forest through the large windows. The driver was droning on about the history of the area. Tarzan had vague plans to look up D'Arnot's brother, Claude, who was in military police work, and he was only halfway listening.

"We will be entering the Sudbury Basin, which is the second largest meteor crater in the world. It was formed when a mountain-sized comet hit eons ago, leaving rich deposits of nickel and copper. It is said that the debris from that impact fell as far away as Minnesota and that the minerals enriched the soil for farming."

Tarzan remembered stories of the largest impact crater being in South Africa, but he heard it referred to it as volcanic in origin. The ape-man's taciturn nature precluded any response, and as an individual learned more with his ears than his mouth, he remained silent.

The driver continued, "In 1856, surveyor Albert Salter discovered magnetic abnormalities that indicated mineral deposits. The region remains unstable because it lies in the Great Lakes earthquake zone. The Murray mine site was discovered when the railroad was blasting there while laying track in 1883."

The limousine drew further into the north woods along unmarked roads little more than dirt and gravel in places. Trusting the driver to know the way, Tarzan found his thoughts drifting back to Jane again and again. Since travel was providing no comfort, perhaps a hunt would take his mind off of his sorrows, and the woods looked cool and inviting. Besides, he was hungry, and the promise of fresh game was a welcome change from all the civilized, cooked food he had consumed recently. Hailing the driver, Tarzan bade him to pull over so he could get out.

As any sane person would, the driver looked at Tarzan like he had lost his mind. The chauffeur implored him to stay with the car because there was nothing but miles of untracked wilderness in all directions. By day, the forest was thick with bears, and by night, huge Eastern Canadian gray wolves roamed in packs.

"Surely Monsieur Tarzan will not last a day out in that wilderness alone!" he cried. Tarzan could not be dissuaded and replied, "It sounds like home."

After leaving instructions on where to take his grip and writing a note explaining his plans, Tarzan rummaged in the bottom of his long steamer trunk to come up with a packet wrapped in a leopard skin. Taking only this, he walked into the forest, letting the driver's continuing protestations fall on deaf ears.

Tarzan's supreme confidence in his ability to survive came from knowing he was self-sufficient in all ways. After almost twenty years of living alone in Africa, he was sure there was nothing in the Canadian wilderness that he could not overcome. Indeed, he was quite looking forward to the challenge.

Once in the privacy of the trees, he quickly shed his suit of clothes, and even that small act buoyed his spirits with a sense of freedom by symbolically stripping away civilization and getting ready to begin anew in an unexplored territory. He left the confining clothes where they lay in the pine straw. Especially satisfying was divesting himself of the choking tie and pinching shoes that fashion demanded; surely no real man thought such effete trappings essential. Even an expensive pocket watch was discarded as the final break with the relentless chains of time society placed on men.

"Ah, this is living again." Tarzan fashioned a loin cloth from the spotted pelt and placed his father's hunting knife in its sheath at his side. The ape-man favored the hide of the Sheeta for its ability to conceal and because it was from another exceptional predator. Slinging his rope and bow and arrows over his shoulders and taking up his spear, he was ready for anything. His primitive clothing would embarrass some, but to Tarzan it felt as natural as the forest surrounding him.

Before striding into danger, Tarzan surveyed the landscape; it was quite different from the jungles of his youth because the more northern clime gave growth to different flora. Relying on his most trusted sense of smell, he was overwhelmed by the fragrance of pines. It almost masked all the other odors and would make hunting much more difficult. In Africa, the powerful smell of the beasts was easy to rely upon except when upwind or on calm days.

All animals, including man, had distinctive scents like plants, and even different emotions could be discerned by the highly trained. Tarzan had spent his years away from city fumes and industrial waste that caused a withering of the sense of smell, and he could detect the species, gender, and disposition of all around him. What he wanted to find now was the sweet odor of Bara, the deer, or the rough undercurrent of Horta the boar for his next repast.

The pines also shed layers of soft needles that made walking as silent as on a carpet. Since Tarzan was already as quiet as the summer breeze, there was no chance his prey would be aware of his approach. Catlike, walking on the balls of his feet and toes, the ape-man advanced through the trees with a spring in his step. His hearing, not dulled by years of traffic noise and the general cacophony of the city, could tell the size, speed, and bearing of his quarry.

Most men rely primarily on their vision since the senses of smell and hearing have atrophied from disuse. Tarzan's eyes were eagle-sharp, but he used them mainly to verify what his nose and ears had already told him. In the hunt, vision was indispensable to making the kill. A poor cast of the rope, errant throw of the spear, or miss with an arrow could cost the hunter his dinner, if not his life.

Touch and taste have been elevated by city dwellers to primary importance, perhaps because of their tendency toward self-gratification. They have elected speech as their sixth sense because most people just seem to enjoy hearing themselves talk about anything, any time, and in any place. Tarzan had a commanding presence when he spoke, but preferred to let his actions speak for him. His sensitive fingers might help in darkness or when his vision was impaired, but smell and hearing usually were more reliable from a greater distance. Tarzan had been raised on a diet of fruit, eggs, insects, and raw meat when he could catch it. He was hardly an epicure and his sense of taste was of the least use to him.

As Tarzan advanced along an old trail, he saw his usual methods of hunting would not succeed. The pines were not close enough to interlace their branches and provide an arboreal highway in the upper reaches. Added to the challenge was the fact that the downward sloping limbs were not strong enough to support his weight except close to the trunk. Finally, the hanging vines which allowed large distances to be covered in a single swing were absent here.

Tarzan usually liked to attain the high ground and use his rope to drop unsuspectingly upon his prey. Even the use of the spear or bow would be difficult amidst the dense pines, which provided much ground cover, so this was going to be a matter of surprise and chase. Caching all his weapons in a tree except for his knife, he searched for a suitable bend in the path to wait.

It was too early for any big predators to be on the hunt with him, as they would all be lying up during the heat of the day. However, where there is forest, there is game, and where there is game, Tarzan could feast. He wet his nose with a damp fingertip, much as a dog does to increase his sense of smell. Now he was assailed by a wave of aromas, similar to the smells of home but different, too. No one but Tarzan could tell the subtle scent distinction between an antelope in Africa and an elk here.

Thinking of home left Tarzan longing for his primeval forest. Filled with old growth hardwoods and well-worn game trails, it was as familiar as a city map in his mind. He could remember favorite ambush points, giant jungle trees with a nook just right for sleeping, and where to get water at any time. The family of apes and Tantor the elephant were his only allies, but they were stalwart companions.

It was a carefree existence. He was seldom troubled, because the strict taskmaster of time in civilization did not intrude there. The simple lifestyle rarely found him uncertain and he never worried because he was the master of his fate. The majesty of the great herds of animals and tremendous size and savagery of the hunters added excitement to every day. Bolgani the gorilla and Numa the lion were admirable foes.

Tarzan had given all this up and tried to fit into Jane's polite society by changing himself into a new modern man with appropriate dress and manners for her. But despite his efforts, the ape-man had come thousands of miles only to be rebuked. Even now, on the hunt, thoughts of Jane intruded once again. Tarzan shook his long mane of black hair to focus on the task at hand. He couldn't let his mind wander, or he would go hungry today. The danger of the hunter becoming the hunted was real if his total concentration was not on his task.

Tarzan allowed the heat of passion to dissolve into the hot blood of pursuit. He was downwind from the fork in the trail and caught the sweet scent of Bara approaching. But it also had a strong musty odor that could denote a larger male. Crouching in total silence, in an instant the ape-man reverted back to a hunting jungle beast.

Next, Tarzan heard the soft tread on the pine threads covering the floor of the forest. His quarry was approaching unaware and would cross his position at an angle that would allow Tarzan to come up from behind. As the animal neared, he got his first look at it through the trees. Not gentle Bara the deer but a huge bull elk with a seven-foot rack of deadly sharp horns! Tarzan had but an instant to gauge the difference in size before the giant deer ran, but it was as if thinking was action, so swiftly he moved.

Tarzan took one step and launched himself from his concealment straight onto the broad back, taking a firm grip on each beam antler. The animal bolted down the trail with all the speed at its command. Hanging on with one hand and his legs locked under its middle, Tarzan's left hand sought his knife to deliver the killing stroke. Whereas Bara would have collapsed by now and given up, this massive creature was fully capable of carrying Tarzan on the ride of his life!

Usually his strong right arm would encircle a beast's throat in a tight embrace to control the fighting fangs, but here he had to hold on from the greater danger of the slashing horns to avoid being thrown over and impaled. Unsure what was upon him, the elk headed into the trees in an effort to scrape Tarzan off. With his knife free at last, the ape-man made a quick thrust to the side behind the left shoulder. It was all he could do before being knocked off by a large pine bough and losing his knife.

The elk was bleeding profusely from his side, but no vital organ had been reached, and now it looked for revenge upon the defenseless man. For his part, Tarzan was scraped and bloodied but stood ready to engage in the final death match. The towering beast lowered his lethal antlers for the attack.

With only a short distance between them, the elk was unable to mount a strong charge and sought to pierce Tarzan with his rack. But before it could close with him and swing the deadly prongs into play, Tarzan leaped ahead and seized the forward pointing brow tines on each antler, just above the eyes, keeping away from the teeth and sharp hooves. Both beasts spread their legs and braced for a contest of strength and will. The elk sought to raise his head and throw Tarzan upwards, to be torn to shreds on the needle-like tips. The ape-man locked his feet in the coiled pine roots below and forced that head ever downward while applying constant pressure to rotate it clockwise. Tarzan tightened his grip until the corded muscles in his arms writhed like snakes. The elk strained with labored breathing and tried to shake loose, but the blood loss from the wound in its side rendered its efforts ineffective against the powerful shoulders of the ape-man. Heavy panting was the only sound from both adversaries as they were intertwined together in a deadly embrace.

This was for the ultimate victory. At the moment of maximum exertion, Tarzan reversed his force to counter-clockwise, using the beast's own energy against it, twisting the neck in the opposite direction and severing the spine with a resounding crack. Tarzan of the Apes held firm until all movement had stopped. Then, placing his foot on the prostrate form, he rolled his head back and voiced the victory cry of the bull ape. For the first time, the piercing yell was heard in the north woods of Canada. But what was that? As the sound came back, was it an echo or an answering challenge?

Tarzan cut off the most tender section and prepared to eat. Even though cooked meat is easier to digest and assimilate, he preferred his raw. Like the King of Beasts, Tarzan did not need to feed often, but he did consume a large portion of every kill to sustain him during the lean times. He would carry a haunch with him for later or bury some on the possibility of his return. The top predator only kills what he needs to eat and does not waste. What is left behind will provide for those unable to secure their own food. As the lion bows out, the lioness and cubs eat next. When the hyena and jackal have had theirs, the vultures and lesser animals consume the rest. In Canada, it is the same, but with bears, wolves, foxes, and buzzards. After all are done, down to the tiniest of creatures, what remains nourishes the earth, completing the eternal cycle.

Chapter Two

THE END OF THE LINE

I n 1885, the formation of the Canadian Pacific Railway made it possible to travel across the breadth of Canada. The Railway previously consisted of numerous smaller lines of variable quality and reliability, but after the bankruptcy of some of these, the government was in the process of combining all the railroads into the Canadian National Railways. Travel was extensive up the highly populated eastern provinces from Toronto to Montreal and on as far as Nova Scotia. But the pride of the line was the trans-Canadian branch that went from Toronto all the way across the country to Vancouver. It traversed some of the most untouched, sparsely settled, and gorgeous wilderness in North America.

Three days after Tarzan had left his touring car for the call of the wild, all this beauty was speeding past the window in a private stateroom, unappreciated by the two occupants inside. They were engrossed in a discussion about where to spend the last days of summer and early fall before the weather made travel too difficult. Eighteen-year-old London, newly graduated from boarding school and with all the confidence and self-righteous importance that implied, was extremely disappointed after not being invited to the Hamptons that summer.

"Mama, I don't understand why we had to take this awful trip north to nowhere when the rest of my class are at the shore," she said with a pouting downturn in the corners of her mouth.

Her mother, only referred to as Madame by everyone else, thought long and hard before answering. Madame was as close to a title as she could get, and she aspired for far more for her only child. The Hamptons or Newport News was where such position was determined and would have been an excellent place to marry up. But with the last name of Gunderson and being from Sweden, there were no invitations from classmates at the private, upper-class finishing school her child attended. Madame had nearly exhausted her funds just to afford the tuition there, and now there was not enough money left to go on to university.

Madame always indulged London in an effort to fit in with society's expectations, even as she had to privately squeeze each penny until the Indian Head whooped. She would not let on to their dire financial situation until all hope was gone. As a last resort, Madame had hatched this crazy scheme to go to Canada in search of nobility. Truly desperate circumstances led to desperate choices. With no thought and a twisted logic, she had arranged this spontaneous trip on a whim and a prayer.

"You know, Canada has Prince Edward Island, which must be full of royalty. I don't fancy living on an island though, so we are going to visit Prince George and then on to Prince Rupert. Surely one of those cities will have plenty of eligible men with titles," replied Madame, unaware that Prince Rupert was also on an island.

"But mama, you know I don't care a whit about those stuffy class distinctions, and I certainly will not be getting married to anyone anytime soon," said London.

Madame had a good heart and good intentions and desired the best interests of all concerned. She disliked this feeling of bartering her daughter for wealth and position, but she realized London was beautiful, young, and spoiled, and didn't understand the realities of life. Madame had been something of a beauty in her day and knew that it was not enough. You needed the extra edge of social class to live well and have security.

"When you come out in society at the tender age of eighteen, you can make a connection with someone near your own age and have a happy liaison. The other less attractive alternative is to wait until your late twenties, when you will need a marriage of convenience to an older man as an assignation," Madame reasoned.

Madame had named London after the city where titles were invented, so intent was she upon rising in status. People who chose names like Paris or Brooklyn for their children generally must be unhappy with where they are in life. Obviously, she seldom thought anything completely through before reacting in a sometimes irrational manner. She herself had always been addressed as Madame by her husband as a term of condescending endearment because it was as close to a title as she was going to get. Madame's choice in names may not seem totally absurd when considering rural roads were named for the farmers that lived on them, New York's Wall Street once had a wall on it, and some of the states were named after royalty.

After losing her husband to the devil's grippe, Madame had immigrated to New York where she led a hard life and it showed in the lines on her face. Unlike the happy upward tilting wrinkles at the corner of the eyes, brought on by a lifetime of smiles, she had the slight beginnings of a downturn around the mouth from too many frowns.

Where there is no man in a family, the woman has to take on both roles. Madame had kept a tight rein on London; any remonstrances were lovingly done and she had never struck the girl. Early in her life she was stern, but now had trouble with discipline as London sought her independence. However, from the beginning, Madame doted on her only child and pampered her as much as possible, using her small inheritance to give London the best.

Madame was still a handsome woman with light hair that had a hint of red in it that she wore up in a bun, which gave her a restrained appearance. Madame's squarish face, with fine-cut features, high cheekbones, and a Roman nose, enhanced that effect. Above average in height and with a slightly stocky build, Madame had the look of someone aristocratic, even if she couldn't maintain the lifestyle.

They both dressed fashionably, but not flamboyantly, in the current style of the early nineteen-hundreds, wearing good conservative clothes that would stay popular and were well-made so they would last. Madame had a thrifty nature but saw the value in presenting oneself properly attired. Similar to the female species in advanced countries, they both enjoyed shopping enough that it was not just a pastime but, when possible, consumed enough of their day to be considered a full-time job.

London favored her father in appearance. He had been tall, fair-haired, and broad-shouldered. Originally from northern Sweden, he was very handsome if somewhat rustic and weathered. Before the illness took him, he worked for a lumber outfit in the timberlands there, and after starting as a logger, he rose through the company to a foreman position. He was a self-made man whose only inheritance was a small pension to London, her good looks and the discordant name, London Gunderson. You would think the first marriage proposal tendered would be acceptable just to change that combination.

A Nordic beauty, London had blonde hair that lay like fallen snow about her wide shoulders. Her eyes were ice blue with a sparkle of mirth in them. An upturned nose and rosebud lips gave her a face that may have been the cause of several accidents in New York City. Added to that were her naturally infectious laugh and bubbly teenage personality which captivated everyone who met her.

London still had the blush of youth, but had recently blossomed into a stunning young woman. Her skin was unblemished, with a lustrous glow that radiated both health and vitality. Possessing a curvaceous figure, she moved with the grace of a dancer. Boarding school gave London the classical education of the day with a fluency in French, the romance language expected by the elite; a fit and proper girl, she was well-versed in all the expected society customs. They had always lived in the city, not ever returning to their forebears' home in Sweden, so London had a desire to see the world and experience the adventure that beckoned from unknown lands.

Life's gifts are often unappreciated by those who have never wanted for anything. The many natural and cultural presents that had been bestowed on London seemed inconsequential to her because all of her peers had the same advantages. So she was not so much spoiled as just unaware that there was another side of life where people fought merely to exist. In the same way, amongst her friends where all else was equal, London was lacking the main essential hallmark of class: birthright. That was not taught or learned in school and could only be inherited by parentage or earned in the past by deeds of great valor. The only other way into that coveted circle was by marriage.

Now there was a knock at the door of their stateroom. As it was nearing dusk, the third member of their party was arriving from his adjoining compartment to escort them to dinner. When Madame opened the door, she invited him in, "Please do come in Mr. Fitch and talk some sense into this child. She refuses to see the advantage of an arranged marriage in the elevation of one's station in life."

Mr. Fitch was a very tall man but sparsely built. He had exceedingly long fingers and a bit of a beak for a nose. His dark hair fringed his narrow head like a laurel crown from Roman times, and he had piercing eyes that took in everything with an analyzing stare. Except for his full lips and warm smile, he could have been the personification of Ichabod Crane right down to his stern, black, formal attire. Fittingly, he was currently employed in the literature department at London's school.

A cross-country runner at university, Mr. Fitch had the characteristic long, lean body. While the hammer and even the discus throw were too heavy for him, he had excelled in the javelin in the field events. Mr. Fitch still maintained an athlete's regimen, believing in the "early to bed, early to rise" adage and maintaining a strict diet that kept him thin.

But it was not for any physical prowess that Madame had retained his services. Although it was prudent for two women traveling alone to have a man to carry trunks and provide some protection from unwanted advances, Mr. Fitch would not be taken as much of a deterrent. His purpose was mainly to continue to provide London with societal training and to help in the acquisition of invitations to the proper upper-class functions.

Originally from England, Mr. Fitch had worked for the privileged well-born his whole life. While he had no title of his own, he could speak their language and move in their circles as easily as a child cutting lines at the carnival. In addition, his university degree gave him a broad base of knowledge, allowing him to converse on any subject with authority. Madame needed him to provide legitimacy and open the doors for London that she could not.

Mr. Fitch, an itinerant teacher, had worked many jobs throughout England and Europe before coming to the United States. Also a man of limited means himself, Mr. Fitch could not hope to see the vastness of North America without finding a way to be paid while travelling. So when he was introduced to Madame through a school official, a mutually beneficial agreement was reached. Though early in the trip, Mr. Fitch had discovered his main duty might be to protect Madame from herself.

"Not hearing the beginning of this conversation, I can only doth quote Marcel Proust: 'Desire makes everything blossom, possession makes everything wither and fade,'" said Mr. Fitch with a learned expression.

"There he goes again, mama, spouting literature like I was still in school. I thought this was to be a holiday," said London, as she rolled her eyes.

"He is actually agreeing with you if you took the time to listen," replied Madame.

"To be in love is like the eternal joy of springtime, while a marriage without it is doomed to become as cold and lonely as winter," paraphrased Mr. Fitch.

"I don't care what season it is, I just want to see the world and have some adventures before I settle down to the drudgery of marriage. It sounds as boring as listening to his nibs here prattle on," teased London.

"You could fall in love with a rich man as well as a poor man," interjected Madame. "Perhaps if I made it a real comparison of an artist marrying a musician and becoming enhanced by her and her by him. Whereas if she was to marry an accountant, she would become a servant to money," countered Mr. Fitch.

"All the nobility I have seen so far prance around like a peacock with a puffed-up chest showing his feathers. A true man leaves gilding the lily to the ladies," said London with a look of finality.

Madame looked at both of them and shook her head slowly back and forth while she said, "Hopeless. None are so blind as those who will not see."

From there, the conversation lapsed to mundane things and eventually ended as they watched the beautiful, but endlessly same Ontario countryside pass by until darkness overtook it. When the conductor rapped on the door with the dinner call, Madame and London got ready to go to the dining car, while Mr. Fitch went back down the narrow passageway to his single room.

The compartments on this train were fairly similar with one or two couches that were pulled out at night by a porter to make a bed. Overhead racks stored the luggage where it was available for easy access, and there were washrooms for general use at each end of the car.

Near the back of the train, there was a special Pullman car in which Lord Bridgestone rode alone. A rotund man with a bulbous red nose, he was full of himself in many ways. He was part of the board overseeing the railroad and onboard to personally observe how the different lines worked together to make a continuous cross-country trip possible. Seated at his dining table, before a sumptuous dinner of pheasant and mixed vegetables served on fine china and sterling tableware with crystal wine and water glasses, Lord Bridgestone was engaged in his favorite activity: eating.

The line out from Toronto had been modern, efficient, and on time. However, the current spur was across older track and far from urban areas. He was not enjoying his dinner in his private car with the jostling that his service was taking. A particularly jarring bump spilled his spirits, and he called for his personal porter, Jeb, to complain about the waste of good liqueur. Unbeknownst to him, his servant was in the main dining car fetching a larger portion of his master's favorite dessert. When no one answered immediately, Lord Bridgestone rushed out, intent on obtaining the service to which he was accustomed.

Unfortunately, he had to pass through a cramped, second-class car to get to the conductor, and Lord Bridgestone had a fairly wide girth. So when he came up to Madame and London as they were exiting their compartment, he brusquely told her to retreat to her cabin, so he had room to pass.

As Madame turned to comply, London burst through and confronted him, "Where are your manners, sir? A true gentleman should make way for a lady."

"You are speaking to LORD Bridgestone. Move aside as I have important railway business to attend to," he said, leaning in with intimidation.

Having nothing of it and not backing down an inch, London bristled back, "If you are truly part of the railroad, then you should see there are wider walkways or lose some of your portly self."

"Harrumph, I can see there are no ladies here," he rejoined.

Mr. Fitch had just caught up from the rear, after retrieving his dinner jacket from his compartment. He immediately apprised what was happening and saw that Madame was trying to rein in London. He pushed to the fore and defused the situation by apologizing to Lord Bridgestone and gathering everyone in a retreat to their stateroom.

As he passed, Lord Bridgestone said under his breath, "They will let any riffraff on these trains nowadays."

Back in the stateroom, Mr. Fitch tried to explain to London that this type of behavior was never allowed in polite society.

Madame worried that this was their first encounter with nobility, and it was a complete disaster. London had the last word this time, pointing out that Lord Bridgestone's rude behavior was a serious breach of noblesse oblige. Even Mr. Fitch was speechless at that bit of classroom trivia, but he was glad to see that some of his lessons had been retained.

The only thing they could all agree on was it was going to be a long trip. Portents and omens are more common in Shakespeare, but troubles usually come in threes and their next one was just down the line. A sudden jolt pitched them forward in a heap. With a screeching of metal brakes and hissing of air, the train ground to a lurching halt. They had no chance to ascertain the cause of anything as the lights went out, and they were pitched into total darkness.

Chapter Three

TRAPPED IN THE PIT OF DOOM

Frankly, after having to sleep on the hard ground instead of up against a comfortable bole of a tree, Tarzan was getting a little bored with this forest. As he walked through the endless pine trees, he noted that it lacked the riot of noise, smells, and vibrancy of life that he had in his African jungle. The sun was only slightly visible above, where the trees tapered to a narrow tip. Below, the dense widespread limbs let in little warmth or light, and these same branches could not support any weight and did not allow for travel between the trees. As a result of this, the birds, small game, and life in general made do in the upper terrace, while the forest floor was dank, quiet, and barren.

In his native jungle, there were three distinct levels. On the upper terrace, like here, small animals, gaily plumed birds, and insects held sway. The middle level provided a highway through a variety of interconnected old hardwood trees that allowed Tarzan to move with rapid speed. At the bottom, the filtered sunlight let a range of undergrowth prosper, from open grass-lands to thick, impenetrable brush. Life in all of its forms thrived throughout.

Lacking a variety of plants here also limited the diversity of the animals. By not providing shelter and feed, the huge herds of antelope, zebra, and larger animals were not possible. This, in turn, curbed the numbers of larger predators and spread them over a wider hunting ground. A country where the giant mastodon and saber-toothed tiger had once ranged would never again support elephants or rhinos.

Of course, the real reason for all of this was the climate. Much further north than Tarzan's tropical jungle, you could not expect the same abundance of life. Here, a tougher existence had to be eked out from the limited resources. Without the perpetual warmth of the jungle, these forest dwellers had to prepare for the lean, cold months of winter or leave. Now squirrels were storing nuts and bears were putting on fat for hibernation, while the fish were swimming downriver after spawning and the geese were flying south for the winter.

While the ape-man was not in a hurry, it would take a long time to get to New York if he had to walk, as the nearest civilization was hundreds of miles away. So sure was he of his sense of direction, he didn't have a compass. Not that it would have worked anyway with the widespread magnetic disturbances caused by the unstable metallic content in the earth. That would also prevent any rescue as searchers would easily become lost themselves.

When Tarzan cast his lot, he never had second thoughts. He was so sure of his abilities to master any situation that the challenges only made life more interesting. Indeed, testing himself had been ingrained early in the daily struggle to survive in a hostile jungle with only Kala, his she-ape mother, for protection. The ape-man had to compete with his far more physically advanced tribe of primordial apes while avoiding the deadly claws and fangs of surrounding predators. Tarzan had proven himself in battle by defeating Kerchak, the head of his tribe, and risen to become the King of the Apes. While he might be unprepared for human deceit and betrayal, in his jungle he was supreme.

Unlike a pride of lions, bears are solitary animals not even staying together after mating. While they will defend their territory, in general, they prefer to avoid conflict. In fact, the bear is related to the canine, but with a nose ten times more sensitive than a tracking dog, a bear knows of any encroachment of his range. So when the hated human smell came to a young grizzly, he got up to investigate. Secure that he was the king of beasts in Canada, the animal carelessly sought his prey from upwind. Humans were stupid and slow and only to be avoided when they carried the long thunder stick.

Tarzan was well aware that he was being stalked from the tell-tale odor on the wind. He had never smelled anything like it before, but the heavy, coarse scent told of a large predator. Soon, his ears heard the ponderous sound of a large body coming through the woods. Finally, Tarzan got a glimpse of the immense bear, Ursa, moving parallel to his path.

Conventional wisdom says that when confronted by a bear, the best way to escape a mauling is to stand still, drop your eyes to avoid confrontation, wave your arms to appear bigger, and make a lot of noise. You might add prayer if you think that might help you on your way to the hereafter, because devotions surely won't stop a charging bear.

Tarzan did none of these things except stand his ground and turn slowly to face the forbidding creature. He knew that any movement away would precipitate a charge, and there were no trees to climb for safety anyway. Were he to charge the grizzly first, it would be considered a challenge that must be defended. So the two beasts squared up and took stock of each other from thirty feet apart.

As the bear appraised the man, it noticed Tarzan was not so puny and didn't cower or run away as other humans had in the past. But there was no thunder stick that spoke death from a distance, so it reared up on its hind legs and gave a fearsome, earsplitting growl. This usually caused the prey to tear away, madly screaming, giving an enjoyable chase with a quick, in-evitable, bloody ending. As with all savage animals, bluster is a part of working up the courage to attack before laying it all on the line in a fight to the death.

Tarzan saw a six-hundred-pound brute with shaggy, deep, brown fur flecked with grey tips. Its head alone was as wide as the ape-man's chest, and the slaver dripping from the fangs told him it was hungry. When it stood up on its rear legs, it towered over seven feet. Tarzan backed not an inch, instead dropping his bow and arrows as ineffective, and took up his knife in one hand and spear in the other. Answering the challenge, he gave voice to the piercing bellow of his own primordial apes.

Ursa dropped down ready for the moment of attack. His massive head moved up and down in warning. He could advance with the speed of an express train and lunge over the man-thing rending it with claws and teeth. But still the man did not run. Where were the fear and splendid race? What are those strange things he is holding and why did that sound invoke an almost primal fear?

Tarzan noticed this split second of indecision and used the opportunity to voice the paralyzing roar of the true king of beasts, Numa the lion. That broke the spell and the grizzly turned abruptly and fled into the forest. There would be an easier meal to be had later at the river, and fish tasted so much better than man anyway.

Ape-like in his ability to mimic most animals and birds, Tarzan had bet that in the posturing that precedes the fight the bear would run from such unknown, terrifying calls. Many fights among equals are often settled this way between males of any species, including the men in civilization's jungles; if every fight had to end in mortal combat, every species would soon face extinction. Often he had bluffed other apes in the daily skirmishes over mates and food. With scarcely a backwards glance, the now undisputed King of the Forest continued on his tedious journey.

After the monotony of miles of woods, Tarzan was surprised when he came up against a dense wall of thicket. Covered with brambles, it was impenetrable. But the change in landscape was also accompanied by a wealth of new scents. A normal person wouldn't have noticed, but the ape-man's sensitive nostrils detected an intriguing new array of smells that piqued his curiosity. It took but a few minutes for Tarzan to scale a large pine to try and verify what his nose had told him was there. However, all he could see were treetops below a low-lying, dense, cloud-like fog.

Upon regaining the ground, Tarzan set out around the thorny barrier since he could not get through it or over it. He followed a roughly circular path around the barrier that seemed endless. Finally, after about an hour, he found a break where an old Ponderosa pine had heeled over and crushed through. Slipping deftly up the trunk and dropping a dozen feet from the last limb on the other side, Tarzan was amazed at the vista.

To each side, the barbed brush extended as far as he could see nearly to the edge of a vertical cliff that dropped away hundreds of feet. Tarzan's vision was limited by the misty cloud that covered everything below and towered up into the sky. Apparently this was caused by a now noticeable draft of warm moist air coming up from below, colliding with the cooler Canadian winds. Brief changes in the currents made eddies in the clouds that allowed the tops of huge trees to fade in and out of view. This temperate updraft was also the source of the variety of familiar smells that were much more pronounced on this side of the barrier.

Tarzan could easily regain the broken pine that had allowed him inside the brambles by using his rope, but the stronger exotic smells were intriguing, making retreat to the boring pines undesirable. The thicket was just as impenetrable on this side, and the smooth rock face of the cliff prevented any downward movement, so Tarzan was forced to follow the edge around. It was a tough go at first since, unlike outside where he had room to skirt the thorns, at times the brush came almost to the edge. Eventually, the beginnings of a path took shape and after a few scratches, the ape-man made better progress.

As Tarzan traveled, he could not see the other side, but he had the impression that this was not a valley but instead a huge pit. Round in shape, with uniformly smooth vertical rock walls, it resembled a quarry. Constantly, he looked for some way to descend, but even with the climbing ability of an ape, he could not find access. Where there was no way down, there was going to be no way back up. By the time the outer barrier finally angled away from the edge on the north side, Tarzan had circum-navigated half of the massive hole. But his curiosity was aroused, so Tarzan continued along the outskirts in an effort to determine why this was here.

Certainly it was not man-made but what could have created such a perfect depression three miles across and hundreds of feet deep? Tarzan recalled the driver's discourse on this whole area being formed by a comet's impact crater from long ago. He had also said there were more recent meteor strikes in De Cewsville in 1887 and again in 1904 in Shelburne. Could this be a part of the original comet or a yet undiscovered meteor hit? This far from civilization, it could have gone completely undetected for ages.

With the afternoon sun, the clouds thinned but never completely lifted, still partially obscuring the bottom of the crater. What he could see was huge, old growth trees like the ancient jungle patriarchs from his home. There were still occasional pines, but these were more the giant, coastal, Sequoia variety that can tower up to three hundred feet and had boles at the base close to thirty feet wide. It appeared the height of all the trees were limited only by their emergence into the colder Canadian air above the pit, stunting their growth at that point and effectively eliminating another way up or down for Tarzan. There were no limbs close to the side of the cliff that he could leap to or from, even if he wished to risk the deadly fall.

As Tarzan continued on, he realized that this depression could have been here virtually unchanged and undetected for a long time. Isolated from outside influence by the unscalable walls, any denizens below were trapped in time, unable to get out. Even were an aeroplane to fly over this area, the semi-permanent cloud cover would obscure discovery from above. That event would be further unlikely due to the magnetic shift and the danger to a pilot's instrumentation keeping him away. Finally, the circular thorny barrier enclosing the entire crater made an impressive obstacle that only the most determined would attempt to penetrate.

By now, the sporadic path had widened to a game trail, and Tarzan was scanning with all his senses alert for a possible place for an ambush to obtain his next meal and a suitable campsite for the night. He was still interested in the crater but becoming more concerned with finding a way out of the sharp thicket, since it seemed to completely circle the hole. Tarzan didn't retrace his steps back to the leaning pine and try to escape there because by now it was easier to continue around and complete the loop.

Just then, a subtle but recognizable smell assailed his nose. Adopting a wary posture, he advanced much more slowly to keep surprise on his side. But Tarzan was totally surprised himself when he came upon a familiar sight. Across the trail, someone had dug a pit trap much like the elephant traps in his native Africa in which the cannibal chief Mbonga had once captured the ape-man. There was a smooth floor here, unlike the native's habit of putting sharp stakes pointing up in the bottom of the hole to impale the elephant, since the hunters were only interested in the valuable ivory tusks, and certainly once trapped, the animal could not be lifted out alive.

Here, Tarzan was looking at a cube, dug about fifteen feet square and of similar depth. The delicate lattice and leaves that had covered it lay in a pile in one corner on the near side. While there were no sharp corners, the walls were cut with precision so that the edge was actually narrower than the base, making an overhang. From the bottom, the walls were at an angle worse than vertical inclining in as they rose. In addition, the composition of the sides was made smooth and damp with the natural ground water. The effect of all this was a pitfall as inescapable as the walls of the nearby crater.

Obviously, the trap was sprung, and the ape-man could walk around it and go on. But he was curious about the scent from home lingering within and why there was nothing now in the pit. Perhaps the game had already been removed, but then wouldn't the hunters reset the mesh-works to disguise it again? In any case, as Tarzan looked around, he found a slender tree beside the trail that had been felled and stripped of limbs. Apparently, it had been used as a sort of ladder for the trap builders to get out when they had completed their task.

Since there were no spikes in the bottom or danger present, Tarzan decided to investigate further. It took but a minute for the strong ape-man to swing the small end of the denuded tree to the base of the far side and create a path he could walk down as easily as strolling along a sidewalk in Paris. As he got to the bottom and leaped off, he sensed, rather than saw, a furtive movement from behind, at the top of the pit from where the trunk depended. Tarzan turned and crouched, pulling out his knife, but there was no attack. Instead, the angled tree was rapidly rising above the pit like a see-saw leveraged on the edge of the trap. Tarzan leaped for the tiny end, but so fast was it withdrawn that he had no chance to grasp it.

Tarzan called out once and waited for whoever had sneaked up the trail to trap him to appear, but no one responded. He checked the walls and found them slippery and weak. His knife merely sliced through and was not able to create a hand hold or cut a step. The sides were too far apart to spread eagle and work his way up even if he laid down. Next, he noticed the lattice and leaves were strewn around the floor on the far end, but they were not of sufficient strength to bear his weight. Even if the ape-man could jump the fifteen feet to the edge, it was too thin and would break away. While looking up, the ape-man saw only the sky above him with no overhanging limbs to cast his rope upon.

Once he saw that he was securely caught, Tarzan did not pace the pit as his jungle brethren are often seen to do when caged in a zoo. There was no screaming at his plight like most men in a useless plea for assistance. The ape-man's stoic nature imbued in him the ability to accept what he could not change and save his energy for escape or revenge when the opportunity presented itself. So Tarzan gathered up the remains of the lattice and leaves, made a pallet, and laid down to sleep.

Chapter Four

The Cajun and the Giant

S kinner was playing the fiddle. He much preferred the fast-paced reels, but this was a slow refrain to quiet Lennie. They had been partners for two years, though you would never picture the two of them together, so unalike they were in every way. Skinner was born somewhere up the backwaters of Lake Pontchartrain, where his father was a traveling man who only stayed long enough for his latest hustle to bear fruit and his mother was engaged in the world's oldest profession. From a young age, he was on his own in New Orleans until he escaped back to the bayou to elude continuing interest from the local constables. Even as a child, he engaged in every swindle and racket he could find to get ahead the easy way. Skinner left elementary school by the third grade, only staying long enough to learn English spoken with his naturally heavy French Creole accent, but he still reverted to his native tongue occasionally when angry or excited. He had no use for society's rules, preferring to live on his own terms outside the law.

Skinner came from a group of proud peoples originating with the Acadian exiles; their lot had been persecuted by the British for most of its existence from back to *Le Grand Derangement* of the middle 1700's. Forced to leave Canada by the English, his ancestors were moved to the colonies. From there they were expelled again, with many returning to Canada or fleeing on to Louisiana. Skinner's family, like many others, intermingled with other immigrants from Europe, Africa, Native Americans, Caribbean Islanders, and from as far away as the Filipino. The result of this great melting pot of humanity was a new culture with a distinctive language that blended a French pride with the Caribbean lawlessness of the times into the Cajun.

Near Loreauville on the Bayou Teche, Skinner operated just under the law, trading hooch and other contraband with the Chitimacha. He had married into this local tribe; even though the indigenous people hated the French, with Skinner's mixed heritage and acceptance of tribal customs, he was grudgingly accepted. The Chitimacha were skilled tattooists and the Cajun rebel learned the craft while having his upper body covered, with their needlework even extending onto his face. Animal claws, wings, and scales embellished his torso, and terrifying teeth with bloody fangs were around his mouth. Beside his eyes, horns radiated upward like the devil's own. While a tattoo of an anchor or bulldog on the arm of a US Navy man or Marine showed service and dedication to country, he had marked himself for the demon he was. His grotesque visage alone guaranteed Skinner would never again be let back into civilized society.

Not that he wanted back in. His mother gave him up about the same time as she had kicked out his father, so he never knew either of them and they had no further interest in him. Early childhood was spent defending himself from bigger bullies and the girls who, at best, ignored him and at worst, ridiculed him mercilessly. Even as a man, Skinner was only a little over five-feet tall and thin and wiry, but what he lacked in stature, he more than made up for in meanness. Add to this his narrow face, thin cruel lips, and stringy hair, and he was nobody's prize. But his worst aspect was the shifty, squinting eyes which never stopped moving in a furtive manner; there was a cold, reptilian look deep down that said, "Born killer of men."

Skinner's weapon of choice was a long, thin, wicked, skinning knife. He always carried it with him on his belt, and it could move from there to his hand in an instant. The blade was always kept razor sharp to be useful in filleting a fish or skinning a deer; he was quick to reach for it in any argument and had no hesitation in gutting a man and letting him bleed out in a slow death. It was this hot temper and general mistrust of all mankind that got Skinner into trouble time and time again with the law and forced frequent moves to stay out of jail. Eventually, it cost him his only attempt at a home and made him a confirmed misogynist for life.

While he was away on a swamp run in a pan boat delivering moonshine to some remote customers, his new wife was being wooed by a handsome native warrior in the tribe. Having been cheated in a past dealing, this young buck had a particular dislike for French white men, and he particularly did not like Skinner for marrying a Chitimacha girl, so it may have been his desire for revenge as much as his infatuation that spurred his lust. In any case, the word got out because gossip between squaws doing the wash at the river spreads as quickly as rumor at any dainty afternoon tea attended by those of more genteel birth.

When Skinner learned of this betrayal, he didn't plot a subtle payback or wait for an opportune time for retribution. Immediate vengeance was achieved by enticing the warrior to an out-of-the-way place with free whiskey where he got him drunk and then went to work with his knife. No duel of honor or even a fair fight, Skinner blinded the man first, for looking upon his wife. Though the Cajun kept him alive for fear of tribal retribution if a white man killed a native, there wasn't much remaining of the man after that craven attack. However, for Skinner, there was no going back; shunned by society, chased by the law, rejected in horror by his wife, spurned through his childhood, and abandoned by his parents, he left everything behind as he fled north.

His given name long forgotten, Skinner took the moniker that came from his skill with a skinning knife. Thus, as there are Carpenters, Taylors, and Bakers, he has ever since been known as Skinner. They say true celebrities in the public eye need only one name, so that must be true for the infamous as well as the famous; for every Aristotle and Cleopatra, there was an Attila the Hun and Bloody Mary though that last pair may actually be considered two names. Then again, maybe not, because surely no one ever formally addressed a Mr. Hun or Miss Bloody. Without a proper name, the authorities found it difficult to follow him as the Cajun worked his way up to the French enclave in Canada. Through the states he moved, trapping and skinning where possible, grifting and stealing when the opportunity presented itself. Somewhere along the Appalachian Trail on the Tennessee ridge line, Skinner met Lennie.

While Skinner never had any love in his life and was stunted for it, the case could be made that Lennie had too much of it and never grew up as a result. Lennie had been protected and indulged his whole life in the Appalachian backwoods. Not that he had it easy in the mountains, where his family scratched out a living working on a truck farm selling produce or deep in the coal mines as these were the only jobs to be had. Most locals added to their larder with hunting, fishing, and of course, the proceeds from the mountain still, both liquid and monetary. It was these common interests, mainly the hunting and running of moonshine, which brought Skinner and Lennie together.

From the start, there was a natural bond between them, as if one complemented the other in a negative way. Where Skinner was diminutive in build, cunning, smart, and naturally devious, Lennie was slow and callow and immature in all aspects of his development except his size. He had been a huge baby and never stopped growing until he reached his adult weight of over three hundred pounds, and was strong as a draft horse. But this was not a well-proportioned, muscular physique; indolence and overeating left Lennie as big around as his six-and-a-half-foot height. Layers of fat starting with multiple chins also hung down the back of his arms and circled his body, overlapping so that sweat constantly beaded in the folds of his skin. Even his face had cheeks so large they dwarfed his tiny features, giving him beady porcine eyes and making channels beside his panting mouth down which drool continuously flowed. Lennie wore coveralls with shoulder straps and went without a shirt in even the coldest weather because so much heat was generated by his bulk, and so few other things could be found to fit.

Lennie was too big and afraid to work in the dark mines, too lazy to work under the hot sun growing vegetables, and too stupid to do anything else. He was expensive to feed and needed constant attention to prevent him from getting into the trouble that seemed to perpetually find him. Deemed feeble-minded, Lennie was seldom held responsible for his actions, because he just didn't know any better. If there was any truth to the idea that some people are born from a bad seed and have an inner cruelty in them, then this was the one thing Skinner and Lennie shared.

As a boy, Lennie pulled the wings off of butterflies and tortured small animals as he went from frying ants with a magnifying glass to killing a neighbor's pet, but excuses were made and his intimidating size made any punishment rare. Eventually, his attempts to defile a young girl led to an altercation with the girl's brother in which Lennie killed the boy with his bare hands. Once he had crossed over into adult crime, he gravitated to Skinner for help in escaping the slow process of the local authorities or the swift retribution of mountain justice.

For his part, Skinner took Lennie under his wing not for any sense of decency or affection but rather because he saw the value of an intimidating watchdog at his side. If there was any camaraderie involved, it was only in the common hatred of mankind and its rules, and their need to escape the law. So they became an unlikely pair, united for evil intent, bent upon self-gratification above all else. There was no fondness between them, not being in their make-up; each would desert the other at the first sign of trouble or profit to be made. But they realized they were stronger as a pair, with Skinner being the brains and Lennie being the brawn, and as they travelled north, they fell into their roles.

All that was two years ago. Their trip went through the Appalachian Mountains until it connected with the Adirondacks, and from there they went west into Canada. Always staying one step ahead of the law, Skinner would set up the scams and Lennie would be the enforcer if things went badly. Most of the patsies kept quiet about their losses and the ones who complained usually ended up with broken limbs; Lennie liked to start with the fingers and work up to arms and legs, and it seldom took long to ensure silence. The pair was easily recognizable, though, and by making enemies, they had to move often, so it wasn't long before they entered the Allegheny National Forest and slipped across the border to Toronto. From there, they drifted up into the desolate north woods and faded from the memory of the people they hurt and the reach of United States justice.

Free from the constraints of looking over their shoulder all the time and waiting to be apprehended for one of their many larcenies, and with the skills to live off the land, they found a comparative peace for once in their lives. After a year on the run, the hobo's life of going from camp to camp following the game trails was easy in the abundance of the Canadian wilderness. But like many who cannot find joy in a simple life or in the pristine beauty around them, Skinner was miserable without the chance for the big score: the con that would set him up for life, where he could get back at all the big guys who had kept him down. Then he would show them all.

That opportunity presented itself when Skinner encountered a lone prospector and invited him to share some rabbit stew. Hopeful of stealing anything the man had of value, he plied him with some of his ever-present moonshine in an effort to determine where the loot was hidden. Though the grizzled old man didn't have any luck in his venture there, he told them of a fantastic lost valley with great riches to be had if one could find a way in. While his woodcraft had been insufficient to the task, he was able to draw a rough map on a piece of birch bark to show the general area where the valley could be found. Skinner was doubtful of there being any truth in it, but the Cajun slit the prospector's throat as he slept, just to be sure the tale went no further.

After burying him in a shallow grave, not for religious purposes but instead to leave no evidence behind, Skinner and Lennie gathered up their gear and headed out, following the crude map. Within a week, their superior tracking skills led them to a massive thorn barrier twenty feet tall that seemed miles across. As they circled it, Skinner became convinced what he sought lay within, so to that end, he began to dig a tunnel under the thicket. This took a week because Lennie was mostly useless except in hauling away the extracted soil, and Skinner had to enlarge and shore up the walls sufficiently to accommodate his giant partner's bulk. Finally, when the roots of the brambles ceased and he broke through to the surface, he found a breathtaking vista that convinced him he had indeed found the hidden valley.

To secure their find, they constructed a cover for the outer entrance of rocks and plants that was undetectable and impenetrable from the outside yet easily removed to allow their egress. Then they set about building a simple hunter's cabin while they explored the area. Much was accomplished in the next year, and now Skinner was close to realizing his dream of wealth and the power that came with it. As he laid aside his fiddle, Skinner looked at Lennie, now sleeping soundly, and thought soon there would be no need to take care of him anymore; the Cajun could use the tunnel to bury him and block the way out permanently when he left.

The next morning, Skinner was remonstrating Lennie for getting into the berries again. Lennie, as usual, denied it, but the evidence, unbeknownst to him, was plain on his face where the customary drool was stained purple as it flowed down his chin. Skinner was cagey enough to know when to stop teasing the giant, so he never provoked him into a fight because he had seen how easily Lennie could break a man in two. For his part, Lennie was not bright enough to challenge Skinner or even understand his own ridicule, and he had an equal respect for the swift and merciless knife that was never far from the Cajun's side.

"Let us go see to the trap line today, eh Lennie?" asked
Skinner. He knew that would please Lennie because he always
enjoyed snapping the necks of any hapless animals unfortunate
enough to get snared. If they were lucky and caught some big
game, Skinner needed Lennie to carry it back.

"Mebbe we get a bare in de big trap," Lennie responded
simply.

"You like to wrestle the big hairy one, eh? But this is not
possible; they are worth much more to us alive. Get the chains,
though, in case lady luck smiles on us," said Skinner.

Lennie carried everything, and they set out to check a series
of snare traps that captured small prey with a noose around the
leg or neck. It seemed fitting that these degenerates would
resort to a deceitful hidden ambush instead of hunting man
against beast with only nature's weapons. Their victim restrained
and hobbled, fearful and injured, Lennie would administer the
fatal blow, hardly a noble contest amongst peers. In this case,
the honor remains with the animal rather than the human. The
complete enclosure by the thorns kept larger game from migrat-
ing and ensured they never went hungry.

At the far end of this line near the exit tunnel, which was
easily visible farther down the path from their approach, Lennie
was like a gleeful child when he saw that the large pit trap
covering was collapsed. They didn't hear the usual bellowing
from the trapped animal, so they hurried up to see what, if
anything, it contained. You can imagine the looks of surprise
when instead of a bear, they found a large, tanned, white man
at the bottom. At the moment, he was curled up on a bed of
leaves looking back at them through appraising eyes, not deign-
ing to talk to his captors.

Skinner was the first to speak and used his broken English.
"Who you be and what fore you do in our territory?"

Lennie, slow as usual, looked to the Cajun and asked, "Wot
is it? Ken I kill it?"

Tarzan remained silent until he could determine their intent.
Skinner's eyes narrowed as he assessed the situation and then

widened as a plan for profit took form, and then he directed Lennie to bring out the chains. These were heavy slave manacles from the Civil War and he tossed them down to Tarzan and directed him to put them on his wrists and ankles.

"Are you stupid? Put the shackles on, and we will lift you from the pit," Skinner said in French in an effort to get the ape-man to comply.

From the unclean and disreputable look of these two and their demands for him to place himself in their power, Tarzan saw that he could expect no help and might have to fight his way free. But he decided to give them a chance to do the right thing and asked in perfect English with a British accent for them to lower the tree that he might walk out.

"*Sacre bleu!* An English pig!" spouted Skinner, and then in English, he told Tarzan if he didn't put on the chains, they would leave him for a few days until he was weak from hunger and thirst and then haul him out with a rope around his neck. Tarzan saw the impasse and felt he might have a better chance to escape once he was out and at full strength instead of after being starved. So he donned the heavy metal bracelets and anklets, closing their locks as a low growl rose from his lips much as any chained animal would emit.

Seeing his captive securely bound, Skinner had Lennie lower a rope with a hook on it and catch the chain between Tarzan's wrists. Then Lennie easily dragged the heavy muscular ape-man up over the edge of the pit to lay on his back on the trail. As the huge man leaned over to remove the hook and fix the lead rope about Tarzan's throat, the ape-man saw his chance and quickly drew his legs up and planted a double kick in Lennie's solar plexus that brought about a whoosh of air escaping from him. While he was breathless, Tarzan threw his arms over Lennie's head and pulled the chain tight around his neck. Normally this would have led to a snapped neck, but the folds of blubber prevented Tarzan from making the decisive jerk and instead left him to slowly strangle this whale.

Before this inevitable end could happen, Skinner had his knife out and was at the ape-man's side threatening to take an eye if Tarzan didn't release his hold on Lennie. Still chained and his own weapons left in the pit, Tarzan saw he could not prevail now and released his captive. Lennie gasped for air for several moments, and, when he had collected himself, turned on Tarzan with the fury of vengeance and began beating the chained and defenseless man savagely. Knowing Lennie would not stop until he killed the ape-man and seeing his profit about to be lost, Skinner had to threaten Lennie and physically pull him off until the rage left him.

Tarzan lay dazed and immobile, unable to rise. The last thing he had felt before he slipped into unconsciousness was being lifted by the chains and slung over Lennie's back as easily as a sailor takes up his kit-sack to carry it away.

Chapter Five

TRAIN WRECK!

After the initial shock of the sudden stop, the passengers began to pour from their cars in search of answers. As the train representative aboard, Lord Bridgestone was going to be the one held accountable and sought out for solutions. He had been in search of the conductor and his private porter for some explanation about the rough ride, and now it seemed he had a bigger problem, though the one might relate to the other. As he made his way through the cars, those who knew of his position on the board accosted him with queries that were dismissed with a wave of his hand to passengers of his status, and returned with a cold stare and a gruff comment to those of the lesser societal ranks.

Using his size to force his way through, Lord Bridgestone eventually reached the source of the trouble and found the conductor and engineer gathered outside examining a piece of track that was obviously detached from the rail bed. The conductor was shaking his head as the engineer said, "This section of track was older than others, but this looks to be pried up and not a matter of wear."

"We couldn't have found a more desolate place on the run for a breakdown. I can't imagine there is anyone around for miles to have either caused this or to be available for repairs. It's a miracle we didn't derail entirely and suffer serious injury," replied the conductor.

"Who's responsible for this delay, and when can we get moving again?" demanded Lord Bridgestone, as he swaggered up to the two men.

The engineer pointed to the loose rails and said, "I barely managed to stop, or we would have gone into the woods. As it is, we will have to send for materials and men to repair this before we can move again at all. We are closer to White River, but the resources will have to come from back in Sudbury Junction up the adjacent spur and may take a couple days to get here."

"This is precisely the sort of thing my fellow owners feared when the government cobbled together these shoddy lines and why I was sent to report back on those who are derelict in their duty. Heads will roll if I do not make it to that meeting on time," blustered Lord Bridgestone.

"Sir, if not for the engineer's alert and prompt action in stopping this train, we could have crashed with many injuries and possible loss of life," countered the conductor.

"I shall hold you to getting us to our destination on time," Lord Bridgestone said, pointing at the engineer and then turning to the conductor. "You are responsible for keeping the teeming mass of passengers under control. Find my porter and send him to my car immediately."

With that, Lord Bridgestone absolved himself of any duty to help in the crisis, and not waiting to brook any questions, he returned to the train, leaving the two men now both shaking their heads.

Solicitous to her health, Mr. Fitch had first helped Madame to a chair and got her some water, and, finding her without injury, had then turned his attention to his charge. He needn't have worried, though, because with the resilience of youth, London was peering out the window excited about some potential adventure on this hitherto uneventful trip.

"I can't see anything from here. I need to get closer. Do you think we are in danger of robbery or under attack?" London said, guaranteeing a negative response to her request to leave by virtue of her suppositions.

Madame was not flustered enough to let her go, saying, "Absolutely not. We must stay together until help arrives."

Mr. Fitch was busy cleaning up and rearranging the personal items that had been strewn around the room from the sudden stop. Once things were in order again, he volunteered to find the conductor for an explanation and to offer his services in any reparations that might be necessary. But before things could progress further, there was a request by word of mouth down the cars for all passengers to come off the train's north side and gather for a general announcement of their situation. Since London could not be trusted alone or convinced to stay with Madame, it was decided best for them all to go together.

This all took some time because there were some minor wounds of mainly cuts and bruises and a couple of more serious contusions and broken bones that needed to be tended to before the train personnel were free to speak. But the conductor commandeered a room for medical treatment and was fortunate to have a traveling doctor and nurse able to treat the injured. Candles had been dispersed throughout the train, along with calm reassurances that did much to allay the fears that darkness and the unknown had brought. He also assigned duties to the porters, housekeeping, and kitchen staff beyond their normal responsibilities, so the passengers could continue to enjoy fairly normal service during the delay.

At last, everyone was assembled outside the train that could get there, and windows were opened for those still inside to hear, and even Lord Bridgestone graced them with his presence. The conductor relayed what he had learned from the engineer about the necessity of remaining here for a couple days while repairs were done and that with everyone's cooperation, there would be no hardships. Most of the crowd accepted their lot and were grateful a worse calamity had not befallen them. But as always there were a few, emboldened by liqueur consumed since the crash, who grumbled and even raised their voices against Lord Bridgestone as the visible face of the railroad authority here.

Instead of handling it with measured poise, Lord Bridgestone took personal offense and riled even more people with his confrontational response. The result was harsh words on both sides that led to shoving and fisticuffs as the crowd surged, trying to either get away from the melee or get to the source of the altercation. The conductor and his staff tried in vain to restore order and did manage to help those trying to retreat to their compartments. Mr. Fitch placed a protective arm around Madame and was in the process of escorting her away when they became separated from London. Madame urged him to find her, but feeling the older woman needed him more, Mr. Fitch continued to guide her back to the safety of her stateroom.

For her part, London was complicit in this separation. Seeing her opportunity to escape the rules and sensing the real excitement of the battle, she made sure she was not easy to see and ducked out the opposite way. This may have been the first time in her young life that she was on her own; until now, she had always been sheltered at home, surrounded with classmates at school, and properly chaperoned elsewhere. As a result of the heightened tensions, there was a bloody nose here and two men grappling in the dirt there, and London found herself eager to drink in the exhilaration of the moment. But as quickly as it started, it was over, and the participants dispersed along the train nursing their wounds and fortifying themselves with more liquid courage from a bottle.

London was not ready to give up the thrill this skirmish had aroused in her and return to the confining stateroom and supervision of Mr. Fitch. As she walked along outside in the darkness, there were some coarse comments from the ruffians who had participated in the brawl; that startled her because she had always been shielded from such baser elements of society. One young man approached her, blocked her way, and got her attention with a nice smile and warm words about her beauty.

As he was fairly good looking in a rough unshaven sort of way and the compliment seemed sincere, she returned the smile with a radiance that shone through the darkness.

Soon a couple of his friends completed a circle around her. What girl doesn't like to be the center of attention? In her naivety, she felt flattered and delighted with the sweet talk. But this was not her debutante ball, and these were not gentlemen asking for a dance. It didn't take long for the conversation to lead to a soft caress of her arm, and then a gentle arm around her waist trying to lead her away from the train to the even darker woods. At first, she followed meekly, unaware of their intentions but then resisted their urgings and tried to pull away. They, in turn, became more insistent and raised their voices to overcome her pleas and began half carrying her off.

London must have been under a lucky star that night, or her guardian angel was nearby, or it may have just been the whiteness of her hair tossing in the struggle that attracted a porter's attention. Fortune had it that this happened to be Jebediah, the personal servant of Lord Bridgestone; almost as big as his employer but all muscle from his heavy duties, this large black man placed an equally huge hand on the shoulder of the nearest rogue and easily pulled him aside, saying, "What's going on here?"

"We're just having some fun," said the trio almost in chorus.

The porter addressed London alone, "Miss, you would be safer in the train at night; there are all kinds of wolves in the woods."

Intimidated by his size but unwilling to give up their prey, the boys gathered their courage with some degrading racial comments and questions about his authority in this situation while Jeb, confident he could handle the three but unwilling to risk the consequences, edged the girl away. Before the rowdies could gang up on the larger man, London finally realized her peril, and free for the moment, seized the opportunity to defuse the situation by rapidly walking back to the train. With a glare to keep them in their place, Jeb escorted London to Lord Bridgestone's private car saying, "I think Lord Bridgestone would like to hear of this incident from you personally."

Meanwhile, Mr. Fitch was guiding Madame back to her cabin through the jostling crowd. Leaving the fighting behind, it became a matter of slow progress with many passengers seeking safety and blocking the narrow corridors. By the time they reached their compartments, Madame was overwrought from the strain of the day and frantic with worry about London's whereabouts. Never before had she been unaccounted for and especially not in such a dangerous place. While the situation was coming under the control of the railroad staff, there were still pockets of unruliness and London was such an unworldly maiden to be alone in the crowd. After seeing to Madame's welfare, Mr. Fitch left her safely behind the locked door and began to slowly work his way back through the passengers to find London.

Since Lord Bridgestone's car was only occupied by him alone, no one else was going that way, and the size of the burly porter made a quicker trip for London through the thin stream of people. Once there, Jeb was dismissed by his employer with instructions to find the conductor and see to the safety of the train, protecting it from vandalism with special attention to his private car, which might become a target considering the mood of some of the travelers. The furnishings in the coach alone were worth protecting, with the front room composed of a dining area for six, still covered with the remains of Lord Bridgestone's dinner. A small table between two sofas rested under a chandelier, and against the wall was an open roll-top desk with his correspondence in disarray, all surrounded by heavy floor-length drapery beside expansive windows and oil paintings with gaudy gold frames on papered walls. In the back room, a large bed and a chifferobe from the latest Sears catalogue were adjacent to a private bath complete with an extra-large tub. Lord Bridgestone's agitated demeanor and pacing showed his concern was mainly for his own safety rather than the contents of his carriage.

London was indifferent to the opulence around her if she noticed it at all, completely unaware of where she was and still trying to compose herself, to come to terms with all the new emotions encountered in such a brief span of time. From the adventure of the crash and excitement of being alone, and then the violence of the fight and unknown danger from strangers, it all set her heart to beating like never before. There was some fear but more a sense of exhilaration that comes from truly experiencing life rather than reading about it in romantic poetry or hearing about it second-hand from older friends. Where some would helplessly faint or dissolve into tears, London found she was made of sterner stuff, with enough courage and boldness to accept the risks and come out stronger and hopefully wiser in the end.

Lord Bridgestone ushered her to a sofa and listened patiently to her story as it flowed out all at once in a jumble of excited teenage jargon, not making a lot of sense. Her beautiful blue eyes told the true story as they flashed wide open in fear and then sparkled with the thrill of her misadventure. Her hands were clasped on her rising chest, as she gasped to get enough air to continue while her foot tapped in a nervous twitter.

Lord Bridgestone recognized her from their previous encounter and remembered his disgust with her lack of respect for his elevated position and biting comments on his size. But presently he saw her in a new light as a stunning young girl, given to him for aid, who was at his mercy. Now that the lower-class hussy had the temerity to ask him for protection, he found it easy to delude himself into misinterpreting her animation as the actions of a coquette and was quick to take advantage of the situation.

Lord Bridgestone brought her a glass of brandy and pressed it into her hands saying, "Drink this to calm yourself. It is medicinal."

London had been on the way to dinner and had not eaten and was dry-throated from relating her tale, so she gulped down all of the spirits only to cough hoarsely from the unexpected contents. She had no experience with alcohol of any sort, and on an empty stomach, the effects would come on rapidly. As she continued talking, her words began to slur, and in time, she slumped back from her usually perfect posture.

Waiting until the opportunity was right, Lord Bridgestone quietly sat down beside her, putting his arm around her shoulders, and took one of her hands in a comforting embrace. He allowed her to relax while speaking soft words of sympathy and commiseration into her ear. Ever so slowly, he began to casually pat her arm with his other age-spotted hand, gradually rising to stroke her neck and finally, upturning her head to face his, he bent down to kiss her.

Mr. Fitch glanced both ways as he exited the compartment, trying to decide where to look for London. Unfortunately, at that moment, there was some noise forward that decided him to go that way instead of to the back of the train where Lord Bridgestone's private car was coupled. Thankfully the crowd was less, as the disturbance had caused most of the passengers to retreat to the safety of their staterooms. When he found railroad personnel, he stopped to question them and describing London was unsuccessful until he caught up to Jeb and the conductor. There, Jeb immediately recognized London as the girl he had left with Lord Bridgestone and directed Mr. Fitch back the way he had come.

Feeling uneasy about the rumors that might come from the situation, Mr. Fitch hurried to get to London, trailed by Jeb. Still dealing with other passengers, the conductor was unable to spare the time and decided to let the other two men take care of it. Upon reaching the heavy door, Mr. Fitch rapped sharply and called out. There was a muffled cry from within. Growing more frantic, he pounded on the wood and then threw himself against it but to no avail, as his slight frame couldn't break the heavy lock. Finally, Jeb caught up and as he fumbled with the pass key, they both heard a piercing scream.

London's first intimation that something was wrong was when she saw Lord Bridgestone's looming big nose and pursed lips. Startled speechless, she pushed away from him with all her strength. But his lust was aroused, and he was not to be denied; he pinned her down beneath his great bulk, covering her mouth with one hoary hand and sweeping up her leg with the other. She beat on his chest with her tiny fists to no effect and twisted her head to scream, but it was muted by his sweaty fingers across her tender young lips. Leaving her leg, he reached for her bodice, and it began to tear. With her legs free, London managed to bring up a knee into his stomach, creating just enough distraction that the hand restraining her head slipped, and she was able to bite a finger. She let loose a scream as the door burst open and Mr. Fitch entered, closely followed by Jeb.

Without hesitation, Mr. Fitch threw himself into the fray and pulled the larger man off London, allowing her to jump to her feet and race from the room. Still in the fever of passion, Lord Bridgestone flailed out at Mr. Fitch sending him across the room into the dining table and chairs. Jeb paused for just a second, unsure about his loyalty to his employer, before he restrained the lord from inflicting further injury to Mr. Fitch.

"Unhand me at once, or I will have you fired," roared Lord Bridgestone at Jeb and then to Mr. Fitch, "What gives you the right to come into my private car?"

Jeb backed away and edged toward the open door. With London gone, Lord Bridgestone's ardor was fading, and realizing he had been caught in a compromising position, he adopted a more defensive strategy. To avoid any stain upon his honor, all the blame must be shifted to London, so Lord Bridgestone explained, "I was helping the girl up after she had taken ill and swooned."

Unsteady but up on his feet again Mr. Fitch said, "Sir, you are a liar and a cad. You sought to take advantage of an innocent

girl by force and I will see charges proffered upon you when
we reach the proper authorities."

"We shall see who they believe when I put my reputation
against that trollop. Best you escape with what dignity you have
left and let it be," Lord Bridgestone countered.

Eager to be out of the argument that placed him between a
passenger and his boss, Jeb had slipped out to the corridor and
disappeared. Seeing no support from that direction and alone
with the larger influential lord, Mr. Fitch had to suppress his
righteous anger and end the altercation. Besides, his responsi-
bility now was to find London and get her back to Madame,
who could best help her through this shocking ordeal. Mr. Fitch
searched the entire length of the train and spoke to every
employee and even knocked on doors in an effort to find London.
His last hope was that London had somehow been missed and
returned unseen to her compartment. Upon entering, his heart
fell and Madame's tears flowed; when they both looked at each
other, they knew they were so terribly alone.

London exploded from the private car, holding her dress
together, red marks on her cheek from Lord Bridgestone's
crushing hand and her own blush rising over the painful experience. She exited the train from the first door she came to,
dashed across the open space, and continued into the forest.
No one on the train saw her leave, and save for a single mechanic who was supposed to be working on the rail but, in
reality was idly smoking a cigarette, no one noticed where she
entered the woods. The mechanic called out, but she was gone
in an instant, and he returned to his smoking and took a nip
from his flask.

Crashing through the trees, London had only the single
thought: to get away from the horrid, leering face and escape
his pawing hands. Twice in one night had she been accosted
and only by the narrowest margin had managed to circumvent
their intentions. First, boys of her own social strata had attempted to take advantage of her inexperience, and then the
noble class had assayed even more vulgar designs on her when

she had turned to their representative for help. How could she explain the shame of it to mama, and what if word followed her back home where people were sure to believe the worst? That she was innocent mattered little when salacious gossip from eagerly wagging tongues spread like butter on a hot ear of corn.

Onward she ran until, exhausted from the trauma, she stopped and placed a hand on a large trunk to steady herself and take stock of her surroundings. It was possible to become lost after taking ten paces into this forest, so alike are all the trees. London turned around several times looking for a path but found none and thereby disoriented herself in the process, making it impossible to find the right direction to return. She cried out for help several times, but there were none to hear; no answer came back save the baying of wolves, so effectively did the dense pines muffle the sound. She clasped her hands over her mouth with the sudden realization that hunting animals might be attracted to the noise and then moved quickly from this area lest they find her. Unfortunately, she took the easier downhill track, which naturally led away from the railroad that had been built on the highest ground to avoid rainwater pooling.

Finally, tired, hungry, thirsty, disheveled, aching both mentally and physically, and knowing she was utterly lost, London stopped and began to sob. For all her courage and self-confidence, she was still only a young woman alone in the worst situation she could imagine. But things could get worse, and they did when a strong arm encircled her waist and a filthy hand with black chewed fingernails covered her mouth while she was borne away deeper into the dark forest.

Chapter Six

CAPTIVES ON THE PRECIPICE

Tarzan was only unconscious for a short time, and at the first sign of revival, Lennie immediately dropped him to the ground, fearful of having that chain used on him again as a garrote. Still suffering from the cowardly beating and now chained at the ankles and wrists, the ape-man decided escape was impossible at the present time. Skinner had tied a lead chain around Tarzan's neck while he was out, taking no chances that his prize would get loose again, and with this, he jerked Tarzan to his feet and dragged him down the path. With the short chain on his ankles, the ape-man could only shuffle and stumble along behind, with Lennie bringing up the rear.

Tarzan recognized that he was still on the same trail inside the thicket, and that it crossed a side branch that led to a large tunnel under the brambles easily visible from this side. Just past this, they came up to a hastily constructed shack made of scrap wood mixed with rough cut trees, with not much more than a lean-to on top serving as a roof. A dirty, stained piece of canvas covered the opening that sufficed for a door, and there were no windows. Hooks on the wall held more chains and some ropes and traps coated with a sinister, brown stain. The wholly disreputable building was perched near the edge of the cliff and looked like a strong wind could send it tumbling down the side. Some tools, including an axe and a saw, lay near a woodpile, and a pot hanging from a tripod was over a fire pit. This could only be home sweet home to a pair such as this.

The inside was worse. A packed dirt floor was covered with debris of all sorts, uncured hides, bones, food scraps and unidentifiable pieces of refuse and human waste. The stench of unwashed bodies and residue from the vermin within permeated the place, contained by the lack of windows and fresh air. The furniture consisted of a bench against the far wall and a small table beside two stools. On both sides of the door were piles of mildewed furs that looked to be makeshift beds guarding the exit, and in the far corner was a heavy rod with a ring on top sunk deeply into the earth. It was to this that Skinner attached Tarzan's chains, effectively securing him on a short length and then placing the key in his pocket. Lennie cuffed the back of Tarzan's head with a cheap shot from the blind side before they both left.

Once alone, Tarzan turned all his energies to where he was and how to escape. The sturdy chains were locked tightly, and even Tarzan's mighty thews could not break them. Holding the chain where it was attached to the stake, he strained with his back, legs and arms but was unable to unseat the stake. When brute force failed, Tarzan thought perhaps if he worked on it, in time it might be loosened enough to be pulled free; so he set to pushing and pulling on the ring in an effort to create a gap between the rod and the soil. Every moment he was alone would be devoted to this task, as the only other path to freedom was to get the key from Skinner, and while he would be alert for that chance, it seemed unlikely that it would occur.

Tarzan's mind was also active analyzing all the information he had about this peculiar area and how it could exist in the frozen northlands. Evidently, the warm up-flowing wind was constant and strong enough to encourage the brambles to grow densely around the crater and allow these two reprobates to live comfortably in a house of sticks. They had breached the thicket with the tunnel he had seen on the way here, and as the only way out, it was guarded by the pit trap on one side and their dwelling on the other. But to what purpose? The only reason Tarzan could come up with was that they were hiding from something outside.

As they came back in, Lennie was complaining that he didn't want to go alone outside the thicket. Skinner also wanted to go see what evil his plan had wreaked but realized the ape-man could never be left by himself. Tarzan could smell the fire from outside and rightly assumed they were preparing food of some sort.

"After we eat, you have enough time to get to the disaster by nightfall and pick over the ruins without being seen," said Skinner, and with a chuckle, "There should be many dead and others you can send to join them."

"Why not jest kill him and den we both ken go?" returned Lennie.

Skinner's plans had changed since the capture of the ape-man, and though he hated to send Lennie on a job by himself, the timing was critical, and it needed to be checked tonight. Knowing he could never trust Lennie alone with Tarzan and unaware he was talking about a true English Lord, Skinner said, "A naked wild man running in the woods is worth no ransom, but we can blow the horn and see what we get."

As always, Skinner had the last word, mainly because he was in charge but partly because Lennie was incapable of having a long conversation or coming up with any convincing arguments. He sent Lennie to tend to the cooking and said to Tarzan, "You be strong as a bear to beat Lennie but need to behave, or I kill you quick."

Tarzan gave no response and left untouched a foul-smelling bowl of greasy soup consisting of turnips and stringy meat with some other unidentifiable bits floating in it. After they had eaten, Lennie made up a small pack and left, while Skinner went outside to smoke and play his fiddle. Tarzan continued to work on the sunken pole.

Once he got to the train, Lennie was disappointed to find there was no crash or field littered with the dead and dying.

Under Skinner's direction, he had previously loosened the tracks for a stretch in hopes of a total derailment and much easy looting. But the careful engineer had managed to stop in time and thwarted their nefarious plans. As Lennie observed while hidden in the trees, an assembly of the passengers was turning into a riot, and the opportunity to mix in with the crowd and hurt someone allowed him to get close enough to throw a few punches and filch a couple of wallets before the train personnel broke it up.

Lennie was about to slip into the forest and head back to Skinner with the pitiful take when he could not help but notice a beautiful girl and overhear the conversation between Jeb and the boys. Lennie was disappointed at the intervention because he could have easily taken their trophy from the young men had they been successful in talking the girl into the woods. And what a prize it was! Lennie was so struck with her beauty that he completely forgot about his plans for robbery and focused on kidnapping. After all, Skinner had the wild man, so why couldn't he take her?

So entranced was he that he stayed watching the train in hopes the girl might reappear or that he could come up with a plan to find her on the train. Neither was very likely and Lennie was just about to give up when she burst from the train and ran headlong into the forest in a blind panic. Silently, the big man melted into the woods and followed. She made so much noise that tracking her was easy, and as she was going the way he wanted, he let her run. He came close when she stopped by the tree to rest, and his hungry eyes again drank in her beauty. Deep amid the trees, no one but Lennie heard her cry for help pierce the darkness; when she moved on again, he was right behind, ready to take her at the next stop. Silently, he crept nearer and swept her up in his arms, easily controlling her struggles and stifling her screams. He wanted to stay and examine his spoils, but it was too dark to see and even more, he wanted to get back and impress Skinner with his resourcefulness.

London's eyes streamed with tears as Lennie carried her deeper into the forest, for she knew she would never see the train again.

After a terrifying journey, being mauled by the huge hands of her abductor the whole way, she was dragged through the tunnel, where she truly thought she was being taken to the eternal fires of hell. Presently, London was being displayed by a triumphant Lennie in the weak candlelight to an appreciative Skinner in the shack. He had both her wrists in one giant paw held high above her head and was twirling her to show every side while she danced on tiptoes. Tarzan let a low growl escape from the corner at the inhuman treatment and London, no more tears left, hung in abject misery, head on her chest, totally defeated, and resigned to her fate. In the candlelight, she had seen her captors for the first time. London knew there would be no swift, merciful end from the grotesque Lennie and the horrifyingly tattooed Skinner, and she promptly fainted from fear and exhaustion. Skinner moved closer and, taking a handful of her hair, pulled her head up and slapped her face lightly to bring her back from her swoon.

Once she was awake again, he said, "What is your name, *belle fille*, and who will pay for your return?" Of course, Skinner was immune to her beauty, as he hated all the fairer sex from his mother onward, and was only interested in the potential ransom.

"She shore purty. Ken I keep her?" Lennie ventured.

"*Non*, you have done well here, *mon ami*, but she is not for play until we get the payoff due, and then you may have your fun," promised Skinner, as he pinched her chin between two fingers, looking for an answer to his question.

"We have no money or titled name, and there is only mama, who cannot afford to pay you," London replied.

Seeing the honesty in her innocent eyes and knowing that if there was any reward to be had, the girl was frightened enough she would surrender it. In a fit of rage, Skinner stuck a dirty finger in her mouth, pulling her cheeks aside while saying, "Then let us see if there is any gold in your teeth to pay for your keep."

At this affront, Tarzan leaped to his feet and came to the extent of his chain, demanding, "Unhand her, you cur, and I will pay your blood money if she is unharmed. Molest her further, and I will see that you both suffer my wrath!"

Lennie dropped London's arms, and she fell to the dirt floor as he shied away from the imposing presence of the ape-man, for he had already felt the power of those muscles and knew Tarzan was the superior man. He cowered, as all bullies do when confronted with their inadequacies.

London looked up at this heretofore unseen bronze Adonis in chains who had taken up her cause and offered succor without even knowing her. New hope sprang into her breast; where before she was totally alone and desolate, now she had a champion.

Skinner, however, was unmoved by the declaration and certainly not threatened by the chained prisoner. "You who have no clothes, how do you expect to pay me? It grows late, so I do what I want with you both in the morning."

Assured by Tarzan's offer of protection for the girl that the ape-man would not harm her, Skinner chained London to the same lead that held Tarzan, and with an admonition to all that there be no funny business, he retired to his bed of furs. Lennie blew out the candle and settled his bulk in his place on the other side of the door. Tarzan took the girl aside and offered her his protection in the corner of the shack.

On the cold earth floor, with the night time chill in the air and nothing but her thin torn clothes to cover her, Tarzan, inured to any temperature, gathered the shivering girl under his arm, his front to her back, to find warmth from each other, and here they quietly traded their stories in the darkness. Tarzan spoke softly with the comforting words of reassurance that while the heart still beat, there was hope. She found strength in his mantra, "I still live," and had occasion to repeat it many times to herself henceforth. Eventually, overwrought from the day, London fell into a fitful sleep, comfortable in Tarzan's secure embrace. Tarzan held her safe with one arm while the other continued to work at the stake.

Morning light gave London a true look at her surroundings and disheartened her once again, as she saw the filthy squalor and smelled the reeking stink that came from her hideous captors guarding the only exit. Yet her faith was somewhat restored when she turned over and looked at the most handsome man she had ever seen, now catching a little sleep after staying awake and wary most of the night. Tarzan was only a couple years her senior, but where she retained some girlish charms in a woman's figure, he was a living personification of Michelangelo's David with straight chiseled features and a muscular physique that could have been carved from stone. London instinctively knew she was safe while in his care, reassured by the strong arms that held her, and when Tarzan opened his steely grey eyes and gave her one of his rare smiles, London could see the purity of his character in his face.

Tarzan was equally impressed by the beauty of the girl, undiminished by her harrowing experiences. She returned a timid smile; awkward in being chained to a stranger and still wary of trusting anyone, she blushed slightly at their closeness. That innocent flush in her cheeks gave her a radiance matching the morning sun, and Tarzan could perceive her inner goodness and virtue. They talked quietly; he sought to buoy her spirits, and she relaxed again, confident in the integrity of his motives.

Soon enough, the ugliness behind them awoke with Lennie making rude noises and Skinner shouting at him to get a fire started for breakfast. Before leaving, Lennie came over to inspect his prize in the daylight, but as he got close, the ape-man rose, let out a fearsome snarl and bared his teeth; that took London aback but accomplished the intended purpose of scaring Lennie out the door. London wondered at the sudden transformation of the gentleman holding her into a savage beast but also thrilled at his power in protecting her with only a threatening sound. Sitting now, she slid under one of his arms, not wanting to break from his safeguarding touch.

Skinner laughed at the giant Lennie scurrying away and then turned to the captives and said with a sneer, "Cuddle close for now, for today we make the plans you will not like," and then he went out with Lennie to have breakfast. None was brought in for the prisoners.

London was infatuated with Tarzan, and if a case could be made for love at first sight, this would be it. With a mane of black hair swept back to his broad, tanned shoulders and a tall commanding stature, he brought to mind the power and presence of a wild, untamed lion. The physical attraction of both was immense, coupled with their common bond in peril and her dependence on him for succor. After their long conversation during the night, which had continued on this morning, she was drawn to him with the admiration that trust produces. Tarzan's chivalry and noble mien were evident from his heritage of the Greystoke line and like a lodestone to London, raised since childhood to respect the aristocracy. Tarzan's confidence was giving her hope and also stirred the close companion sensation of desire. In a moment of sweet tenderness, the inexperienced girl blurted out her feelings.

London's countenance projected a photogenic allure; her form was flawlessly sculptured in the classical mold, and this exquisite beauty was lying in his arms with wide-open eyes. Yet as Tarzan looked upon her, the face of another drifted over the visage, and his thoughts drifted away again to another more natural beauty that he could not forget: tall and trim with an athletic bearing and a vitality of spirit that surpassed all else. The ape-man had left his beloved jungle, learned the social graces, and worn the binding clothes that fashion dictated to be part of her world, so to honor her, he would continue to live life as she would expect.

Tarzan was surprised because, while he also felt a mutual attraction for London, an animal magnetism of two young individuals in their prime, he was still too newly hurt by love's loss to reach out for it again and so had missed her signs. He realized the situation they were in, friends in a nest of enemies, and that his position as protector had prompted her avowal, and he was too honorable to take advantage of her dependence. Not experienced in love himself, seeking to retain her friendship and not wanting to make her feel foolish, the ape-man reverted to his primal nature when civilized words failed him.

"My heart is in the lair of another."

That simple statement did not diminish London's feelings or imply there would be hope in the future and left her with her pride intact. With a child's ability to rebound, London was further impressed with Tarzan's honesty and moral certainty and realized her good fortune to have Tarzan at her side, even if love was premature.

There was no mistaking his intent when Lennie entered alone, leering at London. This time, a growl would not deter him from his reward. He had been thinking all morning of the sweet smell of her hair and soft curves of her body as he carried her last night. Now was his chance, while Skinner was away hunting, if he could only subdue the wild man. To this purpose, he carried a knob club which, wielded by someone his size, would be lethal if it connected. Lennie circled the pair, sweating profusely and drooling his breakfast berries down his chins, with eyes narrowed into slits looking for an opening to incapacitate Tarzan and leave him free to ravish London.

Tarzan did not return to the beast state and threaten with bared fangs and posturing; instead, he stood meekly with his arms at his sides and palms upraised as if he was unwilling to brave the cudgel. London was hiding behind Tarzan, peeking out at the terrible fate that awaited her when Tarzan stepped to the side and said, "Take the girl, she means nothing to me."

Did her champion have feet of clay? London was aghast and reached out to Tarzan as she fell to her knees, begging for help. He appeared indifferent to her fate as he turned aside. On her own now, London turned to face her molester and fight for her honor but could only stare in wide-eyed horror as the repulsive giant approached. All her vows of courage from last night faded as she was sickened by loathsome Lennie.

Lennie was delighted at this turn of events and feeling like a bully again after having intimidated the wild man with the stick. The smile that spread across purple-tinged lips revealed yellow, broken, and missing teeth and did nothing to enhance his appearance. He put the club aside as he fumbled with a cord around his neck from which depended a key. London's head passively dropped, unable to comprehend what was about to occur as Lennie freed her from the chain and pulled her to his furs. His vile fetor was overpowering, and once the slimy Lennie touched her, London came alive and began screaming like a banshee. She fought furiously, beating with her tiny hands and kicking with her feet in an effort to keep him off, but it was like a drop against a dam for all the good she could do as he gathered her in and forced her down, tearing at her skirt.

As soon as London was free from the chain and Lennie distracted, Tarzan leapt to the stake, and his powerful muscles contracted as he lent all his strength in one mighty effort to dislodge it. He had wanted to wait for a better opportunity to get the key first and set them both free, but Lennie's lechery made it imperative to act now. Slowly, the stake came up from the dense, packed soil and the reason it was so difficult to remove became apparent: it was a ship's anchor with the curved prongs buried deep. Suddenly, it burst free. Tarzan let out a length of chain and swung the anchor like his accustomed rope in an ever-increasing circle until he could reach Lennie and then let fly. Unfortunately, it was only the base that hit Lennie and not the prongs that could have impaled the swine, but backed by the centripetal force and Tarzan's strength, the anchor completely knocked Lennie across the room where he lay stunned.

"Run quickly; escape while he is down!" shouted Tarzan.

London hesitated for a moment, not believing she was saved; then, realizing Tarzan's seeming indifference was planned all along to get her free of the chains, she beseeched him to come with her. As Lennie began to stir, she saw the heavy anchor still holding Tarzan and she did not want to waste his sacrifice for her, so London raced out the door.

Thwarted once again by Tarzan, Lennie reached for his club, intent on killing the meddlesome wild man once and for all. Tarzan gathered up the chain, drawing the heavy anchor back, determined to use the awkward tool as a weapon to defend himself. They came together in a rush and Tarzan again had only one cast which he used to disarm Lennie by striking for the club rather than the man. From then on, it was two beasts closed in mortal combat using nature's weapons of fists and fangs. Initially, Lennie had the advantage of his greater size and Tarzan being chained, but quickly the greater power of the ape-man brought his teeth nearer to the pulsing jugular in Lennie's neck and an inevitable end. Lennie, ever the bully, turned coward again and began screaming for help as he frantically clawed at Tarzan to keep him away.

"Release him or she bleeds out," said Skinner, standing in the doorway and holding his well-used knife along London's throat, a thin trickle of blood dripping from the edge. Uneasy on the hunt, Skinner had returned early to check on the prisoners, recaptured London on her way out, and quickly dragged her back.

Tarzan immediately released Lennie from certain death once again, and the giant jumped up and grabbed his club to finally kill the now defenseless ape-man. Skinner stopped him, saying, "Get the horn; this wild man, he trouble us for the last time." As Lennie left, Skinner transferred London back to the anchor chain, keeping Tarzan at bay with the knife. When the big man returned with a huge Manx Loaghtan horn, together they escorted Tarzan outside, still chained at the wrists and ankles.

London watched from inside as they led him to the edge of the cliff and then further out on a precipice that extended some ten feet over the crater. She lost sight of Tarzan for a moment as they came together at the point, but then Skinner backed away and without further ado, Lennie pushed the bound ape-man off the edge to fall silently to his death over a hundred feet below. London's heart fell with him as she saw her last hope drop from sight.

Chapter Seven

THE TORMENT OF SEPARATION

Madame became hysterical as soon as she read the forlorn look on Mr. Fitch's face, unable to function whatsoever on her own behalf or focus on finding the missing London. Who could blame her, the disappearance of her only child was the worst tragedy she could imagine. Once before while shopping, they had experienced this for a brief moment when Madame was distracted for an instant and London had wandered off, a toddler attracted to a bright display. What followed was a gut-wrenching, heart in your throat, frantic search, where time stood still until relief flooded in and Madame's little one was found, having been hiding in a coat rack all along, simply because it seemed like fun at the time. Overcome with emotions, Madame couldn't decide whether to hug her or swat her and ended up squeezing London so tightly she had complained. But to be tormented with this empty feeling going on and on for days with no end in sight was too much for Madame to endure.

The next morning, Mr. Fitch did his best, trying to bolster her spirits initially when there was hope, encouraging Madame that London had to be somewhere on the train and she would eventually be found. Even after a thorough search had been instituted, all the passengers alerted, every compartment and car inspected, and still no trace of her appeared, he continued to maintain the positive attitude that once London got over her embarrassment, she would return on her own. Besides ensuring Madame got some rest and ate to keep her strength up, along with providing a shoulder to cry on, there was little else he could do.

Toward the end of the day, Mr. Fitch had the idea that Lord Bridgestone might have something to do with this, considering he was the last person to see London. So he went to question him and found him observing the engineer and other railroad personnel working on the track, now that the supplies had arrived from Sudbury with the workers and tools necessary to fix the partially derailed train. Lord Bridgestone was hesitant to even talk with him considering how they had last parted and tried to move to a more private area, but Mr. Fitch would not be put off and cornered him amidst the men.

"We have searched everywhere but the engine and your private car, and thought she might have returned to your state rooms," said Mr. Fitch.

The engineer vouchsafed that he had just been through the front of the train, and there was no one there. Lord Bridgestone said, "I vaguely remember the girl, but I last saw her leaving with you and she never returned."

"Perhaps you would accompany me to your car to check?" asked Mr. Fitch.

"My word is good enough, and I have more important business to tend to than an unruly child," said Lord Bridgestone, with his voice rising angrily.

This would have escalated into a heated argument and perhaps more as a tired Mr. Fitch was not going to back off from the instigator of London's disappearance, but the confrontation was averted when one of the workers stepped up and said, "I was working on the track and saw her run into the woods last night."

At this first positive lead, Mr. Fitch let everything else go and, turning to the man, asked him to show exactly where this had occurred. Lord Bridgestone was glad to be forgotten for the moment and permitted the employee to leave the job and walk to the rear of the train with Mr. Fitch.

Once there, Mr. Fitch followed the man to the precise location where London had entered the forest. Neither of them had the least tracking ability and their stomping around searching only succeeded in obliterating any signs that might have been present. Eventually, the railroad man excused himself to get back to work, and Mr. Fitch carried on alone. Finally, darkness settled in, and he was forced to leave the woods himself but not before he resolved to contact some men on the train who were going west to hunt bear and, together, organize proper search parties at daybreak. With this exceedingly slim bit of good news, Mr. Fitch sought out Madame to give her a slight hope for tomorrow.

Lennie raised the foot-long horn to his bulbous lips and blew a single extended blast, much as a triumphant herald announcing a victory march, that echoed back and forth across the crater several times. Skinner wiped his hands together a couple of times, like he was dusting them off after a problem solved, and then they both turned back to the shack. To London, the note signaled the end was near, and she shrank back to the limits of the chain into the corner in a hopeless attempt to hide and be overlooked. But this was not to be, as Lennie had only one thing on his mind and headed toward her immediately upon entering.

This time, relief came from an unexpected source when Skinner called, "Leave her be. I have the idea she will fetch much from the head man if there be no ransom possible."

"By rights, purty girl mine." cried Lennie, like a child denied his toys. As usual, Skinner had the last word with, "Needs she be unharmed to get big money."

For the first time in the years they had been together, Lennie didn't acquiesce and back down from the superior intellect of Skinner. His desire had been aroused and denied too many times to stop now. Reaching for London, he had his back to Skinner and didn't see the long, thin blade slip from his belt, but he heard the familiar rasp as it came free, as he had heard it so many times before to gut a deer or slit a throat. Turning swiftly for his size, Lennie confronted the Cajun with malevolence in his eyes and crouched, ready to take on the small man bare handed.

Skinner realized he had pushed too far. Hating women as he did, he didn't see the power of the infatuation or understand the lust that Lennie felt, instead viewing the girl as an asset to be sold for the highest profit possible, which would be lessened if the giant had his way with her. Indeed, she might not survive physically and her mental state, already fragile, could be irrevocably damaged from the experience. There was more at play here than Lennie's simple mind could understand, and until a ransom or sale could be arranged, Skinner would need to keep a watchful eye on his partner. But right now, he needed to defuse the impasse and regain control over Lennie.

The wily Cajun preferred treachery and, unsure he could win a fair fight, he assumed a lackadaisical posture and began using the tip of his knife to clean his fingernails, as if there was never any threat implied. Speaking in a soft drawl, Skinner sought only to delay the big man from his pleasures and promised he could have her after they checked the train for someone willing to pay ransom and then killed that person to get both the money and the girl. Lennie liked killing more than anything else, so this appealed to him and he relaxed somewhat. Skinner suggested they go hunting to get Lennie away from London and break the spell she had on him, but the Cajun realized this was going to be a continuing problem requiring him to keep a constant watch over Lennie. Though, for the moment, every parents' solution for a recalcitrant child - deny with delaying and distracting tactics until they forget the original desire - worked on Lennie, and after he reburied the anchor, they left her to dread her uncertain fate.

The rest of the day, London was in a constant state of terror anytime she was alone with Lennie, as he would paw at her and then act like nothing was wrong when Skinner returned. She begged Skinner to keep Lennie away, but for his part, the Cajun seemed to enjoy the power over a woman and only stopped it when he feared for his own loss of control over the man-child and to avoid damage to the prisoner. Lennie toyed with her like a cat with a mouse, reveling in the torture so much it saved her from any consummation of his desires. Nighttime was worse, waiting sleepless for Lennie to molest her and then screaming for help that only came because Skinner didn't like to be awakened.

During this same time, repairs had been completed on the train and it was preparing to depart once again to the west. Mr. Fitch had led parties of the traveling hunters on searches during the daylight hours ranging deeper into the forest. From the start, it had been at best a futile attempt, so trampled was the trail and dense the trees that now they mostly were following their own previous tracks in circles. The city-bred hunters were in danger of getting lost themselves; without the paid guides they were accustomed to and with no beaters to bring their quarry to them, they couldn't find their nose if it wasn't stuck between their eyes. Originally, it was a fun exercise to relieve the boredom of the delayed trip and carry a big gun around strutting to impress the ladies, but now with the lack of any positive results, the shame had led to a dwindling participation.

At first, the other passengers were sympathetic, but their support waned as the days dragged on and eventually ceased when a vicious rumor circulated that the missing girl had a wild side and probably got what she deserved running off in the woods with boys. With everyone around them giving up hope, only Mr. Fitch remained stalwart in his support of Madame and untiring in his search for London. Finally left alone in this, he swallowed his pride and returned to Lord Bridgestone for help.

"You must delay the train for a few more days, or London will have nowhere to return to," Mr. Fitch said to Lord Bridgestone in his personal car.

The aristocrat took his time before answering, like he was considering it but in reality his mind had been made up during their previous confrontation. When the train was ready to go he would leave the girl and her embarrassing accusations behind. Lord Bridgestone had been secretly pleased the searches had been fruitless because if he never saw her again it would preclude any inquiry into his conduct in the affair. But he tactfully replied, "I will see that supplies are left for the chance that she may return, but I cannot justify further delaying a train full of already late passengers on that possibility."

"Surely decency demands more to be done for a child." countered a desperate Mr. Fitch.

Tiring of the conversation Lord Bridgestone casually remarked, "When I last saw her, she was hardly a child and not very decent."

Even as his anger rose, Mr. Fitch realized he was powerless here and that further conversation was useless, so he choked down the bile enough to threaten, "You will be held accountable for this, if not in the courts then personally by me." With that promise of retribution, Mr. Fitch turned on his heel and left.

Later, with Madame, Mr. Fitch tried to soften the blow by saying he had spent the remaining time before departure seeing a large cross, made from rail ties, erected marking where London had entered the forest, so they could find it again when they came back for a more thorough search. In addition, a tent had been raised and the promised supplies were left for London should she return. Mr. Fitch tried to smile while surmising what a sight it would be to later find the city girl camping out. While it was the right thing to do, he knew it was not enough, but it was all he had to offer.

Faced with actually leaving her only child, Madame grew silent. In a few moments, she arose, gathered her things, exited the train, and made her way to the large cross. Mr. Fitch followed the whole way trying to convince her to get back on the train, that there was no one who would send back help if they didn't raise the alarm. She didn't hear his words, or if she did, they meant nothing compared to the force of a mother's love for her child. Hers was a simple choice: Madame would wait for London until the end of time.

Mr. Fitch was torn between traveling on to notify the authorities and his duty to protect Madame. In the end, it was simple for him, too; he could not desert these two women who, in such a short time, had taken such a strong hold on his heart. The train left them both standing together beside the cross as it rolled on westward.

At first, London was petrified into inaction with fear, exhausted, thoroughly defeated, and thinking more of a way to end it all rather than to escape. Then with the new morning sun, the words of hope from a handsome young man who had met his fate with courage inspired her to the self-same actions. She would fight back, not physically of course, lacking the size or defensive skills; but with her intelligence and cunning, she could outsmart the moronic Lennie. To this end, when Skinner left them alone the next day to check on the train, and Lennie began his advances, she startled him by turning receptive and complimentary.

"You were so magnificent and strong in throwing that wild man off the cliff," purred London as he came nearer.

This took Lennie aback as he had never had a kind word from anyone, much less a beautiful girl. Starved for affection his whole life, he drank it in like a man finding an oasis in a desert. He stood up straighter, and his massive head tilted to one side with a querulous look on his face.

"Come sit here and tell me all about yourself," said London with a beguiling smile, feigning interest and taking subtle control of the situation.

Slowly, the lust and rage drained away, replaced by a childlike curiosity of a never before experienced relationship, that of friendship. The baser desires simmered just below and could erupt again at any time with the quick changing temperament of the man-child, but for now, Lennie was intrigued enough to put them aside. Instead of assaulting her, he just sat down beside her, and when she didn't draw away in revulsion, he was content for the moment to just listen to her mesmerizing voice.

"Now that we're alone, it's nice to just sit here and talk, don't you think?" London persisted, trying to draw him out.

"You wanted wild man, not me," said Lennie, still distrusting this turn of emotions.

"Not at all. I was just frightened before by the horrid man with the knife and now I see that you are not like him at all, are you?" London continued, sowing a seed of distrust between the two men. "Please don't let him cut me again."

Lennie swelled up, visibly proud of himself in this new role as protector, and promised to keep her safe. Since Lennie had a limited vocabulary and was not smart enough to carry on a conversation, London took to telling him about herself, describing a life Lennie could never appreciate but which nonetheless held him in rapt attention entranced by her melodic voice. Much like Scheherazade with her tales to the King, London kept Lennie at bay over the next days, rewarding his good behavior with her charming dialogue, all the while encouraging him to take her away from the Cajun.

Skinner was aware of the changes in that Lennie had stopped going after the girl at night and treated her differently during the day, but since the conversations only occurred when he was absent, he was in the dark about why. At first it was fine because it lent to a more peaceful existence, but after a while, the Cajun's suspicious nature demanded an explanation. Rather than confront Lennie again, he took to spying, by creeping up on the cabin, after his daily trips to the train, to overhear what the two conspirators might be plotting. With Skinner, lying and cheating were a part of his character, so he could not imagine that anyone else could rise above it.

London had slowly brought Lennie to the point where he was ready to free her and take her away to his promised reward once they were alone. Even though she remained revolted by the odious giant, she risked arousing him with physical contact by finally taking his meaty hand with her delicate fingers. London pressed forward in an all-out chance that she could continue to play him along once free and escape later in the woods by saying, "You have the key to our freedom; let's run away together now."

Lennie feared the wrath of Skinner. He had seen him on the hunt and knew there would be no mercy if they were caught. But the intoxicating girl had woven her magic around him, and he fumbled weakly with the key in the lock of her chains. But even as she was freed, the canvas at the door was torn aside and there stood the Cajun, silhouetted in the sun, with his knife bared having heard all that had transpired within. He had returned early this time, only going part way to the train when he had heard it leaving in the distance.

"So you go agin me for the wench," snarled Skinner.

The spell on Lennie was broken by the ingrained terror of the knife. He crawled aside, feeling guilty at being caught, begging forgiveness, and leaving London defenseless. Skinner glared at them both for a moment and then said coldly, "Go get the horn."

As Lennie scrambled to obey, the Cajun caught up London by the arm and dragged her roughly from the cabin. Blinded by the sunlight after days in the shack, London couldn't see where she was being taken, but her heart sank knowing when Lennie ran up with the horn, it was toward the same end that Tarzan had faced. Determined to meet her fate just as bravely, she didn't struggle or cry out as they all advanced across the precipice.

Chapter Eight

Burned Alive

When Tarzan reached the edge of the precipice, he looked down a hundred and fifty feet at piles of jagged boulders that followed the base of the cliff around the floor of the valley. Only from the north side was this visible, as the constantly prevailing colder winds kept this area clear while mixing with the warm updraft and forming clouds over the rest of the crater. Evidently, except for the mammoth crag they were standing on, much of the rock face had fallen from the sides over the years and accumulated up to thirty feet away from the edge forming a dead zone that circled the entire pit. This also explained why no trees grew near the walls nor vegetation on the sides.

As the ape-man prepared to meet his Maker by being broken on the sharp rubble below, he noticed an extremely long flexible line tied to a sturdy limb on a nearby tree that overhung the valley from above. The other end had a loop fastened to the outcropping they were standing on. He thought it was a lot of trouble to hang him when the rocks alone would be effective as an execution. When Skinner stooped and quickly attached the heavy, elastic cable to the chain about his ankles, Tarzan had only a moment to be puzzled before Lennie pushed him into space and the rough stones below came rushing up to meet him face first.

Just as the deadly edges loomed before him, Tarzan felt the cord about his feet tighten as it reached the extent of its length, drawing him up just short of his demise and leaving him bobbing there like a worm on the end of fishing line. No screams of fear came from him on the way down, and now the ape-man, who was used to swinging across harrowing distances and making death-defying leaps in his native jungle, smiled as he had found the whole experience quite exhilarating. Energized, Tarzan bent at the waist, reached up for the knot attached to the chain, and quickly untied it while holding onto the line until he was upright again and able to drop to the crater floor.

There was no solution for the chains on his wrists, since he couldn't effectively use his confined hands to wield the rocks to break them. Tarzan could only shuffle away with the ankle chains, so he immediately went to work beating on a link there with one of the many stones around him. The echo of his pounding carried across the valley, but much louder still came the blast on the horn from above. Realizing that must be a call to someone or some thing, Tarzan redoubled his efforts to separate the chain.

Too soon, the ape-man smelled the approach of many men and when his ears told him they were near, he desisted in his efforts to get free and took up a sharp-edged rock in each hand, preparing to sell his life dearly. From out of the woods some thirty feet away came eight helmeted, burly men dressed in tunics, carrying round shields with a metal center boss on one arm and a heavy axe or sword in the other hand. Many had scarred, painted faces covered with full beards, while some had dyed, horizontal grooves filed across their teeth, presenting a horrifying sight, and with a bone shaking war cry, they circled Tarzan and closed in.

True to his nature, the ape-man stood stoically awaiting the charge. But the hunting party was evidently surprised at finding their terror tactics had failed to induce fear and paused to take stock and looked to a young leader for direction. One with blood markings on his face spoke in a language Tarzan did not know, but it sounded European, so he tried English in return, but the other only shook his head negatively. When they hit upon a common understanding of French and were able to converse, the soldier explained that past interaction with Canadian explorers and trappers made it necessary for some inhabitants of the valley to be fluent in the language.

The leader assured Tarzan he was not what they usually found when called by the horn, he would be treated well, and his chains could be removed with tools available at their village. Seeing no sense in starting a fight with armed men that he could not survive, Tarzan decided to take them at their word and allowed himself to be led away, still feeling more a prisoner than a guest.

The party surrounded Tarzan as they walked through the woods and he took the opportunity to observe them. Hard, heavy men who looked ready for combat, many carried axes with a ten-inch blade and a four-foot handle. Others had returned their long swords to a baldric; some also carried yew bows with twisted fiber strings and had birch arrows fletched with feathers in a quiver. All had metal helmets with nose guards, and while only the leader had chain mail over a dyed tunic, some of the rest had a boiled leather jerkin for protection. The men's woolen cloaks had various animal embroidery, while the captain's was fur trimmed with braids, and all had a single gold broach clasped at the right shoulder leaving the sword arm free. Goat-skin shoes, wool socks, and tweed trousers, held up with a sash or drawstring, completed the wardrobe.

Most fascinating were the heavy round wooden shields three feet across circled with a hard leather binding edge and an iron boss in the center that provided protection for the hand and a place to hold on. Ferocious animals and hunting birds shared the painted surfaces with fantastic dragons and other unrecognizable shapes; no two alike, each was particular to the warrior who carried it. A few of the warriors had some small gold pieces of jewelry, but as fighting men they had little use for ornamentation, it was their weapons and shields that seemed to be a greater source of pride.

No one spoke further to Tarzan, and as the leader was at the front of the column, the ape-man did not try to communicate either, unsure if his French would be understood and preferring to determine if he was among friend or foe before giving any information. He focused on his surroundings, marking the way back in his mind, since after circling most of the crater above, he was convinced the only way out was by climbing up the cable that had delivered him to the bottom. Even that was unlikely because he had watched the line pulled back to the surface after the head man attached a pair of chains and a leather bag to it.

Aside from the confining chains, the walk was far from unpleasant. Tarzan saw he could easily swing away in this forest, so different was it from the cold pines above. Here, giant oaks shared the path with other trees familiar from his native jungle making arboreal pathways with their spreading boughs. Occasionally, a coastal sequoia reached endlessly to the clouded sky. Game trails led off in many directions covered with signs of prey, both large and small, easily visible to the ape-man. The chattering and chirping of life was everywhere in the lush landscape so reminiscent of Tarzan's home.

A humid warmth pervaded everything, kept in by the clouds above and generated by thermal springs that bubbled up randomly, heated by their closeness to the earth's inner fires. Tarzan first encountered this phenomenon when crossing a small stream that was cooled by pebbles and evaporation but still pleasantly warm and teeming with fish. The ape-man leaned his head back and dilated his nostrils as a plethora of odors assailed his sensitive nose. Indeed, from the luxuriant beauty and massive growth of the profuse vegetation to the abundant wild life in all its forms, Tarzan felt that he had dropped into paradise.

After they cleared the forest and turned onto a well-travelled dirt road, the men seemed to relax their vigilance and the captain dropped back in line with Tarzan. He introduced himself as Erik Wildefarer and explained that his hunting party had happened to be close by when the horn sounded, and now they were en route home, where a fighting man such as Tarzan would be welcome. As they passed farms, Erik pointed out the abundant barley, cabbage and peas in rows plowed by an ard and lava rock querns used to grind the grain to flour. On open grassland, chickens, goats, pigs, and sheep foraged, providing a source of eggs, milk, meat and wool. Tarzan noted some of the sheep had up to six long horns while others were shaggy and ready to be trimmed to make yarn for clothing. Supplemented by the game and nuts and berries from the forest, it was clear this society lived well off the land.

They passed a large stone alongside the road that had cryptic carvings on a flat side. The border looked like an entwining snake and the center was filled with symbols. Asking what it meant, Tarzan learned it was a memorial stone, and the runes were from the Futhark alphabet of twenty-four characters used to depict the bravery and glory of the dead on ancestral voyages. Some commemorative boulders had secret and magic figures known to only a few mystic leaders.

By now, Tarzan was convinced he had been captured by a band of Norsemen but was unable to inquire further because, after a bend in the road, the village came into view and Erik returned to the front to lead the way in. Surrounded by earthen ramparts, there appeared to be a few longhouses made from upright wooden boat staves in the ground, forming a base with posts around the outside supporting the roofs. Long beams that could have been used formerly as a keel traversed the full length at the peak and wood shingles covered some roofs, while green turf grass grew on the top of others. Smoke trailed upward from vent holes in the center that allowed fires for cooking and warmth inside. Barns served the same purpose as the smaller byres on the farms and some tents were scattered randomly about. Iron rivets nailed the wooden structures together, and walrus-hide ropes lashed everything else in place.

Tarzan thought the inhabitants must feel very safe from attack since there was no palisade or gates and only a single sentry with a long warning horn kept watch on the earthworks. Unlike the native villages of Africa where the women subjected an entering prisoner to all kinds of verbal and physical abuse, here Tarzan was merely an object of curiosity, and the people just gawked as he passed. A spectacle taking place near the center of the compound in front of the largest longhouse occupied the interest of many and may have saved the ape-man some of this derision. The hunting party joined the group watching.

A huge man with a great red beard was jabbing his sword in a large iron cage containing an infuriated cave bear that was growling and roaring savagely. The cage was one of two about eight feet apart that clearly were only man-sized and the immense bear couldn't move or turn rapidly enough to defend itself. Two men around the tormentor cheered him on while most of the crowd merely watched, similarly entranced as anyone would be by a traffic accident in a modern city. Tarzan was struck by the resplendent trappings of the red bearded man, which were in the same style as others but studded with precious gems and woven with golden filigree. A cape with a gold-colored bear embroidered on the back was held with a diamond broach, and the hilt of his sword was so encrusted with jewels that it looked ornamental rather than functional. With red leather boots and a huge gold belt buckle, he looked every bit the showman playing the crowd.

As the fury of the helpless bear rose in volume, the man inflicted more wounds now using his sword tip to draw blood. Trapped like a beast himself, Tarzan felt empathy for the vulnerable animal even though the bear would not hesitate to eat him under different circumstances. Before this could go further, the ape-man voiced a call of the wild that immediately silenced the bear as it sought out a kindred spirit. To be sure, the bear did not understand Tarzan, but the ape-man spoke in the first language and the basic guttural sounds were familiar to all of the lower orders.

The crowd turned as one at the sound, also seeking out its origin, and Tarzan found himself the center of attention with even the torturer leaving the bear to confront whoever had caused this interruption. As to what was said next, Tarzan could only surmise because the participants all spoke old Norse and aside from some words that had passed down into other languages, it was unintelligible to him. He did gather from the deference showed the man with the garish clothes that his name was Magnus Red Beard and he was the Jarl, King of these people, and Erik was related to him, even though there was no apparent affection between the two. When Erik explained how Tarzan came to be here, Red Beard glared at the captive who had spoiled his entertainment, while not seeming to hear a single word. Then, cutting Erik short, he dismissed him with a disgusted look.

Then Magnus conferred with the taller of his two aides, a thin, dark-robed man named Wulfstan Forkbeard. The seer pulled an ornate knife etched with sigils from a rune-embossed leather belt and began making strange signs in the air. Dancing around Tarzan, he sinuously waved ring-covered fingers while chanting gibberish. The ape-man was amused by the resemblance of this mage to Mbonga's witch doctor, Rabba Keba, and his zebra-tail totem, and the irony of being cursed on two continents appealed to his wry sense of humor. After a lengthy display of mysticism, the sage whispered a warning to Magnus, who then loudly proclaimed his judgement as King to the crowd and for emphasis at one point cruelly stuck his sword through the cage and blinded the bear in one eye.

The end result was that Tarzan was led to the empty cage and interred there by the other retainer, a disreputable looking, spry muscular fellow with a sword tattoo on his right arm, named Gorm Blacknee, who earned that sobriquet from groveling to do the King's bidding. None dared call him that to his face, for to do so would be to risk him drawing his well-used blade that never returned to its scabbard until it had tasted blood. Of all the Vikings, only Magnus, with his thoroughly functional and undecorated Blood Axe, was the better of him in combat and as the King's lackey, Gorm was charged to be the royal bodyguard and enforcer. Just before Tarzan entered the metal pen, Magnus produced a key that finally removed the hated chains from the ape-man's wrists and ankles.

Even caged, Tarzan felt freer than he had in days because he knew it was only a matter of time now before he would be presented with an opportunity to escape and, once in the closely surrounding forest, not even Usha the wind could catch him again. This was not braggadocio and Tarzan never swaggered, but instead it was a manifestation of his confidence in his abilities, both mentally and physically, to master whatever life threw at him, bred from years of constant, life-and-death struggle to survive in the harshest African jungle, surrounded by savage beasts and fierce native tribes.

Magnus and his close retainers went into the longhouse, and the crowd dispersed to their various tasks, leaving Tarzan alone in his cage next to the one containing the suffering bear. Erik stayed behind and came close to inform Tarzan on his reversal of fortune. Magnus Red Beard, his pride hurt, had declined Erik's pleas on Tarzan's behalf for the lawful right of combat to gain entry into the clan. The bear was meant to be an offering tomorrow for Vetrar, occurring near the autumnal equinox and honoring the harvest; it was the second yearly festival, the others being summer Sigr, and winter Jola. Tarzan's interference was taken as disrespect, causing him to be sentenced to work in the mines. Erik vowed to try to temper his volatile step-father's judgement later when he had cooled down, but there was no hope right now while the Jarl was in one of his dark moods.

After Erik left, Tarzan examined his cage and found the strong iron bars were unyielding to even his mighty thews. Secured with an ancient padlock, he was as effectively held as with the chains before. A thrall brought him some delicious mutton stew at Erik's bidding and well water that was still warm from the earth. At the evening meal time, everyone went into the longhouses for their communal dinner and Tarzan was all alone in the village except for the bear, which was now quietly nursing his wound.

Tarzan noticed no lock was on the door to the bear's cage, relying instead on a slide drop latch to hold it shut. While this provided no opportunity for the bear, it immediately suggested a plan of retaliation to the ape-man. Tired of confinement, he wanted to push the issue, and in turn, the thwarting of their sadistic plans appealed to him much as he had enjoyed baiting the African tribes that tortured helpless victims. To this end, he began pushing his cage back and forth, timing the rocking to a specific point when he could allow it to topple toward the cage confining the bear. The actions caused the bear to look up and emit a low growl when the cage crashed over.

The grass and dirt muted the noise, and no one interrupted their dinner to check. Laying sideways, the six-foot-tall cage had brought Tarzan within two feet of his goal. But when he reached out he was still inches short of the front latch, and now the bear could get to him when he was exposed. The ape-man was undeterred and didn't retreat to the safety of the far end of his cage. Instead, he extended one leg through the bars within easy reach of the long claws. The risk of a crippling wound from the bear was immense, but Tarzan's daily life was always thrilling because of the chances he took. He spoke soothing words in his primitive tongue, probably ineffective on the pain-addled animal, hoping to distract the bear from what his busy foot was doing on the front of the cage.

At times, most civilized men can't even get all their toes into a sock at once, catching some on an edge held by two hands. After years of gripping small branches to avoid a deadly fall from high in a giant jungle tree, Tarzan's toes were like fingers, and he had the latch undone in seconds before the bear could strike at the extended leg. As the door swung open, the animal immediately lost interest in Tarzan, ambled out to the nearby woods, and disappeared without so much as a backward glance.

Tarzan placed both feet on the ground through two parallel bars and grasped the bars on the side close above his head and bunched his massive shoulders. By straightening up and walking with his feet while working his hands down the bars, he was able to tilt the cage vertically again until it plopped back close to where it had stood before. He didn't have to wait long before the first diners came out and gathered around the seemingly mysterious disappearance and speculating about the ape-man's role in it. Soon, the noise of the crowd brought out the King and his retainers, who pushed their way forward.

By now, the many scuffling feet had eliminated any signs of what had happened in the ground around the cages, and Tarzan remained mute, of course, enjoying his little joke. Magnus and his seer had to take charge of the situation and not let this prisoner assume a smug air that was engendering awe in their people. So with much bluster and the support of the mage, Red Beard pointed at Tarzan and declared that if the sacrifice was magically gone, then it was because the harvest goddess Sifa preferred the new sacrificial *blot* that had been provided by Erik. They set the villagers to work on preparations for a ritual burning at the stake that night at midnight.

By using his cunning to escape the frying pan, Tarzan's ruse had truly placed him in the fire. He could only watch in dismay as a tree near the edge of the forest was cut to a height of seven feet and the remaining trunk stripped of all its limbs and bark. This saved the work of digging and left a well-rooted stake, impossible to shake free from, made of green wood that would not burn, and covered with a slippery, flammable sap. Kindling wood was piled around the base and the whole assembly was kept far enough away from the dwellings to ensure no sparks could start a fire.

Once the work was done, the festivities began, fueled by mead made from sweet honey. Just like the African native beer, the potent brew soon had minstrels picking up harps, lyres and flutes to make music, encouraging dancing that grew wilder as the night wore on. Later, more food from cooking cauldrons was served by thralls to the freemen working class, called Karls, and the Jarl class of nobles. A skald recited poetry based on sagas of adventure while men competed in contests of strength such as wrestling, running, jumping, climbing, lifting, and balancing. Tarzan could have enjoyed this Norse festival, but he was being saved for a grand finale that only differed from the African tribal orgy in that he would not be eaten here.

Several of the Jarls questioned him about the missing bear and as that class was all fluent in French, Tarzan was able to understand. Since a true magician never reveals his tricks, Tarzan allowed the already superstitious people to believe that he was privy to the great powers at work here. Clearly dismayed at the turn of events, Erik explained that the only way to reverse the King's decree was to challenge him to mortal combat, the winner becoming the new King, but Tarzan could not do that because he was not of the Jarl class. Even the King stopped by with some private words of vitriol about what a pleasure it was going to be to see and smell the ape-man roasted alive.

Tarzan could not resist and would have been incapacitated had he tried when, led by Gorm, four hearty Norsemen with knives and swords ushered him to the post and secured him about the arms and legs with unbreakable knots as only a seafaring race can tie. Though he struggled and flexed his strong arms, there was no loosening of the bonds and the ropes were too thick to hope that they would burn through in time. Wulfstan again traced mystic runes with his knife in the air and drew a bear sigil on Tarzan's body with charcoal while chanting to accept this *blot* in the place of the great bear sacrifice. Magnus invoked ancient words of thanks to the gods for a bountiful harvest, and then the King took some flint-like jasper and struck fire at the base of the pyre.

The flames greedily consumed the circling wood, rapidly rising to feast on Tarzan. The volatile wet sap and green tree burned slower and with much smoke. Tarzan never ceased in his efforts to escape. Trying with all his might, he could not break free or uproot the well-rooted trunk. Now the fire was licking at his feet, and the smell of singed hair and charred flesh was in the air. The ape-man tried to scrabble up the stake like a lumberjack by pulling his arms tight and pushing with his ankles, but was denied a grip by the slippery sap.

Smoke blackened his eyes, blinding him, and choked in his throat and lungs, suffocating him. The heat was intense and his back burned as the tree sap smoldered underneath. Coughing, he gasped one last time and jumped up in a final effort to clear the flames; but the trunk was too tall, and he slipped back down, only to slump into a merciful unconsciousness as the smoke enveloped him from view and continued to billow up into the sky.

Chapter Nine

SURROUNDED BY VIKINGS

As London was dragged to the edge of the cliff, Lennie was pleading with Skinner to let the girl stay, saying that he was sorry he tried to set her loose, and he would do anything if he could just keep her. Skinner was not hearing any of it, once again confirmed in his belief that all women were deceitful wantons, and since there was going to be no ransom, it was time to get what he could for this one. London was quietly reciting prayers, assured that this was her last moment on earth.

She was as surprised as Tarzan when she first saw the elastic cord and as puzzled when Skinner attached it to her ankle chain. Lennie would not push her off so Skinner did the deed with a satisfied smile on his face making the tattooed horns by his eyes curl upward. As London hurtled to the sharp rocks below, she differed from Tarzan's silent trip in that she screamed the whole way down and continued to shriek for some time after as she hung upside down at the end of the line. The horn sounded above, but she was not strong enough to invert herself and unfasten the cable from the chains, so she was forced to wait for whoever answered the summons.

It had been a couple days since Tarzan had been burned at the stake, and Erik, true to his surname of Wildefarer, was again leading a hunting party when the horn was heard. The wanderlust was a part of his roaming ways, but there was also the desire to avoid his cruel stepfather who, afraid of competition from the popular Erik, never missed an opportunity to put the boy in his place. At first, this was harmless, but as Erik reached his full adult size, the rivalry took on serious implications because Erik sprang from the true royal bloodline by way of his father, Annulf Fairhair, who died in a hunting accident some years ago. Magnus had taken Erik's mother, Freyja, to become King and there were no others strong or brave enough to dispute the title in the Viking way, man to man mortal combat with weapons of choice, the victor becoming the ruler.

London did not have to wait long, spinning slowly on the cable, before a few hideously painted men, brandishing swords and axes and voicing fierce battle cries, burst from the woods. If she had not been hanging upside down, with the blood pooled in her head making it impossible to faint, she would have swooned. Instead, she was forced to make sense of this out-of-time apparition from a most embarrassing position, suspended chained with a red face and hanging matted hair, with a dirty torn dress bunched around her hips, rotating and swaying helplessly. Literally at the end of her rope in many ways, she shouted, "Get me down from here!" not caring what happened next.

Even more surprised this time than when they found Tarzan, the Norsemen once again looked to their leader, but since the girl's command had been made in English, he just stood there uncomprehendingly, trying to think of a way to send her back because this was surely going to be more trouble than the ape-man. After a few moments, his sense of propriety reasserted itself and he directed his men to stack some rocks so he could reach the line and untie it while the girl clung closely to him to avoid falling headfirst. Once down, they stared speechless at each other until Erik, remembering Tarzan, tried French and found a common language in which they could communicate.

Much as the inhabitants of her namesake city in the middle ages, London was surrounded by barbarians. They gave her no choice, but as brutal as they looked, they did not abuse her compared to the mauling she had received by the two above the cliff, so she went willingly with them. Despite the blood on his hands and fearsomely painted face, the leader was respect-ful, at times taking her hand through the rough spots and carrying her over the deeper creeks. But when London asked what had become of Tarzan, her hopes were crushed again when she learned he had been burned alive a couple days ago as a sacrifice to some pagan god. Just to think that magnificent man so full of vitality and hope, who had given her of his strength and courage, had come to such an end made the beautiful natural surroundings lose all appeal, as she silently pondered her fate without him.

The trip to the village was a repeat of the one made by Tarzan, with the only difference being that Erik stayed by her side the whole way, intrigued by London, even though her bedraggled exterior and gamey smell from days in the shack hid any sense of her true beauty. He sought to protect her from the rough men and coarse language of his fellow hunters, and by the time they reached the ramparts, what little conversation they had convinced him she was different, which led to a concern for her treatment by Magnus. To this end, he did not go directly to the King with his prize, instead he left her at his home with instruc-tions to the Queen's retainers to see that she was properly cared for as a guest while he reported in.

Olga, whose main duties were food preparation and cleaning, was clearly annoyed that a captive should be elevated above the level of a thrall, and wanted to put the new slave to work in the skali, or hearth room. Her younger counterpart, Elle, who was the Queen's personal thrall and took care of the household wash, noticed London's ruined clothing and suggested they first find some cast-off pieces fit for her new station in life. Each wanted an assistant to lighten their own duties and were ready to shift the most onerous tasks to the unfortunate girl.

London found both women fairly fluent in French though they spoke in Old Norse at times to each other, while exchang-ing knowing looks that convinced London she was being used. After donning some well-worn shapeless clothes that were not much better than the rags she previously had on and certainly smelled worse, London was given a scraper to clean out the cook pot that hung on a tripod above the hearth. When that was done, they had her at a laundry tub, hand rubbing clothes clean and then wringing them dry for hanging outside to be later ironed with hot rocks. Astonished that she was in a Norse village, she noticed every detail as she worked.

The King's dwelling was no regal palace, but it was separate from the longhouses of the villagers. It consisted of the common skali room with stamped earthen floors around the center fire pit and hearth, which were next to a dining table. Around the walls were platforms that served as seats during the day and beds at night with down pillows. Tapestries depicting scenes of gods and legends hung on the walls and provided decoration and privacy when used to separate a section. In one corner, Elle worked on a vertical loom, making cloth from wool and flax, while Olga used vegetable dyes to color pieces to be sewn into clothing later. Carved wooden panels enclosed the other end, making a private bedroom area for the Jarl.

Taking some dresses to hang on the back of those panels, London found a real feather bed beside a chair and table with vellum paper and writing quills. Three chests lined one wall, which London found later contained all of the Viking's personal possessions, like clothes, weapons, and valuables, and also served as a seat that was often carried with them or buried in a hoard for safekeeping. A game board with some scattered pieces lay on top of one. Combs made from antler or bone, oval broaches, and gold jewelry set with colored glass, jet, and amber lying atop another chest showed the wealth of this house and the pride they took in their appearance.

When London went out to empty some waste in the midden, the people took little note of her; in her used, plain baggy clothing and with soot-blackened hair she looked like any other thrall. A bearing dial from a ship stood outside in the sun acting more as a sundial now, although the concept of time had little meaning here. Men were training hawks and falcons to kill other birds while others worked with some hunting dogs. The youngest male children were playing with balls as their older siblings practiced with weapons. Except for one richly dressed group gathered gossiping by the well, the women and girls were mostly inside or working in the fields.

As the evening meal time got closer, Queen Freyja arrived first and London curtsied when presented. As Elle assisted the Lady in changing behind the panels, Olga explained the duties of a serving girl to London. Erik usually ate his meals and slept at the longhouse designated for single men, but he wanted to check on London before Magnus arrived, so he came early for dinner at his childhood home. Nothing of the original girl remained, so like a scullery maid had the other two transformed her.

Erik was questioning Olga as to why London was being worked like a slave when Magnus arrived and seized the opportunity to assert his authority by claiming London as his thrall to be used or sold as he saw fit.

Erik stepped beside London and said, "She has knowledge from the world above, speaks the noble language, and could serve better as a teacher of our children."

"Why would I want the peasants to learn that which will only make them discontented with their lot? Better she joins them in their ignorance," replied the King.

"It is your ignorance that prevents our people from advancing beyond barbarism," Erik retorted, "My father encouraged men to become more than superstitious fools daily practicing a shield wall where we have no enemies."

"A Viking's first duty is to fight. Your father was too weak to survive a hunting trip and you might do well to hold your tongue before the same happens to you," Magnus said menacingly.

Hearing all from behind the panels, Freyja hurried out before things got worse. As the link to the royal line, Magnus needed her to add legitimacy to his kingship; so while there was no love between them, she had some power over him, especially where her son was concerned. Out of respect for his mother in her house, Erik dropped the argument and they all sat down for a stew of wild boar meat and peas seasoned with garlic and onions. There was also barley bread for dipping and wild berries for dessert. Magnus drank prodigious amounts of huckleberry wine while Freyja and Erik had goat's milk. London served and would eat with the rest of the thralls later during the clean-up.

Since all the conversation continued to be in French, London was able to learn about her captors and observe them closely. Freyja was a beautiful woman, with hair the color of straw and a warm giving face, with broad lips that smiled often; but there was a hint of sadness that never left her blue eyes, especially when gazing at her son. Tall and full figured, she had a commanding presence and looked every bit a Queen. She wore an underdress of soft white fleece and an overdress of royal purple dyed wool with embroidered flowers along the hem of the pleated skirt, and gathered about the waist by a black sash. Goatskin house shoes, rings and gold broaches holding her hair up at the sides completed the ensemble.

Where the Queen was understated elegance and sedate in her conversation, the King was the opposite, a boor monopolizing the table talk about himself and a pig eating his food. His bushy red beard and eyebrows thankfully covered most of his disagreeably flushed red face and beady eyes. New doses of food were added to the deposits of previous meals caked in his whiskers as he slurped his soup noisily, disdaining the use of a spoon. Hair seemed to grow profusely everywhere, from his nose and ears and down his back and arms, but the top of his head had a perfectly round center that remained bald. Magnus was a huge, broad man and strong as a bull ox, taking up one whole side of the dining table and spitting food as he bellowed at his wife and stepson on the other side. He was dressed as flamboyantly as always with scarcely an inch of the richly colored tunic not covered in designs, beads, and jewels. A leather belt and fur-trimmed boots clashed with, rather than complemented, the outfit.

London found her eyes often drifting back to Erik, as he looked completely different from when he had brought her in. Gone were the drab hunting clothes made to blend into the woods, and a bath had removed all the blood from his kills. His golden hair was released from the tie that had held it out of the way, allowing it to fall to the nape of his neck. A square determined jaw, long straight nose, and fearless deep blue eyes gave a regal look to his face, only softened by his mother's same warm smile. Taller than Magnus but not nearly as heavy, he had broad shoulders and a narrow waist, with a lithe muscular build that didn't show the strength it contained. Dressed in a plain, grey wool tunic with a black leather belt and boots, the only things that revealed him of the nobility were his father's ornate sword at his side and a gold broach in the form of the Norse letter A holding his cloak.

The conversation at dinner consisted mostly of Magnus' pompous boasting, but at one point, it shifted to the increasing rumors, passing amongst nobles and believed by the general populace, that their recent human sacrifice had a divine connection by way of the sacred bear. Evidently, after the flames and smoke had died away the next morning, there was not the slightest trace of the offering in the residual ashes. It was as if the bear-marked Tarzan had been completely immolated and then taken up to the gods. Combined with his ability to talk to the sacred animal, as seen by all, the disappearance of the bear while alone with the ape-man lent belief to supernatural forces being at work here. Some fanatics were even comparing it to other religions and waiting for a resurrection to occur.

Magnus could ill afford the loss of the support for Wulfstan, whom he relied on to keep order when the use of bribes, threats and punishment administered by Gorm were not effective. He could state privately here that all religion was poppycock, but in front of the people, a fear of the gods was a useful tool to manipulate them by taking personal credit for good results and blaming the wrath of the deities for poor ones. Erik again brought up the lack of progress in their society because of such tactics and received another dressing down by the King.

Once again, words became heated, and with the dinner over, Erik was forced to take his leave before it became a physical battle. They both knew it would eventually come to that, but Erik was not yet ready to challenge for the crown and Magnus was happy to continue to verbally beat the boy down, building anticipation for the delight he would have when his service axe tasted Erik's blood and permanently ended the royal line. But the mortal combat had to be done in public in the proper Viking way to be right for both the honor of Erik and the vainglory of Magnus.

In a private moment only seen by his mother, Erik told London that he was sorry for her plight and that he would keep working on her behalf. He said he would be by again to check on her well-being and that his mother could be relied upon, too. After he left and the King and Queen retired, London worked into the night cleaning and washing before falling into an exhausted sleep on the bench behind a curtain with the other women thralls.

Each day became a repetition of the previous, rising early to cook the morning meal, make the beds, haul the water and wood, clean the previous day's laundry, work in the garden, and attend to long-term projects like making clothes. Never before had London so missed the conveniences of modern living and appreciated all the unknown workers who toiled to make life easy for others. The King was called away for a problem at the mines the next morning, so the atmosphere was more relaxed and Erik continued to come for dinner, much to the delight of his mother. The other main meal of the day was breakfast, but everyone took a break in the mid-afternoon to have a piece of fruit and cheese and rest a bit.

Erik regularly stopped by each day to spend this break time alone with London, talking while they walked together in the forest. He was fascinated with her tales of the wonders of the outer world, and she eagerly awaited this visit of her only friend to break the monotony of her duties. Erik could listen to her forever because for him it was not just what she said, but how she said it. Her melodious voice was like the first lark in spring, singing in the meadow. For her, there was a price to pay when she got back; Olga and Elle, who were jealous of the attention paid to her, made sure the worst chores were saved for her return. But any backbreaking work was well worth the time spent with Erik because as they discovered the differences in their lives, they also discovered how much they had in common.

Chapter Ten

Final Judgement

The first sensation Tarzan had when consciousness returned was blessed water pouring over his entire body. It was warm water, but his body felt like it was still in the fire, and the swift current carried away the pain. Something was supporting his head out of the torrent or he would have drowned, since his hands and feet were still tightly bound by the ropes. The ape-man decided to enjoy the luxuriant feeling a while before trying to open his painful reddened eyes. His other senses were impaired too, as the smoke had coated his nose and throat, deadening his marvelous ability to smell and leaving a charred taste in his mouth. The water filled his ears so the only sensation left was the feeling of the two hands keeping him buoyed up. Two large hairy hands.

With that realization, Tarzan decided to take a look, knowing that his savior must of had a purpose in taking him from the fire, and, if he wanted him dead, he had only to release his grip and Tarzan, tied and unable to swim, would sink to the bottom and drown. Nothing could have prepared him for the sight of a great, primordial ape looking solicitously back at him in the dim light of the early morning pre-dawn. Tarzan was speechless, and was further astounded when the ape spoke in Mangani and asked where Tarzan was hurting.

The ape-man replied in kind that his main problem was the ropes confining him. To his surprise, the anthropoid carried him to the river edge, gently deposited him on his side, and proceeded to untie the seaman's knots. This took a while as the bonds were wet, complex ties and the Mangani's fingers were huge, but the fact that a primitive ape would attempt to loosen rather than chew through them and could stay concentrated on the task until it was done was beyond the limits of the apes in Tarzan's jungle. Yet he did just that, persevering until Tarzan was free. Then he carefully stretched the hide ropes out to dry on a rock by the river's edge.

Tarzan returned to the water and drank great mouthfuls, cooling his parched throat. He gently washed his eyes, ears, and nose free of the smoky debris embedded there and then carefully removed the soot from the rest of his body, avoiding his back where the skin's surface was scorched. Luckily, the soles of his feet, toughened by years of barefoot contact with rough bark and sharp rocks came away relatively unscathed and once all the blackened stains were gone, Tarzan felt somewhat fit again. When he returned to the shore, the ape motioned him over and, breaking open some aloe vera spikes, spread the cooling gel over Tarzan's back, providing an immediate relief to the seared patches.

After thanking him, the ape-man introduced himself as Tarzan of the Apes since he always considered himself more beast than man and believed that man suffered greatly in the comparison. Without the usual jungle bragging of prowess and kills while strutting around impressively flexing their muscles, the ape simply said that his name was B'yat-zor-hul of the tribe of Zu-yad. An open hand gesture from his heart to Tarzan's accompanied his words, similar to a handshake greeting traded by men. The anthropoid's name translated to Head in Stars and Tarzan wondered if it referred to his extreme height or a tendency to be impractical. The appellation represented a progression toward the given name and surname of modern men rather than the less descriptive single name used by the apes of Tarzan's youth. Now that his vision had cleared, he could see there were many other differences between the African Mangani and this North American cousin.

Of course, Tarzan would not trust his eyes without verification from his most reliable sense of smell, which was gradually coming back after the river cleansing. The ape-man's sensitive nose was still somewhat impaired, saving him from an overpowering stench that seemed to be a combination of wet dog hair, skunk spray, and animal dung. The river had not washed it away, the fetor remaining so noxious that even a civilized man could identify and remember the anthropoid's pungent odor. Tarzan's apes never bathed, avoiding the crocodile infested waters, but maintained cleanliness by sharing grooming, licking the fur and picking the insects off each other in a daily bonding ritual. Their smell was more like the family dog than a farm animal.

B'yat-zor-hul later explained that the effluvium came from a special scent gland so potent that it deterred all others from tracking and hunting them by permeating a large area, making detection of individuals impossible. Except in times of fear or stress, like escaping the burning ordeal, they could control the release of the spray. Since the tribe was mostly vegetarians who also ate eggs and fish, they never had to be wary hunters themselves in procuring food, and no carcasses were left behind to tell where they had travelled. Not fastidious about animal smells, Tarzan supposed the tribe got used to the odor, much like civilized men living near a meat packing plant grew accustomed to the stink or city dwellers became inured to the noise of a nearby railroad.

Although Tarzan was unsure that this ape was representative of the rest of his tribe, there were physical differences in size and stature, too. Standing almost ten feet tall, B'yat-zor-hul would have towered over the African apes, although because he was thinner, his weight was more in line with their usual four hundred pounds. His body was covered in a reddish fur as opposed to a silverback, and there was more exposed skin on his face of a lighter color than the black of Tarzan's apes. The frightful countenance was similar with a pronounced brow ridge and the distinctive crested dome on top of his head but without the sharp fighting fangs extending from the mouth. B'yat-zor-hul had larger golden cat-like eyes and less receding of the forehead, perhaps denoting his obvious intelligence, but his long snout was just as flat as Bolgani the gorilla. Aside from the smell, perhaps the biggest difference was the huge feet that measured twenty inches long and eight inches across and the correspondingly large hands.

The introductions over without the circling and smelling of the lower beasts, Tarzan asked why B'yat-zor-hul had bothered to rescue him. Originally the ape had been searching for his lost brother, Ry-blat, when he had been caught in the pit trap. It turned out that B'yat-zor-hul was returning a favor since Tarzan had unknowingly freed the ape by lowering the tree, thereby allowing him to scamper up undetected and run away. B'yat-zor-hul admitted he had been following Tarzan since he saw him lowered into the crater, feeling guilty for having left the ape-man to the cruelty of the two above, but he explained that at the time, he only saw another Tarmangani, or white man, to be avoided, especially since the trap makers ate some of the Sasquatch they caught and dropped the rest back down into the valley. Later at the Viking village, when Tarzan spoke in the first language of the Mangani to the bear and also helped Ursa to escape, B'yat-zor-hul realized his obligation toward a friend of the forest people, and he became determined to save him from the axe slayers.

Fortunately, the opportunity came when the Norsemen selected a tree close enough to the woods to strip for their stake. This allowed the ape to crawl out on an overhanging limb that sagged just enough under his weight to reach Tarzan and pull him, ropes and all, up off the pole. The sap and sweat provided lubrication and the smoke prevented anyone else seeing from below. After that, it was a simple matter to swing away undetected through the trees with his burden and seek out the restorative river waters to revive the ape-man.

In the midst of the longest and most perceptive conversation Tarzan had ever had with a fellow ape, he was intent on determining how this tribe had achieved such advances. To this end, he questioned B'yat-zor-hul about his origins and history. B'yat-zor-hul turned out to be the Keeper of the Words for his tribe, responsible for remembering the clan's stories, and he was happy to oblige.

Long ago in prehistory, the Sasquatch came across an ice-covered bridge of land from an isolated cold mountain area where their mostly snow-white brothers lived in seclusion, called Yeti by the local natives. Once here, they found a place in the warmer climate and evolved to their present state with a darker reddish coloring predominating, since the apes with lighter colors stood out in the woods and were more easily seen by predators. If Tarzan's own black and grey apes could remember their past, would a similar story of their origins be uncovered, or were they the missing link that gave birth to the rest of the line? Certainly, the resemblance to *Gigantopithecus* was present in all three species. Perhaps only being hunted by degraded, cannibalistic, aboriginal people in Africa, Tarzan's apes had no stimulus to develop higher intelligence and remained closer to the beasts than to the first men. Only recently, Tarzan, with much effort, had taught them to place sentinels to protect themselves when foraging.

Lending credence to that, B'yat-zor-hul went on to say they were close to the Native Americans like the Tali, who drew pictures of Sasquatch on river rocks over fifteen hundred years ago. The apes were revered as forest brothers who had come to watch over the First Nations, protecting them from the rampant bears. The Tali believed them to be a rogue spirit that had been expelled from their tribe and became a shape-shifter who could go from man to animal at will. The name Sasquatch came from another tribe, the Salish, and meant "woodland wild man." Centuries of close relationship with the indigenous peoples helped the apes' intellectual evolution, but eventually the Native Americans left the old ways behind as they became more advanced themselves from association with European invaders, and the Sasquatch, like their brothers overseas, chose a life of solitude away from civilization.

It should be noted that throughout the long conversation between the two, B'yat-zor-hul was well spoken but, limited by the Mangani's language, he resorted to inflections on words, distinctive sounds and gestures to get across more complex ideas. These additions provided a far richer conversation full of imagery and showed a deeper understanding of abstract concepts. Tarzan understood the basic mother tongue as any wild animal would, and his human intelligence allowed him to quickly pick up the variations, and then, ape-like, mimic them back when needed in response. He attributed his knowledge of the first root language for his easy mastery of French and English, but it was a tribute to his linguistic abilities how fast he was able to speak fluently with B'yat-zor-hul.

Somewhat dried in the warm breeze and recuperated enough to want to explore this new country, Tarzan asked B'yat-zor-hul to show him the valley. The ape gathered up the partially dried ropes, wasting nothing, and tied them to a bundle that looked like forest debris in an effort to leave no signs behind. Slinging it all across his back, B'yat-zor-hul leaped up and took to the trees that lined the waterway on both sides. He paused and looked back as if expecting to see Tarzan left behind, but in this it was his turn to be astonished as the ape-man sped by him, flying through the branches with a nimbleness the larger ape could not match. For his part, Tarzan was in heaven, free as the birds above, his lonesomeness banished by his boon companion, swinging through the middle terrace of the trees just like in his childhood paradise.

All day, they just travelled together along the river, reveling in the use of their powerful muscles to master the exhilarating heights in great leaps and bounds. Time had no meaning. First one and then the other would lead, generally wandering except when B'yat-zor-hul would point out something of interest. It was on one of these pauses that Tarzan noticed a well-used game trail crossing the river with a drinking area and mud pit nearby. Feeling hungry for the meat he craved after his days of captivity, Tarzan told his companion he wanted to hunt and dropped down to a limb overhanging the mud wallow, remaining well hidden in the foliage.

B'yat-zor-hul continued down the river until he was lost to sight around a bend. Tarzan was not saddened by the desertion of his friend as most apes are solitary creatures except in mating season. Where there is no time, there is no use in waiting except when stalking a kill, and they would run into each other again or not as fortune dictated. Tarzan was lucky today and his wait was short as a fat two-hundred-fifty-pound boar came first to water and then to roll in the cool mud. The flesh of Horta is best loved by Tarzan, so not a muscle twitched or an eye blinked while he allowed his prey to get in position under the branch.

As far as Tarzan knew, his weapons still lay in the bottom of the pit above the crater, so armed with only his strength and teeth and cunning, he watched Horta play in the mud, rolling and coating itself with the sticky substance until it was half buried in the cool embrace. As expected by Tarzan, when at last the boar was content, it had moved to the deepest spot and was directly below the ape-man's perch.

The curled tusks of Horta are razor sharp and can slash through muscle or rip open a gut, so a mistake here would be instant death since Tarzan would become as immobile as the boar once in the mud. The ape-man waited until the broad hump back was exposed, and, not content to let gravity take him down, launched himself full upon the animal in a fraction of a second. One strong arm circled the head, controlling the tusks, pulling up and exposing the neck, while Tarzan's fighting fangs sought the pig's only soft spot above the jugular to let loose the life's blood.

A boar is a mighty engine of destruction if it is free to bear down and rend with muscles of unmatched quickness, but with its short legs confined by the mud and the ape-man on top, it could not bring much force to bear as it fought to buck Tarzan off. Pressed above the animal's shoulder, his face was protected from the beast's teeth, but neither could get traction as they both rolled in the slop, one straining to break free and the other to hold on. Inexorably, Tarzan twisted the neck trying to break the vertebrae, but with the massive head comprising a full third of the body length, that was not possible for even the ape-man's powerful muscles. The pig's loud squeals were finally cut short as Tarzan's teeth found their mark and ripped out the throat allowing the death throes to begin. As in all fights to the death, in the end it is not only the strength of the combatants but the intelligence of the adversaries and will to survive that determines the outcome.

Tarzan rose, covered in mud from head to toe and, placing his foot on the downed opponent, once more gave voice to the blood-curdling cry announcing to all his supremacy in battle. As he was extricating himself and his prize from the mire, he was taken aback by the sound of laughter behind him. Actually it was more like deep guffaws, and turning, Tarzan found B'yat-zor-hul pointing at him, apparently much amused by the filthy ape-man struggling in the wallow with his slippery burden. Seeing the humor in it, Tarzan gave forth with a rare smile, the only white showing now being his eyes and teeth. Slinging the boar over his back, he trudged to the river to wash, dripping all the way.

B'yat-zor-hul had not abandoned his new friend but merely gone downstream to fish for his own meal, as evidenced by the large trout stuck on a three pronged wooden spear held at his side. Not wanting to scare away the game, he only returned when he recognized the primal scream and knew that Tarzan's hunt was successful. As they came together on the shore, he retrieved from his pack a small flint knife he had used to make the spear and offered it to the ape-man to cut up his kill and while Tarzan sliced away a prime steak, B'yat-zor-hul produced some root vegetables and dried fruit from the same bag.

Unnoticed, the thin veneer of civilization had slipped away from Tarzan, now more beast than a man, as he shared a meal with B'yat-zor-hul, a beast trying to become a man. Neither bothered with a fire, the ape-man preferring his meat warm and red, and the anthropoid just eating the whole fish, head to tail. As they squatted together eating, Tarzan noticed the spear had been fashioned from a six-foot stick split at the end into three sharpened points held slightly apart by a pebble wedged tightly in the middle. Since the spear had served its purpose, B'yat-zor-hul discarded the stone and threw the stick into the woods, leaving no trace of his ever having been there. Tarzan cleaned up in the river after taking food for later and caching the rest for the chance return. Well-satisfied, they lolled back against some trees and Tarzan inquired about the pack B'yat-zor-hul carried.

When unrolled to its full length, it was not a bag, but rather a loosely woven cloak with long strings that could be tied around the neck as a cape or in a number of other configurations useful in holding B'yat-zor-hul's meager possessions lashed to his back. He called it a rem-kut, which loosely translated into "catch-hole," the latter syllable more a noise formed in the base of the throat rather than a word. When the male infant balu leaves the care of his mother, the she-ape makes a small rem-kut for him to carry the rest of his life. Each year, it is enlarged by adding on to the sides and bottom to fit the growing anthropoid and these become events like a birthday celebration although, lacking any sense of time, they occur when needed by growth and not on any certain date.

Each rem-kut is unique, ingeniously sewn with pliable vines, sinew, and hair to hold bits of found fabric, strands of rope, pieces of leather hide, small twigs, leaves, and anything else the owner fancies. The garment has many purposes besides being the Sasquatch's only form of clothing and its use as a carry sack. When warm, it is bedding to lie on, and when cold or rainy, it can serve as a blanket or provide cover. Worn when there is danger of being followed, it is tied loosely so the end drags behind and obliterates all footprints and other signs of passage. After the owner dies, the Sasquatch always retrieve the body and the mantle becomes a funeral shroud to be buried in.

Determined to remain hidden from mankind, no ape bones have ever been found, which is not surprising considering their secretive nature, solitary lifestyle, and obsession with never leaving any trace of their passage behind.

Perhaps the main function is disguise when away from the tribe, because when completely draped over the ape, the rem-kut takes on the appearance of a small tree or bush and blends so perfectly into the surroundings that a hunter could walk within a few paces and never be aware there was a huge beast under-neath. Predators often follow the spray's foul smell thinking they have their quarry trapped, when in reality their prey may be right beside them and well away from the odor, waiting to escape unseen later. The tattered cloak is crudely knit so it is possible to see out, but looking in, the ape's fur appears just like patches of bark.

Scientists just discovered Panda bears and mountain gorillas at the turn of the century so it is not unusual that the large Sasquatch were so elusive. Deer are common everywhere, yet their remains are seldom found in the woods. The rarer Sasquatch prefer the deep forest, physically blending in naturally, having an ape's ability to mimic, and with the rem-kut to conceal them, it is not surprising that sightings are extremely rare. Added to their reclusive temperament, extreme stealthiness for one so big, innate intelligence, and instinctive desire to remain hidden from the outside world, it is no wonder that there is no proof of their existence, yet. Their simple repast done and the day drawing to a close, the ape and the ape-man took to the trees and, finding a comfortable crotch of a tree to settle in, they slept contentedly through the warm night.

Early the next day, Tarzan ate again of Horta while B'yat-zor-hul breakfasted on fruit, and then they swung off to the east until the forest grew thin and they came to a plain of tall grass. Only B'yat-zor-hul's head was visible above and as they walked through, he kept watch and led the way. Tarzan noticed the ape was able to stand erect because he didn't have the huge upper body weight that characterized the African Mangani and he never resorted to using his long arms to amble along quickly on all four feet. At his extreme height, the extended limbs provided needed balance swinging at his side. The large feet and a slightly smaller forward rotated hip joint facilitated a long shuffling stride, not quite a man, but definitely not the lumbering of a gorilla.

About half-way through the maze of grass, they came upon a hollow log with some sticks beside it. B'yat-zor-hul took one of them, pounded on the log once, and then, waiting a moment, hit it twice more rapidly. The booming reverberations would be heard for a long way in all directions but not disclose their location. Soon there was a returning sound that could have been mistaken for an echo but was slightly different in cadence. Satisfied, B'yat-zor-hul led Tarzan on through the labyrinth, eventually stopping and warning the ape-man to stay behind while he went on to announce his arrival. Tarzan understood this precaution as his tribe in Africa would be similarly antagonistic to any sudden entrance of an unfamiliar individual.

Evidently, each member of the tribe used a different sound on the log when returning, allowing the group to know who was coming, so Tarzan heard cordial greetings at first. Then barking and grunting noises rose in volume denoting an argument with more voices joining in until it had a fevered pitch. Tarzan would never retreat through the complex path in the grasses nor could he abandon his friend in a hostile situation, so he strode forward and emerged into a clearing filled with about thirty angry apes. Silence fell upon the assemblage as all looked to the largest male for direction.

This was Zu-yad, who broke away from the crowd around B'yat-zor-hul and strode toward Tarzan. Just under nine feet tall and heavily muscled, he had blackish-colored hair covering his entire five-hundred-pound body and a face more closely resembling his African cousin. The fearsome visage was dominated by a gaping mouth full of fangs under a broad flat nose and then angled sharply up to a bullet-shaped crown with little room for brains. Perhaps this was why the narrow, close-set black eyes bespoke more of cunning than intelligence and had no hint of tolerance. Extending down across the cheek was a scar that pulled his entire countenance to the side, giving him a lopsided look that was accentuated by the big ears that gave him his name. Growling fiercely and reeking like moldy cheese, Zu-yad was as unpleasant to be near as he was to look upon.

Showing no fear, the ape-man advanced also, confronting the towering ape and stopping him in his tracks by announcing in Mangani that he was Tarzan, King of the Apes, Lord of the Jungle, killer of men and beasts alike. Of course, he embellished on this list with details of his victories and prowess in battle, accompanied with appropriate posturing, while staring directly into Zu-yad's eyes transfixing him and the rest of the tribe with the bluster. The ape-man wanted to convince all present that he was more ape than man by using his tribe's jungle invective like a lion uses his roar to paralyze his prey. He ended by making a fist from the chest gesture, similar to the open hand sign B'yat-zor-hul had used but not at all conciliatory. Clearly taken aback, Zu-yad attempted some crowing of his own skills, but he was unpracticed in the fine art of boasting and his efforts fell flat on the crowd. Tarzan baited him further and found that the King was not a pacifist like B'yat-zor-hul and would have attacked him had not the latter ape intervened.

Turning to B'yat-zor-hul, Zu-yad tried to regain the upper hand by accusing him of the treasonous act of bringing a Tarmangani to their hidden camp and divulging tribal secrets. B'yat-zor-hul responded that, as Keeper of the Words, he remembered when they befriended and learned from Native Americans for the betterment of all. After arguing the point back and forth, Zu-yad exercised his authority as King and decreed that Tarzan would have to go under the judgement board to prove his trustworthiness. To save Tarzan from an immediate death dealt by the tribe's bull apes, B'yat-zor-hul reluctantly agreed. Confident he could defend himself in their justice system, Tarzan allowed himself to be led away to a rocky area where he was left unrestrained to await their trial.

Uncertain of his future, Tarzan was nonetheless impressed that he had not been killed outright, as any interloper would have been in his African tribe. By their ability to reason and act as a group, the Sasquatch had leaped forward toward civilization, with B'yat-zor-hul showing some of the finer characteristics like loyalty and kindness but Zu-yad seeming to have learned some of the lesser attributes like jealousy and hate. It remained to be seen which traits would win out under their primitive justice system as the whole tribe gathered to judge Tarzan.

Every ape down to the littlest balu was allowed to speak if they wished. Some were curious about the Tarmangani who spoke in the mother tongue, while others were for strictly enforcing tribal law to maintain secrecy; B'yat-zor-hul was vehement in the ape-man's defense but looked downcast in the end. The discussion carried on until all had their opinions heard and, with a final negative comment, Zu-yad called for the judgement board to vote on Tarzan's fate. Two large Sasquatch carried out a huge oaken door that had to have been previously used on a ship to secure cargo from crashing waves. Measuring six feet square and eight inches thick, it had been cut from a single tree and must have weighed hundreds of pounds.

Zu-yad told Tarzan if he tried to leave, he would be killed, so he could not reveal the clan's location. He would be allowed into the tribe if he passed the trial in which each member placed one rock upon the board as it rested on Tarzan's chest. Rather than the primitive way of the strongest fighting to the death to determine the rules, every ape's vote would be measured by their physical strength and their degree of conviction. Thus the smallest balu with little knowledge or experience was limited by its size to lighter stones, and the older, wiser apes could add more weight to their vote if they wished. This assured fairness in that all had a say, but it allowed leaders greater influence if they felt strongly because each individual could choose the size of his rock to punish or to show mercy.

To Tarzan, the fairness was immaterial because the vote was also the form of execution, but not seeing any lawyers around to voice his side, he laid down on his back and the door was placed on him. Starting with the balus, they brought their stones, tossing them carelessly with a plinking sound, forming a pile on the board. At first, the load was easily bearable and Tarzan could breathe using his arms and knees to create room for his chest, but as the pyramid grew, he began to struggle to draw in some air between each rock after bracing for the added weight.

B'yat-zor-hul came with a tiny pebble in his hand, and some of the younger apes followed his example, but others, at Zu-yad's bidding, carried heavier stone pieces. Tarzan's labored breathing came in fits and stops, the strain showing in the cords of his muscles trying to balance the burden. As the largest apes dropped their metal laden slags on the panel with a thud, a groaning sound came, not from Tarzan who would die before he would cry out, but from the timber itself.

Tarzan realized he had reached his limit, the pressure on him measured by the beads of perspiration on his face. He gathered all his reserves and took a final gasp of air because he could not raise his chest again, so massive was the heap above him. The ape-man knew the only thing stopping him from being crushed to death was that last lungful, expanding his ribs and keeping his own bones from piercing his heart, which was pounding in his ears as the solid oak creaked. And still they came with their stone votes. Tarzan's face was turning blue as his blood poisoned from lack of oxygen. Finally, there was only Zu-yad left. He hefted the largest boulder yet. The king ape knew by waiting he would not even have to cast his rock. The scar contorted his hideous face as he grinned fiendishly.

Chapter Eleven

THE GARDEN OF EDEN

Freyja was fondly remembering Annulf and wondered why such thoughts came to mind as it had been a long time since his loss in the hunting accident. Yesterday, she had found herself humming a little tune from her childhood and spontaneously breaking into a smile over nothing at all. Perhaps it was a reprieve from the oppression cast by the domineering Magnus while he was at the mines that made the whole village more hospitable. Surely the tension was less because with Gorm gone with him, there was no danger of losing a body part to an axe or sword at the leader's whim. Only Wulfstan was left to keep track of things and report any misdeeds for punishment upon their return. But this was more than a shared sense of well-being and came from an inner warmth fueled by reminiscing about happier family times when Erik was a boy and Annulf was King.

She could trace her proud line back to the original explorers who had first braved the North Atlantic seas, noble European stock in conquest of new territories. In 982 AD, Eric the Red had been exiled from Iceland for murder; by decree of the All-Thing, he could be killed on sight by anyone, with the executioner held blameless. Forced to escape to the west, he founded Brattahild, ironically naming the surrounding land Greenland in hopes of attracting more settlers. Blown off course in 1001AD, his son Leif the Lucky, so named for saving his men from a shipwreck, went further into the New World, past rocky Helluland (Baffin Island), and forested Markland (Labrador), to settle on the tip of Newfoundland, establishing L'Anse-aux-Meadows, and opening up the St. Lawrence River to North America. Freyja was directly descended from Leif Ericsson and shared the same name as his sister, so she had subsequently named her son Erik after the original progenitor, Eric the Red.

Because of the animosity between Magnus and Erik, Freyja's time with her son had dwindled, and she realized the recent spate of his visits was responsible for her increased happiness. A mother's joy is exponentially multiplied by the pleasure of, in, with, and through their children, so it was not without a bit of self-interest that she set about to assist Erik's growing fascination with London. To this end, the Queen gathered a small bundle of items from her youth and had Olga prepare a basket of food into which she put some wine and other supplies before his next visit.

When Erik arrived as usual for the midday break, his mother met him outside and gave him directions to an isolated place in the hills that Annulf had discovered years ago, now overgrown at the entrance and hidden from all. When London came out, Freyja gave her the wrapped parcel and Erik the basket and sent them on their way, looking on wistfully as they departed.

On this precious time away from the drudgery of her duties, London was excited by Erik's tales of his family's thrilling history, and he marveled at her stories of modern times. Presently as they walked, he was explaining how they came to be in this valley. The Newfoundland settlement had three longhouses and five small buildings and served as a base for their trade with the "uglies," called skraelings. The indigenous people were descendants of the Thule Eskimos who originally came from lands far past the Northwest Territories, the most notable being the MicMac tribe along the Miramichi River. At first, interactions were peaceful, logging and trading for white butternut walnuts and wild grapes to be made into wine. Later, conflicts developed and by the mid-1400s, with the desertion of Greenland, many of the Vikings in the outlying settlements had been killed or taken into slavery by the natives.

After fighting their way upriver through the MicMacs, Erik's ancestors encountered the Hop tribe, said to be a cannibalistic, one-legged, uniped people. Unable to retreat to the east, they were forced deeper into the wilderness, descending into this valley when it was easier to get down. The steep walls and eventually the thorn barrier protected them from the savages. Leaving the heaviest items like the anchor and chains behind, they dragged their Gokstad ship from a nearby river and used its parts to start the village. At seventy-six feet in length and sixteen abeam, the masts, keel, and strakes provided enough wood for the first longhouse. Everything else came from the abundance around them. Secure and content in their seclusion, there was no reason to ever leave this idyllic society and generations passed.

So engrossed was London in the conversation, she did not notice how far afield they had travelled. Erik usually took London different places in the village on their walks to show her his lifestyle, but this time he had led her past the guard and into the forest. She finally realized they were far beyond the point where she could return in time for her afternoon chores, and when he turned on a scarcely visible overgrown trail leading up a steep incline, she balked at going further, frightened after her recent experiences with men.

Erik was busily clearing some brush from the trail when London raised the objection that she was due to return to the Queen soon. He replied that his mother had given London the day off and didn't expect her back. Not terribly reassured by that answer, London began to draw away and would have dropped her package and run for the safety of her slavery had not Erik looked up from his labors and seen the abject fear in her eyes.

Being without guile himself and sensing the reason for her sudden hesitation, Erik responded with a disarming smile, tilt of his handsome face, and shrug of his broad shoulders while saying, "I give you my promise as a Prince of the realm that your honor is safe with me this day."

London told him then of Bridgestone and Lennie and was further reassured by his genuine understanding and sympathy to her plight. In the end, Erik said that though he could not change the circumstances of their introduction, he was grateful it had brought them together, and he would protect her from any future depredations. After receiving a heartened smile in return, Erik took her hand in hand, and together they advanced up the narrow path.

Steeply rising with switchbacks, the passage required Erik to assist London over some rough terrain by holding her closely on ledges and lifting her up on larger rocks. In climbing, the landscape changed from Balsam fir and birch on the lower slopes to cypress, maple and oak higher up. At points there was no track at all, and Erik led from directions provided by his mother by following the larkspur growing along a small creek bed that wound along with the trail. Finally, they arrived at a level area where it looked like a substantial part of the wall of the crater had broken free en masse and settled above the valley floor but still well below the edge of the rim. Thick vegetation on all sides created a dead end and prevented any, save the birds above, from seeing in or out.

To the left, hanging lianas draped to the ground off an unusual mix of foliage, but when Erik parted them a passage opened up to a pool of crystal clear water fed by a small waterfall from the cliffs above, trickling down the wall musically bubbling and gurgling in a symphony of sounds. The pond was overhung with arching limbs from a diversity of flora allowed by the cool waters from above mingling with the warm thermal springs, and a misty cloud covered the base of the cascade, formed from the steam caused by this same interaction. Red and black berries spotted bushes in the patches of shade; spirea and columbine covered the slopes where the open sky above the still waters let filtered sunlight in. What luminescence got through washed the whole scene in a surreal golden aura much like a painting in a gallery. The sharp, sweet scent of juniper perfumed the air

and the last remaining golden yellow spring pollen fallen from
the evergreens covered everything.

The young pair stood in silent awe of the vista for several
minutes, the first to see its magical beauty since Annulf had
led Freyja here years ago. Then looking at each other, Erik said
it must be the Rainbow Bridge that joins the home of the gods
to the lands of the people in Midgard. London replied that
they were surely in the Garden of Eden. Together they entered,
letting the lianas fall closed behind them like drapes on a portal,
sealing them away from all else that would intrude upon their
paradise.

On a grassy area beside the pond, yet with a huge tree close
enough to lean back against, they deposited their burdens and
rested from the long climb. Presently, with the curiosity inbred
in her gender, London inquired about what was in their packs.
Erik opened the basket and found an abundance of food, ranging
from chicken and vegetables to bread with cheese and honey,
and wine to drink. Plates and silverware and his cloak to sit on
completed everything necessary for the day-end meal. Anxious
to see what her package contained, London was delighted to
find a thin white shift and a yellow pleated over-dress decorated with embroidered bluebirds randomly placed as if flying.
Some leather sandals and a woven blue belt completed the
ensemble. At that instant, she was as pleased with this simple
outfit as with any Parisian couture because also included were
a bar of soap, an antler comb, and a bottle of scented oil.

Leaving Erik to set up the picnic and with an admonition
not to peek, London went around a clump of bushes to a se-
cluded corner of the pond and divested herself of the dirty
slave's clothes that had probably never been washed by its
previous owner. Slipping into the warm waters by the shore she
found the solid rock bottom smooth and moss covered, eroded
over the ages by the cataract's relentless force and without a
hint of soil to muddy the limpid pool. Hers would be the first
as London immediately set to work with the lye soap to remove
over a week's accumulation of filth encrusted in her hair and

on her body from the squalid conditions she had endured in Skinner's cabin and while serving as the kitchen drudge to Olga.

It took three latherings of her skin and four of her hair to get it all out, and when London was done, she had a rosy glow all over imparted by the coarse soap, and shining white tresses which she left splayed out on her shoulders so it would dry. She shook and stripped away the water as best as she could and then rubbed the jasmine oils everywhere before donning the loose shift. Pulling the dress over, London found it to be a perfect fit on her curves but had to cinch it in with the belt on her narrow waist. Lacking any cosmetics, she pinched her cheeks to bring up a spot of red and stepped into her sandals before emerging from behind the bushes.

Erik was busy setting up a board game he had found in the bottom of the basket and didn't hear her approach across the soft grass. His eyes travelled up from London's dainty feet along sculpted legs across a perfectly shaped body and came to rest on an angelic face framed by a milky white halo of hair. He dropped the game piece he was holding, and at the same time, his jaw fell open about the same distance. The transformation was so complete and the difference so amazing that speech was impossible, so Erik merely rose to his feet, bowed and took her hand to assist her to his humble repast. London would not have been happier being seated at the finest restaurant in New York.

Though not down a spiral staircase, London was woman enough to be satisfied with her grand entrance but not advanced enough to know the fascination men take in watching women comb their long hair. As she ran the comb through her flowing locks she was gratified to be appreciated just for herself, in a simple raiment, without civilization's affectations of stylish clothing and slathered with makeup. Norse women had only kohl for the eyes and red stains for the cheeks and lips but largely disdained such except for ceremonial events. Erik was entranced by London's natural beauty alone; the fresh-scrubbed wholesomeness under the intoxicating smell of jasmine and the full, oval face and wide, innocent eyes were prettier without artificial adornment.

The hard climb had made them both hungry, so they enjoyed some hard cheese with the bread and honey, drinking cold water spilling from the cliffs above, saving the wine, chicken and vegetables for later. As they snacked, they played the simple game of merils, which is like checkers, and kennings, a word game that Erik thought could improve their ability to communicate since they were both currently speaking their second language of French. London won at merils, while he did better at his favorite game of hnefatafl, which was played on a board with forty nine holes and had eight pieces defending the King in the center from sixteen circling attackers.

The songbirds and babbling waterfall prompted them to trade personal renditions of their own respectively current, popular songs and dances in the private oasis where only they could laugh at the efforts. Erik's attempt to sing ragtime and dance the reel was amusing but when London tried to imitate a skald she looked more like a jester. Eric explained she needed more growling like howling dogs, and it should sound like a heavily laden cart rolling down a rocky hill. When London countered that he needed to loosen up and get more swing, it led to some gyrations of his hips that dropped her to the ground from the force of her laughter. For the first time, Erik observed a fetching lilt as London walked and wondered why he never noticed it before. London began to see Erik as a fellow teenager, awkward at times and regal at others.

For their dinner, Erik put the chicken and vegetables in the basket and lowered it into the hottest part of the springs where the thermal currents bubbled up directly. London fetched the wine from under the waterfall where it had cooled all day, and within minutes, a hot meal was ready to share. They both picked berries for dessert and lounged on the blanket feeding them to each other, enjoying the gloaming as the dusk shadows fell long. Sometimes it is the little things that count when together; they delighted in the discovery that he liked the small, tart ones while she preferred the big, soft, sweet ones. When a drop of juice from a ripe blueberry fell on the corner of her lips, he tenderly extended his finger, deftly cleaned it up, and then licked it off. Everything seemed to stand still in that perfect instant when the balance between day and night also hovered between friendship and affection, and then evening descends, and you can't go back to the bright clarity of the sunshine.

Erik awkwardly left the possibilities untouched by suggesting they clean up and be on their way while there was still enough light to see. After every trace of their incursion had been removed, and their paradise was once more pristine London, not wanting the day to end, suggested a quick swim to cool off before the trek back. Erik welcomed a chance to try the warm pond, stripped down to his breeches and dove in. London carefully folded her dress and climbed the waterfall in her shift. Taking a seat on the smooth, moss-covered waterway, she threw her arms up and rapidly slid down the natural chute, laughing like a child until she hit the bottom with a huge splash. Awakened to the new game, Erik quickly followed her lead, and soon they were both taking turns until the excitement and colder water left them giddy and shivering.

Erik wanted one last trip, so London swam to the shallow side of the pool where the warm updrafts heated it to a bath-like temperature. Ducking under to take off the chill, when she broke the surface again, she was lightly covered by the floating yellow flecks of pollen that, unnoticed by her, caught the newly risen full moon and sent its beams scattering in a glittering array across the water. Erik emerged from the mist at the bottom of the falls and threw his golden hair back like a lion's mane and strode forward to join her.

Her alabaster skin glowed like moonlit snow, and she looked like such an angel she should have had wings. In the magic of the lagoon, Erik cast a figure like the gods from his legends. As they came toward each other in the shallows, they glanced down at their reflections in the still surface, not yet sure enough to trust the truth, but when they raised their eyes to gaze together, all doubts were gone. Erik bent down, bringing his lips nearer to hers, and London arched upward, closing the space with love's first kiss. In this perfect moment, it became the tender caress of pure love, with the fresh drops of water on their lips tasting like the morning dew from a rose petal.

Erik broke to remind London, "M'lady I promised to guard your honor this day." London's eyes betrayed a hint of mischief when she replied, "M'lord, it is now night." Smiling, he covered her face with his kisses.

Later Erik made a torch to lead them back and gave London his cloak against the cool night air. When they arrived, all were asleep so after a parting kiss, Erik went on to the men's quarters, while London, not wanting the magic to end, waved yearningly before turning to enter the King's lodge.

Promptly on the next day's noon break, Erik was at the door calling for London, but when he entered, he found that Magnus had returned and she was gone. Hoping she was on an errand but fearing the worst, Erik asked as to her whereabouts. Magnus retorted that his pretty little thrall had run off that morning, considering herself too good to do the assigned chores of a slave. Seeking confirmation of this, he looked to Olga and Elle, but they became suddenly interested in their work and stared away. Turning to his mother, he saw that she was marked by a fresh bruise on her left cheek, and she shook her head as if to say this was not the right time.

Drawing himself up and placing a hand on his sword Erik glared at Magnus and said, "I go to find her and then I am coming for you."

Chapter Twelve

BETRAYAL AT THE DUM DUM

Moments before unconsciousness took him, Tarzan
decided to risk all in a desperate gamble. Was not
his daily life a constant throw of the dice every time
he cast himself into the deadly struggle to determine the survival of the fittest? From infancy, the ape-man was either the
predator or the prey, nourishment for oneself or sustenance for
another, and only the strongest and most intelligent lived to
walk the next day. Over territory, tribal dominance or a mate,
blood was routinely spilled, but even a trivial item like a log full
of succulent grubs could initiate a dance to the death among
these high strung primordial apes. So without a thought, Tarzan
allowed the massive weight on the board to crush down on his
heart and begin to squeeze his life away when he used his last
lungful of air to malign the towering Zu-yad by hurling vicious
taunts about his origins and manhood.

"Pastar dango por kalu ungo, pamba lot, bu lano blat!" hissed
Tarzan.

His victory was already assured by doing nothing, but Zu-yad
could not let the aspersion on his ancestry and masculinity
stand unanswered and taint his supremacy over the puny Tarmangani. Already worked into a fever pitch by the tribe around
him and straining under the huge stone he held aloft, the
temperamental King was instantly provoked to throw his boulder
on the pile and in his madness also jump on himself. A tremendous cracking sound ensued, though not of Tarzan's ribs,
but rather, the judgement board itself split lengthways allowing

the rocks to cascade to the sides carrying Zu-yad into the rubble and leaving Tarzan unscathed in the middle.

Still in a frenzy and covered with dirt, Zu-yad would have pounced on the gasping Tarzan before he recovered and finished him off had not B'yat-zor-hul intervened and, in a rare show of aggression for him, shoved the heavier King back into the dirt. Assuming a protective stance over the ape-man, B'yat-zor-hul, as Keeper of the Words, cried out that Tarzan had passed the judgement board and was now a member of the tribe and due protection from all. When Zu-yad would have continued his attack, other Sasquatch held him back while B'yat-zor-hul shamed him for breaking the rules and the judgement board itself by jumping on.

Once resolved, the Sasquatch dispersed as quickly as they had gathered, for such is the way of the apes to focus on one task at a time and when diverted, they quickly forgot the past and never worried about the future, existing only in the present. A possible exception to this was Zu-yad, who glowered at Tarzan and his benefactor for some time thereafter because while an ape's memory is not as long as that of Tantor the elephant, a grudge must always be repaid. Any king's throne is never secure, requiring constant defense, and this episode was a pain in Zu-yad's royal seat.

B'yat-zor-hul came to Tarzan's aid as soon as the danger from the other bull apes had passed, but found him already sitting and breathing normally for such is the amazing recuperative powers of the ape-man. Aside from some scrapes from the board and falling rocks, Tarzan was none the worse for wear and evinced a desire to see around the camp of his new, hard won home. This was a step back in time for him, like his simple childhood amongst the apes of Kerchak, and still wary from his treatment by civilization and the rejection of the one he loved, Tarzan was happy to be back with his "people".

The encampment of the Hohotan, or tribe, was along a bend in a creek that provided water and fish on one side and, on the opposite side, the tall grasses through which Tarzan had initially entered. Trees interspersed throughout, some producing fruit and nuts, but most were mainly for shady cover and a quick escape route if necessary since all their belongings could be carried away in a personal rem-kut. Grass had been cleared in a broad common area and made into matted pallets used as beds. Small paths in the remaining tall grass interconnected between trampled sections, which were sized to fit the number of Sasquatch in each Hotan or family, making a warren of individual rooms open to the occasional tree above but providing some privacy and protection.

Divisions marking territory and giving directions were bounded by stick-stacks, several branches leaning in upon the base of a tree or freestanding like a teepee; these also were used to announce one's presence by hitting them together before entering. Unlike the itinerant African apes who moved with their solo foraging, the Sasquatch sent out large bull ape hunters each day to bring food back while the she-apes tended to the young in the camp, establishing this as a semi-permanent dwelling place. Simple rules governed interactions in their daily lives to settle differences, protect the group, and establish tribal customs much as an organized society that worked together for the betterment of all.

As B'yat-zor-hul led Tarzan among his tribe, some of the Sasquatch came to see the new member, with most touching and feeling in curiosity, and while a few growled in disapproval, none smelled him like an ape would. When asked about it, B'yat-zor-hul explained that with their ability to produce an overpowering scent, they had little need of using odors that were dependent on the vagaries of the wind to identify individuals like the lower animals. Instead, by clicking their tongue against the roof of their mouth, they made a low, repetitious sound that their extremely acute hearing used to discern surroundings by listening to the echoes. From the pattern and angle of the reverberations, the qualities of size, consistency, direction and movement were perceived with an uncanny ability to recognize variations among living things and inanimate objects. Zu-yad boasted his hearing was so sharp with his big ears that he could hear the clouds moving above the wind.

This adaptation intrigued Tarzan; he later enlisted B'yat-zor-hul to teach him the fundamentals and found that the separation of the ears on the head did enable returning sounds to be heard individually and interpreted in depth, much like a stereoscope allowed pictures to be seen dimensionally. Already possessing keen hearing, Tarzan was a quick study, but when he tried to return the favor by explaining how the two nostrils could be used to a similar effect, B'yat-zor-hul found his years of avoiding detection through the use of his foul odor had dulled his ability to smell to worse than that of a human's. The Sasquatch was so impressed with the ape-man, though, that he asked Tarzan if he could smell fish underwater. Giving a rare laugh, Tarzan replied, "fish, like visitors, only began to smell after three days."

After so much time away from the apes in his jungle home and feeling lost and alone in civilization, Tarzan was enjoying this camaraderie with the more intellectual, but still emotionally simple, Sasquatch. Except for Zu-yad, they had gone from screaming for his death under the judgement board to forgive and forget, and in time, they would come to accept their new member. On his own most of his life, the ape-man picked his friends carefully and, though he was happy to be part of the tribe, he knew that staying in the camp would be like living in a crowded city. Too, his love of the hunt and desire for fresh meat was best indulged away from the vegetarian tribe. One bold she-ape in particular made eyes at them from afar, and when Tarzan noticed the unusual behavior, B'yat-zor-hul pulled him aside. He quickly explained that Koho-lul was best to be avoided because she was considered the property of Zu-yad, and her mother, Litu-lus, let any other apes know it. However, the warning was in vain as the forward Koho-lul came directly to them.

As B'yat-zor-hul made introductions, Tarzan beheld a young female Sasquatch in her prime of life, strong-limbed and well-shaped, and covered with a glossy light red fur. Prominent on her face beneath a broad nose was a wide mouth that turned up insincerely at the corners, and equally large, round, brown, doe eyes with long lashes that rendered the normally well-spoken B'yat-zor-hul tripping over his words like a balu. As Koho-lul teased the tall Sasquatch, her mother hurried over and soon ended the conversation by letting B'yat-zor-hul know the young she-ape was not for him, and then gave Tarzan a piece of her mind for embarrassing Koho-lul's future mate, Zu-yad. As Litu-lus led her daughter away, one had a glowering scowl while the other turned back with a fetching smile.

Tarzan felt his friend's discomfiture and suggested they take to the trees and enjoy the freedom of two young males on the hunt. Before leaving, Tarzan gathered grasses to make a long rope, his first and favorite weapon; later he could replace his spear and bow and arrows as he came across the proper materials. They were almost constant companions thereafter, traveling far and wide, finding easy hunting and fishing and safe sleeping on crossing branches in the trees. Tarzan pleated his rope when they camped. Where comfortable trees were not available for sleep, B'yat-zor-hul showed Tarzan how to make an arboreal nest by bending three saplings together to create a platform at the junction. They communicated with the tribe, and each other when apart, by whacking on hollow logs.

They were a good pair, with the taciturn Tarzan finding the loquacious B'yat-zor-hul so eager to speak of the tribe's traditions, that, in the following days, he had the finished rope wrapped around his body and was well-versed in the Sasquatch religion before they returned. Lacking any formal religious training as a youth, Tarzan had decided that in the beauty of the world, from the flowers to the sunset, in the natural order determined by the life and death competitions of the jungle, and even in the good actions of loyal companions, God's presence was made known, and here the ape-man discovered common ground with the Sasquatch.

The duties of B'yat-zor-hul included religious leader as well as historian, although a better term for it might be moral compass because he was totally unlike the savage witch doctors of Africa and their more respected counterparts in civilization, who both barter a pathway to heaven, in that he was only responsible to fairly discern the right of matters and not to judge his fellows. Man's dominion over animals was always in God's plan because the lower orders were not aware of His hand in the wonders of nature, but man has left this same simple beauty behind as he glorifies the Divine with imposing places of worship and complicated rituals. The peaceful Sasquatch are unique in being able to appreciate the majesty around them, but not civilized enough to fight wars over it.

Based on Native American culture, their religion embodied all living things with a spirit that can be good or evil depending on how it is nourished, which is remarkably similar to man's 'do unto others as you would have them do unto you' principle. While they retained some primitive mystical beliefs like that of the Thunderbird beating his wings to make thunder, flashing his eyes for lightning, and shedding tears to fall as rain, they also embraced the tree as a symbol of life's cycles, from spring's budding rebirth, through summer's prodigious growth, to fall's slow decline and into winter's long death. Annual rings in the trunk marked the passing years of each individual and the leaves did not compete for the sun but worked together by arranging themselves to share the rays equally with all. The tribe's sacred totem pole was considered the tree of life.

With this simple symbolism encouraging a peaceful coexistence, the Sasquatch never embraced the human blood sacrifices practiced in primitive cultures and still represented in modern religions by the sharing of bread and wine. While they do not have one Supreme Being or many small gods to be feared or worshipped, they come together on the full moon in the Dum Dum and dance the kordo around the totem pole to celebrate the living, mourn the dead, and elevate the spirits of all. Reclusive tribes meet to rejoice in what they have in common, providing a release of energy that could otherwise have been turned into war. Even without the pagan African sacrifice, the drums speak so deeply into each heart that none could say that the beasts that walk like men do not have a soul.

On the day that would turn into a night with a full moon, the same moon that would witness Erik and London's commitment to each other, the tribe of Zu-yad headed to the sacred place in the densest grove in the forest. From near and far, all the large bands and smaller clans would be joining them during the day when peaceful interaction was possible and staying through the night in their ancient Dum Dum. This shared time allowed trading of goods and, as natural tensions eased, some courting for mates took place. She-apes frequently went willingly home with a different tribe, thus preventing inbreeding by providing diversity to the lineage. The males demonstrated feats of strength, performed acts of dexterity, and staged mock battles to gain acceptance of a female and once secured, a primal force reasserted itself as they dragged their struggling new mate away. Aggression was not allowed at the Dum Dum, and no one was ever harmed in this primitive charade.

It was late afternoon when Tarzan and B'yat-zor-hul arrived in the central clearing surrounded by trees so dense the only way through was by the arboreal route. His sudden appearance by dropping out of the trees gave a start to the assembly, and were it not for his companion, he would have again been beset by a crowd of angry anthropoids. Fortunately, tales of the Tarmangani's triumph under the judgement board had previously circulated and most were ready to accept him with the widely respected B'yat-zor-hul at his side. An array of food was available, consisting of fruit and nuts, eggs and fish and some grains formed into a hard loaf which was mostly tasteless and almost inedible. Not yet able to ferment alcohol, the apes would rely on the drums to fuel the night's revelry. As B'yat-zor-hul tended to his duties, reciting stories in preparation for the Dum Dum ceremony, Tarzan drifted off amongst the other young bulls.

At first, Tarzan was excluded from the pompous display of courage and outright bragging that young males display anywhere there are females to impress. But after he bested two apes at one time with some civilized wrestling throws, a group gathered around him eager to learn the moves. Soon, even some of the truculent older bulls began to welcome Tarzan, impressed by his prowess, and the fact that he discretely stayed well away from the she-apes. The ape-man immensely enjoyed the contests too, so similar to those of his tribe in Africa but with a sense of camaraderie never possible there.

As the day grew late, many of the apes retired to depressions under shady boughs to sleep and await the coming of night, while others sought places of prominence according to the degree of their participation in the ceremony. The Dum Dum of Tarzan's youth celebrated an important victory for the tribe, usually a battle that had resulted in a new King, elimination of a despised jungle predator, or the vanquishing of an encroaching enemy group. Doubtless this bloody sacrificial ritual had been passed down from the earliest dawn of time when the first pre-men learned to assemble for warmth around a fire and subsequently formed a basis for all manners of ceremony practiced today, only differing in the savage intensity of our shaggy ancestors versus the refined sophistication of today's well-coiffed gentry engaging in a social function. Both gather in a special place, for a rite of passage, augmented by ample victuals, with an excess of spirits in modern times sometimes allowing those same nobles to surpass the wild ferocity of the pre-men from the distant past.

Likely the only man to ever observe the Dum Dum and live to tell about it, Tarzan found the milieu much the same as in Africa. A heavy undergrowth in the thick forest surrounded a natural declivity on all sides leading to a central depression where an earthen drum was formed by a hollow log partly buried in the soil. But here, in the exact center of the grassy clearing, stood a three-foot-thick stake made from a single tree over twelve feet high and carved with totems depicting all manner of flowers, trees, fish, birds, animals, apes, and even men, the only criterion seeming to be that each was a living entity. The only exception was at the top, which was shaped into a ball that had been dusted with some common white chalk that B'yat-zor-hul had brought with him, giving it the appearance of a full moon. If there were ever any other colors on the pole, they were long since gone as it showed signs of great antiquity, but nowhere was there the tell-tale dark brown stains signifying past use as a sacrificial tether. None present could recall how it came to be here, but to the apes, the circling totems leading up to the moon on the pole represented all living things in their ascent to the stars and heavens above, with the moon's soft benevolent rays watching over the whole living world.

In the crater, the transition from day to night was early and swift once the sun passed beyond the edge of the rim, and tonight Goro the moon was rising early in the twilight. Before, the quiet had only been disrupted by the cracking of some hoary old jungle giant sending a dead limb crashing to earth or the cawing of crows and the melody of songbirds; now, the great apes began to assemble with grunts and other rude sounds. Soon, all the females and young squatted in an outer ring, while the adult males formed a similar circle just inside, and once again, quiet settled over the clearing with even the birds ceasing their chittering, perhaps sensing the solemnity of the occasion.

Three old females carrying heavy sticks with knobs on the ends took up a position along the earthen drum and began a slow, steady beat, the first strike louder and then followed by three softer ones, with all equally spaced. This progenitor of modern quarter note rhythm became the name of the dance as the log amplified and projected the sound through the forest: Dum-dum-dum-dum. As Goro rose and its light played across the sward, the speed and loudness increased, mesmerizing all within and filling those without with dread. The uninvited knew that the pounding signified the strength of the united community of great apes and so slunk away, none wanting to risk the madness that descends upon those participating in the primordial scene. The drumming increased to a frantic pace though still in the same basic beat, and the volume rose to pierce even the farthest reaches of the woods: DUM-Dum-Dum-Dum! At its peak, Zu-yad leaped from his place in the circle into the center, and facing a full Goro now over the totem pole moon, he threw back his head and voiced the victory cry of the bull ape while beating on his chest with both fists. Two more times, he howled into the darkness lest any mistake who was King of the Apes here.

Then Zu-yad began a dance around the inside of the circle and as he passed, other huge males rose and, after bellowing their own yells, joined behind him in the kordo, each trying to surpass the one before in ferocity. Soon, all the great apes were on their feet moving in a continuous circle inside the females, with Tarzan also taking his place in the line, leaping as high as the tallest Sasquatch while adding his cries to the cacophony. In the bright moonlight, his supple body danced gracefully while his smooth skin glistened with sweat in stark contrast to the ungainly hairy beasts around him. Any sense of order was lost as the tireless vibrations of the incessant pounding and continuous screaming of the frenzied bulls combined in a wild din that had the females up now.

For a half hour, the feverish pitch continued to build, leaving all the Sasquatch with crazed eyes and saliva dripping from their shrieking mouths. Following a sign from Zu-yad, as the mated males passed their partners, they joined together in the primitive gyrations, suggestive and provocative in nature. Once they were paired off, the single bulls began to pull females of their choice from the crowd, beginning a courtship dance that was as old as time itself. Huge males would jump from the circle, roar horribly, and confront their intended in the attempt to capture them. The she-apes would dance away and allow themselves to be caught many times again before they permitted the male they desired to claim them. Instead of a violent, bloody end as in Africa, this Dum Dum revered life in all its forms.

Realizing he had no place in this and feeling again his loss of Jane, Tarzan slipped off to the side, content to watch the proceedings and reminisce about his first Dum Dum with the apes in the tribe of Kerchak. The males presented themselves before all the females many times with only Koho-lul receiving no interest. Assured she would be there for him in the end, Zu-yad danced before many others, enjoying his power, for as King, he could have his choice. Being taken for granted would not do for the lovely Koho-lul, who shared the need of "women" everywhere to be fought for and won. As the comeliest she-ape in the tribe, her vanity demanded attention, so she turned on all her feminine charms in a kordo to the next male in line before her. Most males would be smart enough to beware the danger there, but unfortunately for him, it was the already smitten B'yat-zor-hul who, in the charged atmosphere, thrilled by her selection of him, leaped in front of her to realize his dream. He lost all sense of time and place and his infatuation truly had his head in the stars as she danced encouragingly.

Just ahead in the circle Zu-yad happened to turn away from his current prospect and catch a glimpse of this affront to his pride. He was in an equally intoxicated mood, but his passion turned in an instant from love to abject hatred when he immediately launched himself across the space to land on B'yat-zor-hul's back and drive him into the ground. Not giving him a chance to rise, Zu-yad commenced to flail and tear at the flesh of his surprised and helpless adversary until B'yat-zor-hul was quickly rendered unconscious. Then Zu-yad arose, looming over B'yat-zor-hul, and kicked the prostrate ape over onto his back to expose his vulnerable jugular and the drumming suddenly ceased at this breach in the ceremony. Standing astride the mutilated and defenseless body, Zu-yad reared back his head while baring his fighting fangs, and voiced a frightful call as he prepared to make the fatal bite.

When the drumming stopped, all present stood paralyzed, looking at the violent spectacle about to unfold. Only Tarzan had the presence of mind and ability to instantly react to save his friend. From far across the clearing, it was an almost impossible cast to any other than the ape-man, but without hesitation, he had his new rope sailing through the air to settle neatly around the throat of Zu-yad and, with a tug, choke off the challenging cry. As the King grasped futilely at the unfamiliar noose shutting down his air, Tarzan pulled him off his feet and commenced to drag him, sliding across the grass on his back, away from his intended victim. Before Zu-yad could upright himself, the ape-man was upon him and, with several deft loops of the line around his feet and hands, had the King as securely hog-tied as any cowboy dropping a calf in the rodeo.

Though he roared loudly and threatened profusely, Zu-yad could not move and no one moved to help him. Tarzan stood above him, and with the authority of one who had twice bested the King, announced the Dum Dum was now over, resulting in the tribe beginning to disperse through the trees. The situation well in hand, Tarzan went to B'yat-zor-hul and enlisted some others to help carry him home and tend to his wounds. The ape-man was the last to leave the natural amphitheater except for Zu-yad, who finally stopped bellowing when he realized he was alone and helpless and could attract a hungry predator.

After a painstakingly slow trip to the camp, while checking on his friend's care, Tarzan was assured that B'yat-zor-hul would survive, though it would take some days; then, the ape-man swung back through the trees, intent on releasing the King and recovering his rope, the latter being his primary concern. Re-entering the clearing, he was assailed by the overpowering stench of the Sasquatch's defensive odor, evidently released by the King in fear of attack in his helpless position, which had the additional effect of rendering the ape-man's acute sense of smell useless. By now, the moon was passed the rim and again the crater was in darkness, so Tarzan did not notice that Zu-yad was gone and his rope was severed and laying in pieces until he got closer to the center of the amphitheater. Assuming the ape had gnawed himself free, Tarzan was disappointed in the loss of his weapon, but as he turned to leave, he was surprised to see men bearing arms closing in on all sides, cornering him without a path to the trees. As they drew nearer, he saw drawn swords, axes, and spears bristling everywhere, led by Magnus and Gorm.

Chapter Thirteen

REVOLT AT THE MINE

A common misconception abounds that diamonds were made from coal compressed deep in the earth, whereas the truth is that almost all were formed eons ago, long before plants even existed to make coal. The primary source was from other common carbon-bearing rocks, such as imestone or dolomite already in the core, that were placed under tremendous heat and pressure when the planet formed. Volcanic forces brought the diamonds to the surface from the center of the earth in vertical shafts that have been exposed over time from natural forces like erosion and earthquakes. Coal on the planet's surface had little chance of being carried deep enough to form diamonds unless it was subjected to colossal astronomic forces, like in a comet or asteroid strike from outer space. Indeed, these heavenly bodies could also be a source of gems created in the energy of their own formation or in interstellar collisions before arriving here.

In this crater, all these circumstances had come together to provide the perfect setting for diamonds. Originally formed from some massive hit when the solar system teemed with debris, the resultant depression fell further from still active geologic and volcanic forces, making a fertile caldera and capturing the wealth from the heavens. Warm thermal springs bubbled upward and cold northern rain and glacial melt flowed downward, causing fracture and erosion of the surrounding rocks, forming natural tunnels and caves like a maze in the crater walls and exposing veins laden with raw diamond ore.

Initially, the underground passageways gave the Vikings entry into the safety and abundance of the valley but now the shafts were being mined to satisfy the greed of a few.

Tarzan remained silent, and realizing there was no help to be had by calling out and that any resistance would mean instant death, he allowed himself to be bound, ironically with pieces of his own grass rope, which he had made well and had been proven strong enough to hold a full-grown Sasquatch. Having previous experience with these seafarers, he didn't strain testing the complex nautical knots, knowing full well that escape was once again impossible. Surrounded by the guard, he was led to the far side of the amphitheater, away from where the apes had come in, to a place where, by sliding sideways for twenty feet, a man could enter the forest unseen, heading laterally until he reached a small path extending into the forest. After the trail meandered quite a ways through the dense grove, it eventually opened up into farmland and connected to the main road to the Viking village. Once they were clear of the ape's territory and unafraid of detection, Magnus could not resist the chance to gloat over Tarzan's recapture.

"We come at the sounds of the drums to collect an ape selected by their leader, to work in the mines and replace the ones that escape or are lost in accidents," said the Jarl in explaining his presence to the bewildered Tarzan. "Our surprise at finding the big one all trussed up for us must equal your own in finding us here," he continued. "We had to let him go so the supply could continue and were just about to leave when you showed up, so it looks like we won't go home empty-handed after all. The arrangement works out well for both sides, as we continually get free labor and they don't have to worry we will hunt them."

"You were lucky the big monkey missed you on his way out because he had blood vengeance in his eyes. Even though Gorm would have liked to cut you to pieces, I have a use for you in the mines to direct the workers since you can talk to these beasts. Though a few French explorers over the centuries discovered the tunnel down into the valley and may have taken some gemstones out, Skinner found the diamonds and stayed to set up the mining and refining, but we have been limited by the number of ape workers. With your help, we could finally communicate beyond physical threats to their leader and get more laborers to expand the operation," offered Magnus, who had been dazzled by the Cajun's tales of the luxuries in the modern world that this wealth could buy and planned on leaving with him.

The sullen Tarzan shook his head in what Red Beard thought was a denial, and while it was that too, it was also in disbelief that Zu-yad would willingly betray his people by allowing them to be taken into slavery. It was an easy way to get rid of challengers to the throne, but selling out the tribe was the worst possible treachery, because in primitive societies where they have so little, the reliance upon each other is the unifying factor that defines the difference between single animals and community. Without trust, a descent into barbarism is assured in even the most advanced civilizations. Truly Zu-yad had now reached a level of deceit well beyond his animal nature and approaching that of the distinctly human ability to kill their own kind.

The moon had set and the road was dark when they stopped by the village on the way to the mine. Not able to enlist the ape-man in his nefarious plans, Magnus sent Gorm on with the prisoner to avoid letting the people see Tarzan returned from the dead and adding credence to the rumors of his supernatural abilities. Red Beard headed to his lodge, wanting his bed and his wife after being away, but when he heard voices by his front door, thinking quickly, he pulled up short behind the edge of the house. Unobserved, he witnessed the tender exchange between Erik and London and watched him back away after a final kiss, and her, lingering and following him a few steps, waving until Erik entered the men's lodge and was lost to her sight. As London slowly turned to the Jarl's abode, Magnus noiselessly snuck up behind her and swept her into his power-

ful arms with a strong hand over her mouth to silence any
possible outcry. It was but a matter of moments to catch up to
Gorm and after some instructions, add her to his prisoners on
the way to the mine.

To be allowed such magnificent happiness for just one day
and then to be again thrust into such extreme despair, London
did not bother to look at the hulking shadows of the men around
her in the gloominess of the night, and did not realize that one
was a fellow captive, tied and recently gagged to prevent any
trouble so near the village. Roughly dragged along by Gorm,
she trudged to the crater wall a mile away, in darkness and in
quiet, hopelessly resigned to her fate. The bonds on Tarzan
denied him any communication with her but even in the ten-
ebrous night, his sharp eyesight perceived that London was
once again a prisoner with him.

Just within the entrance to the mine, the party split, with
Gorm hustling London, still unaware that Tarzan was alive, up
a smaller tunnel to the right. The rest of the men, after lighting
pitch torches, took the ape-man deeper into the mine, always
descending a long twisting shaft with many branches until they
reached a padlocked and crosshatched iron door securely built
into the rock walls. It took two men to pull the heavy metal
portal open as it squealed on its rusty hinges. Still without a
word, they pushed Tarzan headfirst into the murkiness and
slammed the door shut behind him; the last sound Tarzan heard
was the snap of the lock and retreating steps of his jailors as
they took all the torches away and left him in utter blackness
and silence deep within the bowels of the earth.

Though there was no sight or sound, Tarzan immediately
knew he was not alone when he was assailed by the overpowering musty odor of the Sasquatch around him. There was a
rustling sound as the apes began to stir awake at this unexpected interruption of their monotonous lives in slavery. Fortunately for the ape-man, their poor sense of smell prevented
them from noticing his different Tarmangani scent which would
have provoked an attack in the darkness if the simple apes

assumed they had one of their captors in their power. As it was, when Tarzan spoke in the language of the Mangani and assured them he was a friend, they believed he was just another unknown ape doomed to share their servitude. As the Sasquatch settled back, Tarzan found a spot against the wall and promptly fell asleep on the cold, hard floor in order to be properly rested when the opportunity for escape should come again, for such was his faith in himself that there was no wasted time in worry over that which cannot be changed.

There is no morning in the blackness of a cave, but eventually the guards returned and brought a meager breakfast of bread and water with a piece of fruit. A riot almost ensued when the light from the torches revealed the nature of their fellow prisoner to the five Sasquatch, but Tarzan was able to diffuse the situation by again speaking in the first language and invoking the name of B'yat-zor-hul as a friend. That brought an immediate end to the hostilities when the largest ape and apparent leader gave the hand from heart greeting and introduced himself as Ry-blat, the lost brother of B'yat-zor-hul. There was little time for conversation then, but when the prisoners were divided into two work groups, hunched over in the narrow mine shafts, the two stayed close together when they were led down a side tunnel with another older ape to work at a diamond site under the watch of a single guard.

They were each given a short, heavy sledgehammer to crack the diamond-bearing ore from the walls and then further smash it to loosen the valuable stones from the slag. The rich pieces were placed in a barrel to be carried away by the older ape and further refined outside. Not hard work for a strong man or bull ape and their echolocation talents served them well in the dark mine, but the loss of freedom and confinement quickly broke their wild spirit and led to a resignation of their fate. Tarzan was able to see the whole picture now since he knew the gems were sent up the cable to Skinner and Lennie when they sent the recaptured apes back down. The ape-man surmised that besides the rarely escaped ape, only the two above, Magnus,

Gorm and possibly Wulfstan would know the path to the surface, and he guessed they planned to leave the few other henchmen and Sasquatch dead when they had enough riches to rejoin civilization.

Simple repetitive labor, easily accomplished by the powerful apes, allowed Ry-blat to query Tarzan about B'yat-zor-hul and news of the tribe. The big Sasquatch proved to be the polar opposite of his brother, quick to anger and prone to fight rather than pursue an argument with reason and thoughtful logic, and Tarzan could see why Zu-yad had betrayed this potential rival into slavery. Ry-blat had a nose frequently broken in past quarrels that flared widely with piercing eyes under furrowed brows when angered, like the scar from Terkoz on Tarzan's forehead that blazed red under similar circumstances, and when he heard of the King Ape's latest transgressions, Ry-blat was primed to escape to seek revenge for his brother.

Even before the Norsemen had brought light to see by, Tarzan had examined the iron bars and metal lock that were a barrier to freedom and tested them with his mighty thews and found them too massive to yield to even his great strength. Traveling to and from the work tunnel, the guards were alert and ready with lowered pikes to prod the apes, so the best opportunity to escape seemed to be when the monotonous daily toil also infected their watchman, leaning on his spear to stay upright, his only fight being against boredom in the effort to stay awake in the dim torchlight.

At the end of the day, Tarzan and his fellow apes were again restrained behind the prison door and, after a bland meal of vegetables mixed with some grains washed down with warm water, the torch was extinguished and the guards left. Like any wild beast, the ape-man was loathe to be re-locked in a cell, so he and Ry-blat immediately tried to enlist the others in a plan to escape on the morrow. Only one young bull showed any enthusiasm and joined them to plan; the other three seemed too cowed to help. Lack of knowledge of the tunnels and an inability to coordinate timing left much to chance so it was decided that, since the ape was on the upper work party, he would wait until Tarzan and Ry-blat broke loose from below and freed him on the way up.

Early the next day, they were able to hatch their scheme right under the guard's nose by speaking in Mangani while working. The older ape would not help, accustomed to his bondage and in fear of the Vikings' sharp weapons, so Tarzan picked up the barrel the next time it was full and feigned to trip, thereby spilling the contents on the guard. Ry-blat used the distraction to seize the guard and cave in the man's skull with his sledge, but unfortunately, the single torch was knocked from the wall in the struggle by the falling pike and the flame guttered in the dust before extinguishing itself. The old ape would not move in the utter darkness, so they were forced to leave him behind with the dead body. Now they were committed to escape because if they were caught, their punishment would surely be death. Tarzan led, holding the spear, and Ry-blat followed, more comfortable with his hammer than the guard's sword.

Totally blind, Tarzan placed a hand on both walls alternately to keep him in the center of the wider main passage and avoid missing a turn, and slowly ascended, knowing that the way out was up since the path on the way in had constantly sloped down. He cautioned Ry-blat to remain silent lest his clicking alert the other guards. Ruling out the smaller side tunnels that descended or were narrow and had less headroom, and by following the slightly fresher air flow and the scent of the other work party, the ape-man eventually was rewarded by a faint glimmer of light around the next turn.

Again warning Ry-blat to follow quietly, Tarzan closed one eye to preserve his night vision because if this torch should also go out, he would have the advantage of several seconds of night vision in that eye while the guard floundered. The ape-man extended his head just enough for his opened eye to see this guard, alert and forty feet away at the entrance to a side tunnel, but the main passage was too narrow to chance a throw of the spear. Withdrawing, he gathered some pebbles from the floor, and when he tossed them out in the darkness, he was rewarded to hear the Viking coming to investigate but dismayed when he stopped well short of the fugitive's hiding place.

Risking all on a desperate attack, Tarzan leaped around the corner and confronted the startled guard, who was holding the torch in one hand and his pike in the other. As the ape-man charged, the Viking threw his spear, which bounced harmlessly off the wall while he desperately attempted to draw his sword, dropping the torch in the process, and plunging them both into darkness. Tarzan closed his light-blinded eye and opened the other and was still able to see in the shadows, enabling him to reach the struggling guard and finish the battle with one thrust of his spear through the Norseman's chest.

Ry-blat caught up just as the other three Sasquatch were stumbling out of their mine shaft, and with Tarzan, they explained how now that there were few guards left, escape was possible. Despite vigorous urging, only the one young ape joined them, so great was the fear of these older apes, their spirit broken after weeks in the dark mine. As they continued to advance slowly up the dark tunnel, a muted light from the entrance filtered down, allowing them easier progress, but still they moved warily hoping to slip by the remaining Vikings.

The plan was for the two apes to elude their captors and make it to the forest, where travel through the trees assured they would make it back to the tribe. Tarzan's task was much more daunting as he would attempt to rescue London, find the passage to the surface and leave the valley. If either party was seen, it would provide a distraction for the other. So at the entrance, no words were necessary as Tarzan split off to the left and the two Sasquatch slunk toward the light.

Tarzan's path continued upward, giving strength to his supposition that the way out of the crater lay in that direction, and the low tunnel was lit with occasional torches wedged in crevasses in the wall. Soon, he came upon three openings on the right side that debouched into rooms that had been dug out of the rock and contained the beds and extra clothing of the guards.

Luckily the first two were empty, but the ape-man smelled trouble in the third when he caught the scent of Gorm and London together. Silent and sinuous as Hista the snake, Tarzan pressed against the wall and slid into the final opening, raising his pike for a deadly throw, the occupants totally unaware of his presence.

The ape-man would have cast his spear except that Gorm stood just behind London in the sparsely furnished room and the risk to her was too great. Just then, shouts of rage and screams of pain arose from the outside and the two within looked up and espied Tarzan at the same time. To London, the sight of an apparent ghost left her stunned and speechless, but Gorm reacted instantly, whipping out his sword and placing the razor sharp edge against her soft white neck.

"Drop the spear and back out of here, monkey man, or she dies," Gorm threatened as he advanced, pushing London in front of himself.

Tarzan did as he was told, descending backwards almost to the entrance when his way was blocked from behind by the two remaining guards who had just entered, forcing Ry-blat ahead of their extended pikes. Looking past them, Tarzan could see the other ape and the last guard lying dead outside.

"So it's you again causing trouble," Gorm said to Ry-blat, who didn't understand a word, and then to Tarzan he added, "I knew I should have killed you in the forest." Finally, to his men he ordered, "Tie these two up and load the dead bodies on the ore wagon, no point in Magnus coming here again, when bribery and threats didn't work the last time."

Tarzan relayed what was said to Ry-blat and after the bodies had been retrieved, the remaining apes locked up under the supervision of one guard, and London taken back in the cave with the other guard, the anthropoid and the ape-man were tied to the front of the cart and, with Gorm prodding them along, they pulled it to the village.

A crowd gathered following the strange procession in, many of the farmers having never seen a Sasquatch up close before and others mystified about the reappearance of Tarzan after they had watched him burned at the stake as the harvest sacrifice when last there. Surely many came for explanations, but like mobs of spectators anywhere, from the days of the gladiators in the Roman Colosseum to the modern prizefight, they were expectant of seeing some bloody torture and punishment to vicariously enliven their mundane lives.

Once in the town center, Gorm put the prisoners, still bound, in the two cages, displayed the dead Vikings on the ground in front of them, and awaited the Jarl to rule on their fates. Wulfstan arrived first and was stirring up the assemblage like a Shaker in a southern congregation, so by the time Magnus arrived, the thirst for retribution was running rampant through the masses. Gorm privately apprised his King about what had happened at the mine during a heated discussion with a clearly disappointed and angry Magnus. Next, Wulfstan broke from his rabble-rousing and conferred quickly aside with his Jarl before Red Beard, resplendently dressed and enjoying the big stage again, addressed the throng.

"There are those among you that thought this man supernatural with the power to speak to the animals and come back from the dead. You see in front of you the evidence that he is no better than an animal himself, joining with this beast to wantonly kill your brothers. Let us rely on the greater power of our mage to determine their guilt."

After the Jarl introduced the seer, he stood behind Tarzan as Wulfstan began to circle the two helplessly tied and caged captives, darting in and out, touching them through the bars with long boney fingers covered with rings, all the while waving his rune-covered knife, making designs in the air while blathering nonsense in a rising and falling voice. In a few minutes, he reached a crescendo and stopped in front of Ry-blat, striking a pose with one hand extended pointing at the Sasquatch, and the other weaving the knife in mesmerizing gyrations above his head, drawing everyone's attention for the culmination of the spectacle. Suddenly, Wulfstan lurched forward and slammed the palm of his bare hand flat against the chest of the ape, who immediately began to shake as with the ague; and as the mage moved his hand in a circle, Ry-blat fell to his knees twitching spasmodically. Within minutes, he was lying still on the floor of the cage, dead at Wulfstan's feet. The seer had killed the giant ape with only the mystical touch of the gods; the knife, constantly pointing to the sky, seemed to be the conduit for this magical force from above.

Tarzan saw everything from the side and even though he was bound, he moved to help his friend the instant the mage touched Ry-blat, but Magnus cracked him sharply on the back of his head with the hammer side of his axe, bringing the ape-man down. Then the Jarl stepped forth to address the superstitious and now fever-pitched mob again.

"The great god Odin has spoken through our seer. Death to the killer beast! By my royal decree, the man shall meet the same fate in the Viking Gauntlet!"

Chapter Fourteen

THE KIDNAP OF MADAME

Surrounded and alone in the dangers of the woods left little hope that London would be found or return on her own, but not knowing what had happened made it worse. A perpetual, heavy, sense of doom pervaded the camp leaving Madame feeling like her heart was wrapped in barbed wire, piercing it with every beat, and making it hard to breathe from the pain. Mr. Fitch's heartache also grew every day as he watched Madame decline but his hope never died. The fear that this will go on forever caused a vicious cycle of praying for the best but dreading the worst, but at least they had each other.

Mr. Fitch still ventured forth to search every day, ever expanding the area until he fared quite deeply into the forest, but it was mainly done now to fulfill a man's need to try and fix things, and to feel useful, because he couldn't stand to just sit in the tent with Madame and wait. His expertise in the woods did not improve, blundering noisily and getting lost himself more often than not, but it kept his mind busy and spirits up which was needed each evening when his lack of success saw Madame sink a little deeper into depression through the long nights. To bolster her then, Mr. Fitch taught her a symbol he used with his school children; when putting your hands together for prayer at bedtime first touch just the ends of the eight fingertips together and hold them up in the light of the full moon and you will see three diamond stars shining through, representing the Divine Trinity watching over everyone, and to remind you of the blessings of faith, hope, and charity.

Morning was better, when the new day brought renewed hopes, and, as Mr. Fitch prepared all their meals, he used this time to try and draw her out of her melancholy. He would not leave until he got a smile from Madame with tales of a newly discovered trail or signs of a campfire by a source of fresh water that surely must mean he was close now. These white lies ensured that Madame would still be here when he returned and not surrender to an easy way out. Catastrophe can bring out great strength in some and selfish weakness in others. It remains to be seen as to how these trials would affect Madame and Mr. Fitch.

Happy events can easily bind people together, like the shared joy of a vacation or participating in a wedding party, and be remembered fondly for years later in photographs of the times. Tragedy can also forge an everlasting bond that will either tear a couple asunder irrevocably like a divorce following the loss of a child, the pain seen constantly in each other's eyes never allowing any healing to take place; or, if the child is found unharmed, it can unite them forever, because after having weathered the worst disaster, only smiles are possible every time they are together thereafter.

The fall weather remained fair and warm for the time and summer still held sway as the days passed. The beauty of the forest, with its autumn colors, scent of maple and pine in the air, and sounds of squirrels at work getting ready for winter, was lost on Madame, as she could only see the woods as the evil place that took her child. So she brooded in the tent, while Mr. Fitch camped outside between her and the woods, keeping a fire at night for warmth and protection. The hand axe that was never far from Mr. Fitch served to procure the firewood and was their only weapon.

Mr. Fitch replenished their water supply every day from the clean creeks he passed on his searches and he was able to forage occasionally for some nuts the squirrels left behind, but that was the extent of his hunting skills. Native edible plants and tubers were unknown to him, and such lowly fare as insects and caterpillars too distasteful. All men become hunters when they get hungry enough, but in a forest with small game to be trapped, fish in the streams, nuts in the trees, and eggs in the nests, he could easily starve to death.

Enough food for a week had been left for London, along with the tent and cot Madame was using, and some blankets, candles, matches, toiletries, cooking and serving utensils and other items useful for camping. The problem Mr. Fitch faced was that, with their impulsive exit from the train, nothing extra was added, and the supplies designed for one person were now being consumed by two. He was astute enough to realize this early on, and by scrimping on his own needs, and with Madame's malaise causing her a loss of appetite, he had managed to stretch their larder well past a week, but as the days wore on, the end was in sight. Reluctantly Mr. Fitch broached the subject with Madame when they grew near to their last meal, hoping she would agree to try to stop the next train and go to enlist the services of a properly equipped search party. As the trains ran infrequently and at odd times, even this might be difficult to manage.

Madame took the news stoically before entering her tent for the night, but Mr. Fitch could see that the last straw had fallen as the final remaining light of hope drained from her eyes. She seemed better in the morning, sharing their final meager fare as if a great burden had been lifted and her determination was back; encouraged, Mr. Fitch set about gathering wood for a great fire to put near the tracks, in the chance the smoke and flames would bring someone to investigate. When he returned from the forest with the last bundle, he called to her to watch the lighting, and when Madame did not come, he entered the tent, only to find it empty.

Lennie waited by the precipice and watched the Vikings below take London away. To the man-child, she was both an object of lust and the first playmate he had ever had. Lennie's mind was sluggish, and he was even slower to act unless directed, but powerful emotions he had never felt before raged inside him and would eventually come out in the violence of an adult or the tantrums of a youngster. The only person around for him to focus those malevolent thoughts on was Skinner, the cause of his loss.

Skinner only returned when the signal from below announced that the reward was attached to the line. As the Cajun never thought of anyone but himself, he was totally unaware of the changes in Lennie and wouldn't have understood them or cared if he did, and certainly he wasn't about to help anyone nurse a broken heart. As Skinner pulled up the line and gathered in the large bag of rocks, he told Lennie to set the big pot over the fire and bring some water to a boil while he got the caustic solutions needed to refine the glistening kimberlite stones.

The apes were useful to do the hard work of mining and crushing the ore, and the Vikings had always known how to separate the valuable metals by panning the dirty tailings away with water and leaving the heavier gold and silver behind. So Skinner let them keep the tiny bits of precious metal and the tons of slag but kept the refining process to himself, so all the diamonds ended up with him. Lennie moved slowly to comply and glared at Skinner as he went by. The Cajun didn't notice a thing, so engrossed was he in the fine quality of the latest haul from this exceptionally rich mine.

Over the next couple of days, he would balance the heat and pressure and watch carefully as the mixtures dissolved away the remaining waste and left the hard diamonds behind. Timing, temperature and concentrations were critical in cleaning the stones without damaging them, and rotating between the aqua regia, water baths, and other caustic chemicals needed his constant attention.

Skinner was so busy he did not notice Lennie brooding all day, the giant having little to do other than lift the heavy pots and keep the fire fed. Finally, the stones were in the last water soak to cool until morning; the two retired to the cabin for some jerked meat, and Skinner opened a bottle of whiskey to celebrate.

"This be the richest batch so far. Soon, we be gone from this pit and livin' high in Montreal or Toronto. We eat steak, then sleep in feather beds, and I can gamble while you have fun with the painted ladies, eh?" dreamed Skinner aloud.

"I want white hair girl who tells stories," answered a down-cast Lennie.

"We go to Montreal, get nice blonde Frenchy girl, and you forget all about her," said the Cajun, at last seeing the reason for Lennie's despondence.

"Not have soft skin and nice talk," continued Lennie.

Skinner never had any intentions of taking Magnus with him and Lennie was a liability best left behind once he had served his purpose; the Cajun was too callous to realize the depth of Lennie's feelings and too self-centered to care even if it was in his own benefit to string the big man along.

"You want soft skin, I skin her next time I go down and bring her hide back for you, we use it to cover door and you see her every time you go in and out, what you think about that?" sneered Skinner, clearly at the end of his limited patience.

Those were the last words of the night, as Lennie did not reply, but his eyes narrowed and the putrid air in the cabin was charged with tension from then on as something changed between the two men at that point. The giant was slow to reason, but the idea that he might go his own way without Skinner was taking root, and in time, it might bring action if he was continually pushed.

At the end of the process, they set up the greasing table and, for a time, things were back to normal because Lennie enjoyed this final stage. Based on the fact that newly excavated diamonds will not hold water but will stick to grease, a table is covered with petroleum jelly and the slurry is spread across it and slowly washed down while vibrating. Lennie provided the motion and lifted the heavy table so the water would run off, carrying away the debris while leaving even the smallest diamonds remaining stuck in the grease. A final soak in boiling water removed the oil and produced uncut diamonds sparkling in the sun.

This work served to keep them busy for a few days, and they occasionally had to hunt and check the traps to find food, so several more days passed in boredom with Lennie sulking and Skinner on edge with a surplus of nervous energy as he contemplated the wealth in his growing pile of diamonds. At first, the system had worked well, providing regular shipments of raw stones, but lately, the bags had become more sporadic, which could only mean trouble in the crater. On Skinner's last visit down, Magnus had been at the mine dealing with a recalcitrant ape, and the Viking complained about the monkey man making problems in the village and escaping to places unknown.

How much was enough? While presently there was not enough to split, there was plenty for a normal man, but like many men consumed with greed, Skinner was hesitant to end it until he had milked every last stone that he could from the mine because there would be no coming back. He planned on collapsing the tunnel with some sticks of dynamite already in place in a narrow passage, preventing pursuit by trapping the Vikings below and then killing Lennie on the way out. So while the answer to the question for the avaricious Cajun was always "not enough," he realized all good things must eventually end and the important thing was to get out alive before the problems in the crater became his problems too. Partly to get away from the morose Lennie and partly to try to secure one more big score, Skinner resumed his habit of waylaying human targets outside the safety of the thorn enclosure.

Ever since he entered the wilderness of Canada, he had taken advantage of any lone hikers, campers, fishermen, or prospectors he came across, killing them and using the spoils to finance his venture in the crater. The Cajun allowed vigilant heavily armed hunters to pass unmolested, but occasionally they would see him creeping through the woods and, with the increasing number of disappearances in the locality, they began to rightly attribute the problem to him. Since no bodies were ever found, rumor had it that he ate the lost victims, but in reality, it was because he meticulously buried all traces of his crimes, although since the Cajun had no problem with dining on Sasquatch meat, some of their bones may have fueled the tales. Due to his small stature and practice of crouching low while slinking through the forest, the hunters called him the Dog Man, and as his reputation spread, Skinner's usual weak quarry stayed away from the area.

That was why Skinner was forced to try to derail the train as his source of prey dried up; it was an attempt to create a disaster full of easy pickings, enough to assure the continuation of the diamond mine and possibly be the last big score he so badly wanted before he cleared out. With that thought in mind, the Cajun roamed back toward the railroad again, sure that enough time had now passed for it to be safe, to see if it might be worthwhile to undertake another larger train wreck.

The moon had been full some days past, but it still shed enough waning light to see by when Skinner arrived at the railroad. He knew these woods even in the darkness - which caves could be used as shelter versus those that contained a sleeping bear, the shortest paths when in a hurry, the trails that led to food and water, and where the wolf pack laired. As he approached the tracks, he noticed the trampled undergrowth as if a herd of buffalo had wandered through, so he hunched down, drew his knife, and stayed behind cover in a slow advance until he could observe, unseen, a single tent with a campfire alongside.

Skinner's caution proved necessary, as a man was tending the fire and watching the surrounding area, awake and alert even though the hour was late. The Cajun watched the scene for a while, but not knowing if the man was armed or who else might be in the tent, he decided to withdraw to the forest for the remainder of the night and return in the morning when the camp activity would give him a better idea of who and what this was.

In the light of day, Skinner spied on a tall, thin man and a fine-featured woman at breakfast, chatting about getting on the next train that stopped like they were sitting outside a

Parisian cafe waiting for the *Gare de Lyon* to open. The unexpected and bizarre nature of the situation gave the Cajun pause, but he saw no guns and the lone couple were dressed in fine clothes, though somewhat bedraggled from camping. A perfect set-up for robbery or ransom but still Skinner waited, as he mistrusted things too good to be true, having lived long during his life of crime by the dictum that while the early bird gets the worm, the second mouse gets the cheese.

After their short meal, the woman retired to the tent while the man made repeated trips to the forest, gathering and chopping wood with a hand axe that appeared to be their only means of defense. Skinner was just about to use one of the man's forays to sneak in and abduct the woman when she emerged from the tent and walked purposefully into the woods. Unable to believe his good luck, the Cajun quietly followed, expecting her to stop at any moment, but she seemed determined and hurried further away from the man who happened to be getting wood from the other side of the tracks at the time.

Once they were far enough away that there was no chance of the man hearing or coming to rescue her, Skinner closed in on his prey. She appeared winded from the unaccustomed exercise and was slowing down to catch her breath when he broke from his cover and said, "What's yer story, why the train leave you behind?"

Madame almost swooned from the shock of finding another human being, and so weak was she from lack of food and the whole ordeal that it never occurred to her that he had stalked her. She had entered the forest with the single purpose of finding London or dying in the attempt, not telling Mr. Fitch her plans so he could not dissuade her. As this motivation was uppermost in her thoughts, she overlooked his disreputable appearance and blurted out, "My daughter, she is lost. Have you seen her?"

"Might be that I have. Follow me," answered Skinner, and with a wave of his hand he turned and headed deeper into the woods. Madame looked around at the forbidding emptiness surrounding her, realized because of her impulsiveness she was totally lost, and, desperately needing to have some hope no matter how slim the thread might be, followed meekly to her doom. She tried to engage Skinner in conversation with a barrage of questions about London, but he largely remained silent.

Skinner knew instantly that London had to be the girl that Lennie had previously abducted, and, now that he had revealed himself to her, there was no way he could let this woman get away to inform the authorities. The only reason he did not let her die in the forest or, more assuredly, kill her on the spot was that the well-dressed man left back at the station could be a source of ransom, a last big payment on his way out, or he could always drop her in the crater in exchange for the next bag of raw diamond ore.

Not having Lennie to carry her, the Cajun kept up this pied piper charade all day, enticing her with occasional bits of information about how London looked or what she wore so that Madame fairly rushed along to keep up with him, sure that her daughter was just around the next bend in the trail. She even followed through the tunnel under the thorn barrier, convinced that the briars were what had kept London from returning, and entered the filthy shack anticipating a sweet reunion. The anticipation had built to such a level that when Madame saw that the repugnant Lennie was the only occupant in the reeking squalor, she collapsed in a faint of total despair.

When Madame awakened and found herself chained to the same ring in the dirt that had held London, she screamed and cried endlessly and would have done herself in had there been a means to accomplish it. The men gave her no details, seldom speaking to her, but as time wore on she realized her fate would be the same as her daughter's and that no one would ever find her. Mr. Fitch had been kind and faithful but the schoolteacher had no further obligation and would surely pursue his plan to leave and send a search party back, which would be too late if they came at all. Why hadn't she followed the prudent man's advice in the beginning?

It was easy to lose track of how many days passed when the only measure was the sun and the moon, but having Madame there added to the strain that Skinner and Lennie both felt since London had been pushed into the crater. Her constant moaning and sobbing and endless questions disrupted the usual quiet that had existed previously between one who chose not to talk and one who wasn't smart enough to talk. The men each took the opportunity to leave when the other was on guard duty, only staying together at night, sleeping fitfully with Madame's commotion.

Being around Madame was disconcerting for Lennie, not from any sense of guilt but rather because it kept him thinking about London and in his mind, the loss of his girlfriend, so he spent his time hunting and checking the traps. Where he might have eventually forgotten the girl, now he was forced to constantly hear about her, thereby intensifying his desire to possess her again. Lennie had been with Skinner on some of his treks down the dangerous tunnel to the valley floor, but the tight places petrified the giant, and he had never made it all the way to the bottom. Even so, his lust was overcoming his fears and he finally settled on the idea of making the arduous trip by himself to see if he could find London.

Skinner went back to the railroad a couple of times in an effort to meet with the well-dressed man but was disappointed to find him gone and with him any possible ransom payment. Madame confirmed that Mr. Fitch was but an employee and had wanted to leave from the beginning, but the knowledge of the fact that he had actually done so was devastating to her. His last chance for a big score lost, the Cajun decided that he would exchange the woman for a final bag of gemstones and then leave everything and everyone else behind as he made his escape.

Chapter Fifteen

The Viking Gauntlet

Madame would probably die from the fall if thrown from the cliff by Skinner for want of ransom money. Mr. Fitch had abandoned her plight and Lennie was the most dangerous when off in his own private fantasy. The situation was as grim in the crater, with Zu-yad's ongoing betrayal of his tribe and Ry-blat killed by Wulfstan while his brother, E'yat-zor-hul, lay beaten in the Sasquatch camp. Further travails awaited London, still held prisoner in the mine, while Erik searched endlessly in the valley, having left the village the day before Magnus had sentenced Tarzan to the gauntlet.

Tarzan was only briefly stunned by the blow from Magnus' axe and found he remained bound and in the cage when he awoke. He observed his surroundings with seemingly casual indifference while actually training all his faculties on the festive preparations for the gauntlet in search of any advantage he could exploit to escape. Luckily, the gauntlet was to be run in the broad town commons area right in front of his locked cell, and he could concentrate on the intended placement of each participant and their weapon of choice.

The ape-man ignored the party atmosphere with the free-flowing ale and feasting turning the crowd into a bloodthirsty mob, showing off their skills with pikes, hammers, swords, axes, and even a mace. Each hoped to be chosen to be in the select line of twelve and then vie to be the one honored later after delivering the killing blow. While these might be friends and neighbors tomorrow, today they were a murderous throng. Most were farmers, and while they had never seen battle in the peaceful valley, they were nonetheless large powerful men who retained a Norse pride in war-craft, practiced regularly with their favorite tools of warfare, and were very capable of execution in the name of the law.

The Viking heritage ran deep in all these Norsemen, so this was not a throng of rabble rousers on the edges urging on a few principal fighters in hopes of some carnage. Much like the Sasquatch and their judgement board, this was a form of justice, equally primitive and cruel, but to them a fair test in which the accused were set free if they emerged alive from between the killing lines. No one could remember anyone on trial ever successfully running the gauntlet and gaining their freedom, but the fact that there was a chance it could happen made this an honorable method of enforcing the law to these brutally simple men.

Tarzan watched closely as his would-be death squad poked and prodded, thrust and thrashed, slashed and slit, and generally flailed at each other working themselves up into a physical frenzy to match their current mental state. Wulfstan kept agitating the crowd, and the women present showered oohs and aahs on their favorites, encouraging more feats of bravado while they kept a steady stream of food and wine available to fuel the men. Magnus and Gorm stood apart because, as judges of the event, they would select the other nine men to join themselves and the mage in the two columns. Red Beard's local supply of loyal men was dwindling with the loss of three in the mine fight and the necessity of the two remaining guards staying behind, so they were also watching the best fighting men in the search for new recruits.

One in particular showed promise with the mace. Ulf the Giant was a huge bear of a man almost as wide as he was tall, his body covered with so much thick bristly black hair that his eyebrows seemed to flow up over his head and across his back while his mustache and full beard did the same down his powerful chest and arms. The oaf was as stupid as he was big, but even in his current drunken condition, he was able to swing that spiked ball with awesome force in wide lethal arcs on the end of a heavy chain. Magnus had already decided the first in each row would be Gorm and Ulf to try for a quick kill, while he and Wulfstan would anchor the opposite ends to ensure Tarzan died if he made it that far.

The course was set up straight in front of the cage so when the door was opened, there was only one way for the prisoner to go, with the crowd completely encircling the arena and leaving only a small opening at the far end. Two barrier rows, about nine feet apart, were formed when the selected Vikings established their places in the lineup by placing their shields in front of themselves in a groove dug in the earth that was designed to hold them upright. The six Norsemen on each side were evenly spaced every four feet and had to stay behind their respective shields, making a killing zone almost forty feet long with a deadly overlap in the center because of their combined reach across space. The weapons were randomly dispersed according to each man's choice and looked like this:

Axe (Magnus)	Knife (Wulfstan)
Pike	Sword
Sword	Axe
Axe	Pike
Hammer	Axe
Sword (Gorm)	Mace (Ulf)

Tarzan

Tarzan intently took in all the preparations, paying special attention to each man's position, weapon, and reach, coming to the conclusion that there was no way to escape this trial without being slaughtered, as the Vikings began to cheer for the victim's release while banging their weapons on their shields to further excite the crowd. The unarmed, almost naked ape-man realized he would need more than his mighty strength here and that this task was one of quickness and cunning using strategy and tactics to make his foes use their superior power against themselves if he was to have any hope at all.

An onlooker reached in the cage and cut the cords from his wrists. At least they were going to let him have his bare hands to defend himself although there was no doubt as to the outcome as Magnus, breaking the rules, moved out from behind his shield to stand at the far end of the path and blocked the exit, tapping his simple unadorned axe in time with the chanting mob, the rib splitter's blade gleaming in the sunlight. Next, the cage was unlocked, as the shouting from the assemblage rose to a frenzied pitch calling for the ape-man to make his futile dash. If they expected the fearful mad rush of a rabbit flushed from his warren and dodging deadly blows, they were to be disappointed because Tarzan strode out with his arms crossed across his chest and with a level gaze scanned the field one last time, his noble mien silencing them like a lion before jackals. The ape-man's sleek muscles rippled under his sun-bronzed skin much like a thoroughbred racehorse at the starting gate.

Only for a moment did he wait thus before he burst into action, taking advantage of the quiet from their temporary indecision, and so quick it was done that none present had time to react. Indeed, merely recounting the path he took through that tortuous maze of slashing blades and chopping axes cannot do justice to the speed of his attack because the reading of it takes so much more time.

First, a feint to the right drew the giant Ulf into swinging his mace in a high arcing blow intended to crush the ape-man's skull into his body, but by the time it arrived, Tarzan was no longer there, having dived in a roll toward Gorm, and the spiked ball bit deeply into the ground. Gorm delayed in unleashing his own stroke because of the deception, and by the time he did, it was too late to correct the slash downward, and it sailed above the balled-up Tarzan, who uncoiled at his feet grabbing the shield with a hand on each side as he rose and thrust it upward into Gorm's face, the reinforced edge leaving a red ruin f his nose with blood spurting everywhere like a fountain while driving the man backwards.

In the same motion, while still on the left side, Tarzan twirled to his right, catching the next man's hammer on the edge of the shield and using his own force against him, pulled the hammer up and out of his descending hand. Not stopping there, the ape-man finished his turn, and, concentrating all the energy of his spin into the now-leveled shield, spun it like a saucer across the field to catch the opposite second man in his throat, so surprised was he by the unusual missile that he was unable to raise his axe to defend himself as he dropped like a rock in place.

Scarcely had he thrown the shield and Tarzan was leaping after it toward the pikeman on the right, who responded by leaning out and thrusting to impale the onrushing ape-man. In response, Tarzan twisted and dove, sliding on the grass flat on his back right up to him, presenting an easy target. But the spear fell short and the eager smile was wiped from the man's face because Ulf, who had struggled to pull his mace free from the sod, was finally successful, and seeing a chance at a second shot at the crossing Tarzan, swung a massive blow that safely passed over the prone ape-man and took off the pikeman's head, while the axe man between them frantically clutched at his throat, making his last gasps through a broken neck while he turned blue in the face.

The pike would have landed harmlessly on Tarzan's chest where he could have used it to defend himself, but with seven adversaries left, he caught it out of the air as he jumped to his feet and re-crossed the gauntlet, engaging both the axe and sword men next in line. As their weapons slashed downward simultaneously in murderous cuts, the bent low ape-man turned the metal pike sideways and held it with both hands in the middle and bracing himself, caught both blades on the long pole and with a deft movement of his hands to each side, shed the ax off the end to his left while the sword slid off to his right. Their powerful strokes dissipated, Tarzan dropped the pike and sprung upright, grasping them alongside their heads before they could react, he cracked their skulls together so hard it left them laying on the ground looking up at the sky through vacant eyes. But Tarzan did not even see them fall, since he had already picked up the pike again and launched it across the arena as the two were wobbling behind him on shaky knees.

It flew true, but not as would be expected, at the next axeman on the right side who was crouched behind his shield; instead it struck the fifth man in that line, piercing the shoulder of his sword arm, and as the blade fell out of nerveless fingers, the last swordsman tottered back into Wulfstan. Tarzan then made what appeared to be a fatal mistake when he stood still as if indecisive, with his back turned to the axe man rising from behind his shield, and kept his eyes on the final pikeman on the left side close in front of him. As the Viking gathered himself for a fatal jab, the ape-man focused intently on his eyes, and at the moment the pupils dilated, Tarzan quickly twisted sideways and leaned backwards causing the point to slide along his stomach leaving a thin red line oozing from a shallow wound. Call it luck or some sixth sense, which many believe is the sum of all our other senses, but precisely as if planned, the axe from the right side spun end over end just above the extended pike, narrowly missing the ape-man before burying itself in the pike man's chest. The axe man, furious at missing his chance to slay Tarzan, had thrown it at the perfect target, the broad exposed back of the ape-man, but whether it was due to the fates or Tarzan's uncanny abilities, no one could tell, for by the time it arrived, the mark was not there, but all present were later sure it represented further evidence of Tarzan's preternatural powers.

Wulfstan had seen enough when the Viking next to him toppled over on him, smearing him with blood, and he broke from the line to take refuge behind his Jarl. Magnus was weaving his axe in figure eights before himself, eager for his opportunity to finally kill the elusive ape-man. The King sneered at the cowardice of his mage and then, with a Viking yell, charged at Tarzan intent on a massive, sideways, disemboweling stroke.

Tarzan picked up the second pike, the tip wet with his own blood, and voicing his own challenge of the bull ape, he raced to do battle, carrying it pointed straight at the Norseman's chest.

No Olympic track and field star could do what happened next, so precise was the timing and magnificent the balance. Instantly gaining the speed of a gazelle, Tarzan stuck the tip of his spear in the ground right at the feet of Magnus as they closed together, timing his jump perfectly to when the axe would be fully extended toward him and holding the pike on the end, hurdled up above the Jarl. The pole was not long enough to vault him completely over, so Tarzan used the flat top of the passing blade as his first step and then planted his toes in Red Beard's face as his second to accomplish the maneuver, causing the Jarl's axe to dig into the dirt when he reached to cover his blinded eyes. Not done yet, Tarzan used his momentum and height to clear the space behind to where Wulfstan was turned away and cowering, and landing squarely on his back with both feet, pushed the Mage face first into the dirt, knocking the wind out of him, and jarring the rune-covered knife free.

The whole town was in shock at what had just happened and they stood in silent awe as Tarzan picked up the knife, scampered to the nearest edge of the beckoning forest, and disappeared from sight up into the trees. Then, all bedlam broke loose. The babbling of a hundred voices all at once made an undercurrent over which the moans and cries of the wounded resounded loudly, but the rage of Magnus was heard above all as he shouted blindly for men to pursue the ape-man. But of the twelve best fighting men in the village, half were wounded, three were dead, and only three remained unscathed from the gauntlet, and there were none left in the town who could be convinced to take up arms in search of the ape-man.

As Tarzan swung through the middle terrace, he was already too far away to be caught. He did not believe the fates had anything to do with his escape, and he gave no thanks to luck for stepping in on his behalf, for he had plotted a path through his enemies and used all his resources, both mental and physical, to wend his way. Avoiding the deadly center overlap, engaging one side at a time, and using their own weapons against them were superior tactics, and the ability to move like lightning, strike accurately with power, and sense danger before it arrives were innate to the ape-man's abilities. Talent is not so much accomplishing a task as it is making it look easy in the process. Tarzan visualized the impossible and made it so.

When Erik left to find London the day before the gauntlet, the first place he went, after thoroughly searching the town, was the mine because Magnus had just returned from there. As a child, he had rarely visited and remembered it only as a place where the Viking artisans went occasionally to obtain gold to use in fabrication of jewelry and art since, even in a valley of plenty, a unique handmade gift is always valued for a special occasion. Anyone was permitted to work the mine, but the hard labor involved deterred most from a large, coordinated enterprise, and it received only intermittent use from those who understood the processing technique. Erik was aware that the bag of rocks he sent out of the crater from time to time over the past months came from the mine, but understood nothing of their value or the purpose of the exchange.

The reclusive Sasquatch Erik knew from distant sightings on his many days hunting in the woods, and he thought of them as extremely intelligent animals that kept to their own, so like the sacred bear, he did not hunt them and would not kill one except in self-defense. Recently, his closer contact with the apes when delivering them to Magnus reinforced that opinion, but since he could not talk with them, in the naivety of youth, he assumed that his part in this was just to bring the wayward beasts back home and that the Jarl was setting them free later in the deep woods.

So Erik was genuinely surprised when he got to the mine and was confronted by a few burly Norsemen led by Gorm. All were well-armed and they formed a wall across the trail some distance from the entrance, not threatening at all to the Jarl's stepson, but obviously blocking him from advancing further.

There was no open hostility, but the lack of welcoming smiles led to a desultory exchange of greetings, after which Erik got right to the point of his visit and asked if any had seen London.

Gorm did all the talking and, lying glibly, responded, "Nay, a mine is no place for a woman, only us here on the Jarl's business. He wants enough gold drawn out for a tiara to be made for your mother."

Erik could hardly argue with a motive like that, but he pressed further, "None have seen her in the village and with the ramparts guarded, this direction may have seemed the only way out."

"This is a dead end here and if any of us had seen a runaway thrall, we would surely know what to do with her, right men?" chuckled Gorm, as the Vikings around him laughed in agreement.

Eric was offended at the implications, but with the odds against him, saw no point in precipitating a fight. However, he did admonish them that if London was seen, to return her to the village unharmed because she was the King's slave and any punishment must come from him.

As Erik turned to leave, seeing no possibility of help there, Gorm called after him saying, "I would check the deep woods, maybe one of those monkey men got her."

Having to pass through the town once more, Erik wanted to be sure he had left no stone unturned before he attempted to search the vast crater bottom land, so he questioned everyone he had missed before but with the same results. No one had any idea where she might be. Lastly, on his way out, he paused to query the guard at the ramparts, who happened to be Ulf the Giant.

Unbeknownst to Erik, the clever Magnus had anticipated the path the boy would take in his search for London. Magnus had seen him depart for the mine and knew Gorm could handle things there, so he used the time to convince the stupid Ulf that he had seen the girl leave the village and then install him as the guard before Erik returned.

The giant performed admirably after Red Beard's indoctrination, so dumb was he that he truly believed that he had seen

London leave, and, because she was the Jarl's thrall, did not stop her. Eager for any positive news, Erik was quick to believe the fabrication, and as he was jogging down the road, it was with renewed hope because he now knew where she had to be, waiting for him in their private place, Eden Falls, named by them after their visit.

He was also kicking himself for not thinking of this destination initially, as it was the most safe and secure and logically the only one London could find by herself. But his first thought had been that Magnus was behind the disappearance, and Erik wanted to save her from harm by thoroughly exploring the locations closest to the treacherous King early on. Now there was a bounce in his step and joy in his heart as Erik fairly raced along the path, sure he would soon be reunited with his first love, but unaware he was leaving her with Tarzan, trapped in the mines behind them.

From the heights of happiness when Erik parted the dangling lianas and entered their sacred site to the equal depths of depression did he fall when finding it empty. It was a bitter pill to swallow, but Erik did not wallow in self-centered misery or abandon his quest. He would pursue his love until he knew her fate, whether she had been taken from him or left of her own volition, he had to know, even if either of these now most likely futures might break his heart.

So it was a dejected hunter who began the quick search of the valley, first to where the bags of rocks were exchanged because London might look there for a way out of the crater. Adding to the heaviness in his stride was the thought that she might be trying to escape him. Then, rapidly through familiar woods, where Erik's tracking skills rarely let him down, he would hopefully find her lost but unscathed. And finally into the deep woods and the lands of the apes where none had gone before; if he found her in that last place, his mission would become one of vengeance instead of rescue, so horrible was even the contemplation of that destiny.

Chapter Sixteen

BATTLE OF THE KINGS

As a child, the defining moment of Tarzan's passage into adulthood came when he found his father's hunting knife in that mud-plastered cabin on the western shores of Africa. He had spent endless hours there, learning from the letters that resembled little bugs running across the pages of the few simple primers that constituted his library. They formed the ideas about his place in the world: that he was a Tarmangani and different from his fellow apes, the Mangani, and that as a man, he could aspire to loftier ambitions, complete tasks with the purpose of personal betterment, and champion noble causes. These ideals became imbued in his persona, which already benefitted from a noble English heritage, but when he left, the only physical objects he took away from the place of his birth was the knife of his long-dead sire and his mother's golden locket.

The ape-man's first and favorite weapon was his homemade grass rope that provided endless amusement by tripping and tying up his foster father, Tublat, and eventually was used seriously to capture big feline carnivores and even cruel men, drawing them helplessly screaming up into the trees to meet their end. From these local native tribes, the ape-man later stole simple garments, copper ornaments, and the spears and poison arrows that eventually became part of his basic armament. But that knife from his unknown father gave the youthful Tarzan his first chance to overcome the terrible jungle beasts with their greater strength, long fighting fangs, and sharp talons and claws.

That blade had proved the difference between certain death and barely surviving in the battle with Bolgani, provided Tarzan with a coveted leopard loincloth, garnered the respect of the apes in his tribe, and eventually made him King of the Apes.

So as Tarzan swung through the trees, naked except for a loincloth with his only possession an ornate ceremonial knife stolen from Wulfstan, he did not feel vulnerable because he had excelled for almost twenty years alone in the jungle thus equipped, since all else could come from that one tool. With the knife, he could cut grass for a rope, hew a sapling for a spear, fashion a bow from a yew tree, and strip cedar branches for arrows, but that was all for later; right now the ape-man was hungry for meat after the meager fare in the mines and his recent exertions in the gauntlet. Waiting in a tree over a trail for passing prey could take too long, so he kept his nostrils dilated to catch any drifting odor of game in the winds, while keeping a sharp eye for tell-tale spoors on the forest floor as he travelled rapidly through the lower terrace.

After he had crossed several likely paths and still was unable to detect any promising vagrant smells, Tarzan picked up the strong scent of water and as this was often a common gathering place for a variety of quarry, he detoured in that direction. Intent on catching any drinking animals by surprise, the ape-man stealthily approached and, quietly parting some branches, found himself looking out on a large steamy pond surrounded by a rocky shore. Here again, he was disappointed when his nose could not detect a single whiff of a potential meal and the pebble-covered beach vouchsafed no signs from recent use.

Tarzan silently watched the unchanging scene for a while and then broke from cover when he became thirsty and convinced that further waiting would be fruitless. As he crouched for a drink at the shoreline, he noticed some turtles downwind in the mist, on a partly submerged log across the still waters, warming themselves in the heat of the day. Normally not found above South Dakota in the Missouri river, it is hard to say whether these turtles were trapped here after coming up through the Great Lakes in a warmer pre-history or were transplanted by a roaming Native American to this hydrothermally heated pond. Though not a common prey in Africa, Tarzan knew Kota had very tasty meat if he could catch one, but as soon as he put his foot in, sending ripples along the surface, the turtles all wiggled off the branches and dropped quickly into the water.

With no better options at hand, Tarzan was unwilling to give up his intended meal, and since he needed to wash off the dirt from the mines and blood from the gauntlet anyway, he continued into the pool. The water was initially clear, but as he advanced, his feet stirred up the silt on the bottom, so he did not see the sudden drop off which occurred after a few steps, and the depths closed over his head. Unperturbed since he was an excellent swimmer, the ape-man put the knife between his teeth and struck out with strong strokes, quickly reaching the partly submerged log where he had last seen the turtles and grasping a branch while planning his dive for dinner.

Tarzan knew Kota was a meat-eater that liked to hide on the bottom, unseen because the algae growing on their dark, greenish-brown backs and the red and yellow striped colors around their heads provided a natural camouflage that enabled them to catch unsuspecting fish, snakes, and even small opossums or raccoons with a quick snap of strong jaws that could easily amputate fingers. Because he was in their element, it would be hard to catch one swimming, and having just taken in air, they would not need to surface for a while. The water below the ape-man was murky from the recent passage of the turtles, but he could discern a spot on the muddy bottom with a circular outline that seemed promising. Even with close observation, the position of the dangerous head was not apparent until a thin stream of exhaled bubbles rose to the surface, marking the placement of the nose.

The turtles were unlikely to surface while he was there, so if he wanted to eat he would have to go to them. Not wanting to risk his hands probing the depths, Tarzan broke off a branch from the log and, taking a deep breath, dove down the remaining ten feet with the stick extended to where the trail of bubbles originated. At first, there was no response to his tickling, except that the silt was clouding the water and he could no longer see the bottom, but then, with a violent explosion of mud, something that looked more like a prehistoric creature than a turtle burst upward with gaping jaws extended on a long neck right at the ape-man's face. Thankfully the knife was clenched blade outward in his teeth because there was no time to make sluggish defensive movements with his hands constrained under the water. Only the ape-man's lightning reflexes enabled him to tilt his head and point the tip of the knife, where it extended from the right side of his mouth, at the only soft spot on the well-armored beast, piercing it in the eye and deflecting the brute past himself.

This was not the peaceful Kota of Tarzan's youth but rather the heaviest freshwater turtle in the world, Lukota, the North American alligator snapping turtle that can grow, for its entire life of one hundred and fifty years, up to two hundred and fifty pounds in weight and four feet in length, and is named for the three rows of gator-like spiked ridges along the back of its shell. Not about to let his catch get away, Tarzan grabbed the sharp barbs on the carapace only to be raked with claws along his side as the injured turtle sought to escape. When the snapper turned to fight, the ensuing furious struggle forced Tarzan to put his feet on the rocky bottom to get leverage as blood from both parties filled the water.

Just when he began to gain control over the weakening animal, a new factor came into the battle when Tarzan felt iron jaws painfully fasten around his shinbone anchoring him to the floor of the pond. Now trapped between two of these mighty beasts, the ape-man was swiftly using up his last breath and likely to be eaten himself by all the turtles for his temerity in invading their domain. Quickly, he let go of the lesser danger above and that turtle swam rapidly away, equally tired of the fight. Taking the knife from his teeth, Tarzan bent to the greater danger below and, putting his other foot between the prongs on the back of its shell, he pulled his legs apart, suffering excruciating pain from the beak clenched on his leg but extending the monster's neck in the process. Rapidly running out of oxygen, the ape-man commenced to saw on the tough hide and bony vertebrae while straining to keep it from withdrawing inside the shell, but unfortunately the mage had never kept a sharp edge on his ceremonial knife. His lungs burned as he worked furiously with the dull instrument in a deadly underwater, slow-motion race before time ran out. Even in a fight for his life, the snapping turtle never lets loose once it has fastened on, so Tarzan had to completely sever the head before he was able to shoot to the surface gasping for air.

Once he had rested on the log long enough to resume normal breathing and let the muddy water settle some, Tarzan went warily down one more time to claim his prize and then swam back to the shore, pushing the shell in front. As he exited the water, he found the decapitated head was still hanging on his ankle as fixed in death as it had been in life because of its hooked beak, but thankfully there were no broken bones or damage to the muscles, tendons, or nerves, because while it is true a snapper can hold on forever, the force of its bite is no more powerful than that of a human. It took quite some time to pry off the jaws and break open the shell, which was useful as a serving bowl and storage receptacle for the leftovers. By the time he was done, the additional exertion and delay convinced the hungry ape-man that the meat tasted even sweeter than that of Pacco the zebra. But perhaps it was triumphing again in the constant struggle between predator and prey that added the sweetness of life to the meal.

Tarzan had almost been bested by the lowly Lukota, and just as in the jungles of home, where the bite from a small spider or fly could prove fatal, he learned once again to never underestimate a foe. To be careless can be deadly when most potential repasts can bite back. In respect, the ape-man voiced no victory cry over this kill and spent considerable time using a coarse rock from the shore to hone the edge of his blade razor sharp before taking to a comfortable bole in a nearby tree to sleep for the night.

Kudu was coming over the rim of the crater when Tarzan awoke and stretched luxuriously in the new day. The ape-man consumed more of Lukota for breakfast in the morning sun and then drank and refreshed himself in the pool of water before leaving to take care of unfinished business. A good night's sleep in the crotch of the tree and the hearty servings of raw meat had restored him to full strength, which would be sorely needed for his next task.

For some animals that understand the universal language of the first men, there is no word for friend, though these are generally lower on the evolutionary scale and commonly thought of as prey, and, since all the other beasts seek to devour them, this is understandable. Among the anthropoids, little Manu the monkey has friends, even though he is constantly pursued and barely maintains enough weight on his small body to make it worthwhile to be eaten by another. However, it is interesting to note that in many so-called more advanced species, up to and including some humans, while they may acknowledge friends, the word for stranger is the same as for enemy.

The Sasquatch were historically isolated and naturally reclusive, and they never needed a word for stranger, but if it was up to Zu-yad, it would be the same one they used for enemy since his power over the tribe was greatly diminished after the advent of Tarzan. The Vikings were bad enough demanding an ape levy, but they provided an easy way of getting rid of troublesome malcontents and challengers to his supremacy. But the ape-man had embarrassed him in front of the whole clan during the Dum Dum, and if he ever had another chance, Zu-yad would make sure the only word used for Tarzan was bund.

The King Ape had been in such a hurry for revenge when he rushed away from the amphitheater after being set free by the Norsemen, expecting to find the ape-man back in camp with B'yat-zor-hul, that he just missed the returning Tarzan. Zu-yad did not know the ape-man had been taken to the mines, successfully fulfilling last month's toll according to his original plan, and he raged and fumed for two days at his inability to wreak havoc on the absent Tarzan. All the members of the tribe felt his anger as he struck out at the other bulls and scared the shes and balus into hiding. Even Koho-lul and her mother were not spared from the King's fury for her part in his humiliation by dancing with another ape.

Unable to vent his wrath on Tarzan, Zu-yad eventually needed someone else to blame. Who had brought the hated Tarmangani into their midst, breaking clan customs; who had allowed the ape-man to escape from the judgement board; and who had danced in the Dum Dum with Koho-lul? The King focused his ire on B'yat-zor-hul as the readily available source of all his trouble, and he decided to seek immediate satisfaction by calling out the injured ape to meet him in the common area. B'yat-zor-hul had only regained consciousness yesterday and today could just barely stagger out in compliance with his King's command. As Zu-yad worked himself up with vile words and fierce postures while circling his intended victim, the hapless B'yat-zor-hul stood proud even though he knew that this time, the King would finish the fight.

Like all the other apes, Tarzan had been given a specific drum signal to announce his entry into the camp and to use with the stick-stacks between rooms while there, but he did not bother with it today. Nor did he approach cautiously, as his mission was not stealthy; instead, he came in the fashion of his arrivals in his own tribe in Africa, calculated to instill surprise and consternation among the apes. Tarzan could see he was just in time as he dropped from an overhanging tree in front of B'yat-zor-hul and roared his own challenge, bringing the rest of the apes out from their hiding places.

"Zu-yad is like a toothless Numa who can only hunt the weak and the old!" exclaimed Tarzan.

Zu-yad was initially taken aback by the interjection of Tarzan into the fight and did not know what a lion was, but he understood the insult about having to gum your food. The crowd that quickly gathered around the combatants, eager to see blood spilled, was about evenly split in their partiality between their King and the ape-man and added their own disparaging comments to the mix. Koho-lul, seeing an opportunity to get back in the good graces of her intended, was particularly vocal in support of Zu-yad, matching even the heckling that poured from the mouth of her mother, Litu-lus.

"See these sharp fangs," shouted Zu-yad as he grimaced hideously. "Soon they will taste the hot blood pouring from your throat." He beat on the great slabs of muscle running across his massive chest as he threw his scarred and horribly disfigured head back and shrieked forth the bone-chilling challenge of his kind. After further displays of his mountainous shoulders and bulging sinew-laced arms, the King focused his beady red wicked eyes on the ape-man and contemptuously glared down at his comparatively diminutive rival.

Tarzan used the pause to usher B'yat-zor-hul to the side, explaining to his friend that this was his fight for the kingship of the tribe and not to interfere with the challenge. The tribe historian understood the need for a fair contest and yielded the field to the ape-man. As Tarzan turned to face the gigantic ape, he left his knife in its sheath in order to fight not as man versus ape but instead only with nature's weapons of teeth and claws, pitting his speed and cunning against the brute force of the King in a primeval battle to the death. Since the dawn of time it has always been thus, leadership of the strong, who are willing to risk all to take all, with death the only reward for failure.

Zu-yad had anticipated the easy kill of a debilitated ape, but now faced an audacious, puny Tarmangani who was the real source of all his troubles, so it took little of the blustering that usually preceded a fight to regain the blood-crazed fervor needed to charge. With a ferocious scream, he rushed arms held high, intent on using his superior size to crush the impudent ape-man, who crouched ready to defend himself. Just before delivering the killing blows designed to drive the enemy into the ground, the King raised up to gain the maximum downward impetus, but as his arms descended, the victim was not there. Tarzan had dodged to the left with the lightning quickness of Ara, but not before delivering a tremendous blow with a right cross directly into the exposed gut of Zu-yad that knocked the wind out of the ape, and left him doubled up on his knees trying to catch his breath.

The ape-man, while considered a giant among men, realized he could never let the enormous ape close with him, or he would be overwhelmed and at only a little over six-foot tall, he could not reach his opponent's head three feet above. So while he had Zu-yad bent down and within range, he threw a thunderous left to the side of the King's ugly face that further stunned the immense ape. Tarzan had been exposed to the science of boxing while in Paris and now thanked the fact that "Gentleman Jim" Corbett had invented the left hook in 1889 when he broke both his hands during a heavyweight prizefight and that British champion William "Iron" Hague demonstrated it while the title-holder was visiting in France.

"Kagoda?" asked Tarzan, giving Zu-yad the chance to surrender as he sought to rise.

In answer, the ape swung out viciously with the back of his long arm, swiping the ape-man across the side of the head and leaving him reeling in place. If he could get the Tarmangani in his grasp, it would only take seconds to rip off an arm, so Zu-yad pulled the dazed Tarzan close with one hairy arm and sought a grip on the ape-man's shoulder while lifting him up so his feet dangled uselessly. Instinctively, Tarzan put both hands around the King's throat in a suffocating squeeze also designed to keep those lethal jaws away. Now it was two beasts locked in a deadly embrace, one wincing in pain from the wrenching and the other spraying slaver while gasping for air. Zu-yad gave first and encircling Tarzan with his brawny arms began crushing the life from him while seeking to bring the ape-man's throat within reach of his snapping fangs. Tarzan locked his elbows as his muscles rippled under his bronze hide, barely maintaining enough distance from the fatal bite. His bones beginning to bend, the ape-man trusted to the strength of one mighty choking hand as he used the other to rip one of Zu-yad's big floppy ears half off his head.

Dropping Tarzan as a result of the sudden intense pain, Zu-yad was growling terribly and as he shook off the effects of the punches and lacerated ear, he hunched over, preparing for another charge. Animal sounds issued from the ape-man's throat as well and it was hard to tell which were more terrifying. Not wanting the ape to fully recover, Tarzan quickly launched himself, leaping high at the beast this time, sailing feet first as he doubled up his legs and then kicked out violently at the King's face with his full body weight behind it like a jackhammer that sent Zu-yad to the ground on his back, spitting out broken teeth from behind shredded lips. Before, the King was merely ugly from where Magnus had scarred his cheek, but now with his jagged fangs, hanging bloody lips and ear and red-rimmed eyes beneath bleeding brows, it was a horrible visage to behold.

Zu-yad rallied quickly, seething at his inability to catch his elusive foe, and came roaring at Tarzan again. Parrying the outstretched arms with his own, Tarzan again dodged low and, with a sweep of his leg, tripped the huge ape, sending him sliding forward on his stomach from the momentum. Seizing the opportunity, the ape-man jumped upon Zu-yad's back and quickly insinuated his arms under those of the ape's, and with his hands clasped together on the back of the neck, Tarzan began to apply pressure as he once did to bring the mighty Terkoz to submission in Africa. Slow, relentless force caused vertebrae to creak and groan from the tremendous strain and Tarzan, from right behind the ape's head, asked once again, "Kagoda?"

Zu-yad felt his spine about to break and thrashed furiously, trying to dislodge the ape-man from his back, flailing his arms and rolling over and over, but was unable to break the death grip. Desperate and unwilling to surrender, his pain-addled eyes twitched back and forth, seeking any avenue for escape. Then a crazed gleam flared in his fear-maddened gaze as he saw the knife hanging at Tarzan's side. The King knew the power of the human weapon, and it took but an instant to swing the ape-man's body to one side and pull the blade free with one of his extremely long arms. Awkward in his huge hand and still caught in the hold, all Zu-yad could do was slash blindly at the swaying body of Tarzan in hopes of a score. Unaware of this breach of honor, the ape-man had to abandon his position and roll off the ape when he felt the knife bite into his side, leaving a shallow but jagged wound.

Once again they faced off, but now Zu-yad retained the knife, brandishing it underhanded and point up, low in front of himself, and sought to jab forward into Tarzan's neck as, due to their height difference, that was the most natural killing stroke while also protecting his own body. Even though the ape was clumsy with the unfamiliar weapon, the ape-man was forced to give ground, dodge left and right, parry, and roll away. Tarzan sustained several defensive cuts on his arms and knew it was a matter of time before he would fall to the monster, as Zu-yad was gaining proficiency with every pass.

Now bleeding in multiple places and desperate himself, Tarzan saw no help forthcoming from the crowd as they were shouting for his extermination, eagerly awaiting the inevitable end. Both combatants were worn and tired from the heat of battle on the warm day. Before he got cut on his hands and the blood or sweat made them slippery, the ape-man had one last maneuver to try. Instead of constantly backing, he feinted left and drew the right-handed thrust that way, then sliding under and turning in, Tarzan grabbed the extended wrist with two hands and threw his hip hard into Zu-yad's midsection while pulling with all his strength down on the arm of the much taller ape. In this position, the top heavy size of the King worked to his disadvantage and he found himself flying over the ape-man's back. But as Zu-yad swung by, Tarzan continued turning the weak wrist joint up until his sharp knife found a home in the King's belly and then kept pushing it until it was stopped by the ribcage, the point deep in Zu-yad's heart still held by his own hand. This had started out as a noble contest between two beasts for the leadership of the clan, but even here the treachery of man had insinuated itself when the knife was introduced into the fray.

Shocked by the sudden reversal the assembly grew quiet, but only for a moment, and all present became riveted on the spectacle as Tarzan, placing his foot on the inert body of Zu-yad and beating his chest, roared out the victory cry of the bull ape that proclaimed him King of the Sasquatch.

Their leader gone and his power over them broken, most of the apes milled around, uncertain what this meant and unsure about a Tarmangani as King. Some general muttering was heard after Litu-lus goaded the group to punish the stranger. Taking charge of the volatile situation, Tarzan pulled his knife from the dead body and holding the bloody blade aloft cried, "I am Tarzan, mighty killer, let any come forth who would challenge and feel my wrath."

Zu-yad had previously so effectively eliminated most of the competition and their blood lust sated for the moment, the apes began to dissipate, content to go back to their simple lives and leave well enough alone. Other than one to turn to for occasional tribal guidance and to settle disputes, the King rarely interfered in the daily activities of the community. B'yat-zor-hul ambled up and bowed to his new King, finally free from Zu-yad's lifelong sword of Damocles hanging over his head, and in another very human gesture tried to grin, making a grotesque caricature of his face in the process. But Tarzan understood, smiled back and suggested they get cleaned up and tend to their wounds if they were to lead this tribe together.

For a couple of days, the friends recuperated while Tarzan solidified his hold on the Sasquatch, not with fear and force, but with reason and fairness and with B'yat-zor-hul at his side, he won them all over. Just as a knife can be used as a weapon or a tool, so can a stranger be an enemy or a friend, depending on their intentions, and the ape-man had found both among the Sasquatch. Unlike Zu-yad who gravitated to the dregs of society, Tarzan brought the best that civilization had to offer and, having been raised as an ape, knew just how to introduce it. Soon though they were back in fine fettle and the ape-man, chafing under the constraints of leadership and needing to feel the freedom of the woods again, took on the hunting duties with B'yat-zor-hul and together they swung off into the woods. Tarzan had other scores to settle, so the search was not entirely for four-legged prey.

Chapter Seventeen

THE CHALLENGE OF MAGNUS

Erik had been searching for three days. The rope that dropped from the crater wall was pulled up in its usual position, so it seemed unlikely London could have escaped by climbing out, and from what she had said about the two fiends residing above, he was sure she would never willingly go back there. His search of the familiar woods also included stopping at a couple of outlying farms and questioning all the travelers and other hunters he encountered, while alerting the countryside of her description. But it had been to no avail, and he found himself alone, sitting beside a campfire, grilling venison from a deer brought down earlier with a lucky arrow, thinking morose thoughts about London's probable fate if she had been abducted by the hairy wild men of the deep forest; self-destruction or a quick merciful end from a bear would be preferable. So profound was his dejection that he thought not at all of any dangers to himself, isolated so far from home. Since Erik had quickly checked everywhere else, she must be somewhere in this last place, but despite all his hunting skills, he had not seen any of the elusive monkey men that Grom had joked about and the trees were so thick that capturing one seemed an impossible task. Unlike his usual quarry, he knew so little about the Yeti's habits that he was uncertain if he was looking for solitary animals in caves or a group in a camp, yet he must go on because to admit failure was to live without her and that was unthinkable. Adding to his depression was the pervasive gloom and silence under the towering giant trees that let in little light and allowed no sounds to get out.

Far away, a different atmosphere reigned in the lofty heights of the same forest, where Tarzan and B'yat-zor-hul clambered amid the birds under a dappling sunlight in the upper terrace exploring their kingdom. With no need for a fire for eating, there was seldom a reason to descend since even their beds were easily made with some branches and soft leaves spread between sturdy boughs that forked appropriately. The trees also provided fruit and nuts so the only needs from below were for water and Tarzan's need to hunt. After seizing the leadership from a corrupt ruler and easing the transition of his fellow apes while healing from his many wounds, the problems of other people did not seem so pressing. Who can blame Tarzan for taking time to enjoy his new home since that cruel and relentless taskmaster of civilization did not intrude here with its clanging alarm clocks and shrieking factory whistles, and the ape-man, completely reverted to the beast again, gave no heed to its demands.

But often time teams up with fate to create circumstances that can produce tremendous changes in results, like when a driving error causes two automobiles to collide, or a chance meeting brings future mates together. So it was when an ephemeral breeze brought a faint, drifting scent of fire to Tarzan's sensitive nostrils. Of all the risks in a forest, a fire is the most feared because of its wholesale destruction, but more dangerous still is man, who is usually to blame for starting the conflagration. It was enough of an intrusion for the ape-man to immediately swing off toward this potential dual threat to his domain. B'yat-zor-hul followed but could not detect anything until they grew much closer, and Tarzan adapted a hunter's posture by silently stealing up on their prey from above to surreptitiously learn the nature of the menace.

The only low point in their time together was when Tarzan, after announcing Zu-yad's plot and the fate of the missing apes to the whole tribe, had to tell B'yat-zor-hul about meeting

Ry-blat in the mines and his demise at the hands of the Vikings. Death is such an everyday part of life in the wild that the grieving was short and then internalized, and since the betrayer had been an anthropoid, revenge was not paramount for these generally peaceful creatures. But B'yat-zor-hul's hair bristled and Tarzan's eyes narrowed when they saw a lone Norseman had invaded their territory and was cooking deer over a fire, totally unaware he was being stalked. Both ape and ape-man had deadly grudges to settle, so with petrifying howls, the hunters dove on their quarry, intent on tearing the interloper apart for his temerity, and Erik was never closer to death than at that moment.

Recognition snapped in Tarzan an instant before the killing blows landed, and he quickly instructed B'yat-zor-hul to hold the Viking while he questioned him. Erik had been so deep in his thoughts that he was caught completely unaware, and now he dangled helplessly, lifted off the ground with his arms pinned to his side by the powerful nine-foot Sasquatch behind him. The surprise and relief at finding Tarzan alive was evident on the Norseman's face. The ape-man remembered Erik's previous intercession on his behalf and knew he was not present during the gauntlet. As Tarzan's hot blood cooled, he gave Erik the benefit of the doubt while listening to his reasons for searching the deep forbidden woods. This prompted Tarzan to inform Erik that he had seen London in the mines recently, and the Viking became so volubly agitated that Tarzan believed him and had B'yat-zor-hul set him free.

Wanting every detail and hoping to enlist the aid of Tarzan, Erik invited them to share his camp and partake of his meal, though he was still somewhat wary of the huge Sasquatch. He was even more disconcerted when the ape declined the meat, instead eating some wild turnips and onions from his pack while the ape-man used his knife to cut a steak from the deer, which he then proceeded to eat raw while sitting on his haunches. As Tarzan was the only interpreter, the conversation around the campfire was a bizarre mixture of French between an English noble and a Norseman, and the Mangani's animated barking grunts and growling between the ape-man and the anthropoid. Truly a more improbable group had never before assembled.

As it was getting dark, they decided to stay together for the night, and over the course of the evening, Tarzan learned of Erik's noble birthright and how Magnus had usurped the throne, and he again felt the passion in Erik's voice when he was speaking of London. Erik was finally able to put together everything from the degrading use of the Sasquatch in the mines, payments going out of the crater to the villains above, and Gorm kidnapping London, with Magnus being responsible for all of it. B'yat-zor-hul was not interested in all the human intrigue, but was drawn into it when Erik was recounting the loss of his father on a hunting trip. The ape remembered that about the same time clan members began disappearing, he had found the body of a Viking near where the Dum Dum was danced, and, as it was their way of respecting the dead, he had buried it in the forest near the arena. Erik became extremely excited at the prospect of finding his father's grave when Tarzan translated that B'yat-zor-hul could take them there tomorrow.

Man, beast and one linking the two ringed the fire that night; mighty fighters all, they slept well, secure that their combined skills were invincible should any dare to approach. After a breakfast of venison for Eric and Tarzan and foraged nuts and berries for B'yat-zor-hul, the three set out to solve the mystery of Annulf's hunting accident. Near the entrance to the secret long narrow path that led to the back of the amphitheater, the Sasquatch detoured to the left and came to an area of soft grass where he had interred the Norseman in a shallow grave. Eric used his sword to reverently open the grave, unearthing the bones of a tall man with a few scraps of fabric and leather and a tiny golden necklace clinging near the center. But it was enough to tell the tale of what had actually happened on that fateful hunting trip.

Erik recognized the workmanship of the leather and colors of the cloth as Annulf's hunting apparel, and the gold pendant was in the form of the Norse letter F, a gift from his mother to his father and always worn close to his heart, evidently overlooked in the looting of the body after the violent killing. The proof of murder was in the bones because when Erik uncovered the skull, a deep wide split in the back with sharp edges was revealed; it could only have come from an axe from behind. Erik cried tears of rage and vowed in the names of the gods of vengeance, Vidar and Vali, that he would seek revenge on Magnus for this foul deed and forever rid his people of this blight upon their honor. Moved by his anguish and nursing grudges of their own, the two beasts with him, one retaining the chivalry of an English lord in his soul, and the other a historian responsible for justice in his tribe, both pledged to join in his quest.

Once he had regained his composure, Eric put the necklace in his pocket to be returned to his mother and gathered the bones in his cape to take home so his father's spirit could enter Valhalla in a proper King's funeral fire. With his jaw set in grim determination, Erik accepted his companions' offer of help but explained that while they each had a grievous debt owed to Magnus, his was one of honor and he needed to settle it alone, in the Viking way, in single combat to the death. Tarzan acknowledged the integrity of the duel and B'yat-zor-hul understood the concept of a battle for the kingship of a tribe, so they both agreed to not interfere and would delay their revenge until Erik was satisfied with his own retribution. It was a formidable trio that was forged that morning, bound by a common resolution and intent on seeking justice in the valley.

Magnus was in his lodge in a warm bath with a cloth soaked in cool water covering his blackened, but now fully healed, eyes. It had been a few rough days since the gauntlet and the populace was angry, so he had been content to remain inside and let Gorm handle the aftereffects. Most of his fighting men were dead or wounded, so it was an ill-tempered Gorm, himself nursing a broken nose, that pressed the farmers into service to tend to the injured and build the six funeral pyres while Wulfstan, with his sore back, consoled the grieving and performed the final rites. Added to their woes was the almost universal sentiment among the superstitious Vikings that Tarzan was a demigod who had mystical abilities with animals and could come back alive after disappearing in flames; and now had demonstrated intrepid courage and daring skills before their very eyes, proving beyond a doubt that he could not be killed by mortal men. The mage did his best to counter this but could not command much esteem hunched over and hobbling through his duties. More than anything, the Norsemen respected bravery and expertise in battle.

The first intimation that something further was amiss was when Gorm pounded on the Jarl's door announcing the approach of the odd threesome. Magnus was left to dress himself when Freyja hurried out to see her son, and the servants joined the excited crowd quickly gathering outside. As in the case of the gauntlet, word of mouth spread swiftly, so everyone in the village and most from the surrounding farms and even Ulf, the guard at the earthen ramparts, deserted his post to join the spectators. Here was excitement: Erik was leading the supernatural Tarzan and the largest ape they had ever seen up close toward what could only be the expected and long awaited confrontation that would decide who rules the Norsemen! How would Magnus deal with the upstart Prince; would he have any better luck in his third clash with the ape-man; why was that huge ape along with the men? The large crowd gathered down the street with children perched on brawny shoulders, women craning from the windows, and people even on the rooftops, anywhere they could see and hear. They did not have to wait long for their answers.

With the assemblage behind him, Erik left Tarzan and B'yat-zor-hul on one side with the woods on the other and stood alone facing the Jarl's dwelling, his childhood home, and called for his mother to join him. Pulling the necklace from his pocket he held it high and proclaimed, "I offer my father's pendant as proof that these bones are his," as he spilled the contents of his robe on the ground. Freyja gasped, the tears in her eyes verifying Erik's assertion, and then took the jewelry tenderly in her hands, moving aside to stand next to Tarzan.

Next, Erik raised the skull over his head while turning in a circle so all could see the fatal cleft and exclaimed, "Annulf was killed, not in a hunting accident, but instead by Magnus, in a cowardly act of treachery with his axe from behind; he then sought to hide his perfidy and claim the kingship. As true heir to the throne, I challenge the illegitimate Jarl and demand the satisfaction of a fight to the death to avenge my father!"

Wulfstan had joined Gorm with Magnus as he dressed in his battle gear, including a full suit of chain mail. Confident he could handle this, the Jarl gave instructions to his cronies, sending Gorm to the mines to destroy the evidence by killing the remaining guards and Sasquatch. Then, he was to take London up out of the crater to a prearranged place where they could all meet later. Caught by the accusations of cowardice, which alone were enough to ensure his rule was over, Magnus wanted to enjoy one last pleasure by disposing of the upstart boy and his companions before quickly leaving in the aftermath. Before answering the call, he consulted with the mage while the jeering mob outside, eager for some bloodletting, grew in size and loudness as they shouted derisively. Taking up his well-used axe, Red Beard presented a terrifying figure when he exited with Wulfstan behind him, and the throng fell silent, in awe of his menacing presence. Magnus addressed the multitude by directing Wulfstan to sanctify the King's challenge before proceeding. The mage postured and chanted around Magnus before pronouncing him a fit champion and then moving to Erik, repeated the same routine, except at the end he cried out, denouncing him as unfit in the eyes of the gods to challenge!

Wulfstan had his arm extended and was about to lunge forward and place his hand on Erik's chest when a golden handled knife covered with runes flew in from the side and buried itself in the mage's throat, dropping him in a pile at Erik's feet; the seer's blade had been returned to him by the ape-man. The crowd roared at the intrusion, and Magnus blustered for the ape-man to be killed on the spot for murdering Wulfstan, but Tarzan calmly walked up to the body and pulled a ring-covered hand up for all to see. The ring on the first finger had a long needle-like extension that was held out by the thumb, easily visible to everyone now, but normally unseen as it would rest along the palm of the hand until deftly flipped up when needed, to pierce between the ribs and into the heart of its victim, causing uncontrolled spasms and death.

"Here is the mystery of your Mage's touch. A deadly trick I saw used to kill Ry-blat and intended today to cheat you of a fair fight to determine your Jarl!" shouted Tarzan, and the crowd murmured in comprehension while Magnus was left speechless, his treachery exposed again. After whispering something to Erik, Tarzan rejoined Freyja and B'yat-zor-hul on the side.

"Come and meet the battle axe that tasted your father's blood and I will bury all your bones together so deep the Valkyries will never find them," goaded Magnus as he played the rib splitter back and forth, confident in his abilities against a sword and securely cloaked in steel links.

Erik, without similar protective mail, foolishly took the bait and, leaping over Wulfstan's body, charged the burly Viking. It was almost his undoing as Magnus, seeking an early end to the fight, easily deflected the sword and drove the challenger back on his heels with a series of two-handed hammering blows that Erik barely defended until he tripped over the mage and fell on his back totally exposed. Unencumbered with heavy armor, Erik was able to quickly roll away when the vain Magnus, sensing an easy victory over the boy, could not resist savoring the moment and said with a sneer, "Your momma made you weak by sparing the rod, so I'll take one to her when I'm done with you."

Springing to his feet, the agile Erik now crouched in a defensive stance awaiting the fury of the axe once more. Weaving a web no sword could penetrate, Magnus came on anew and forced the nimble boy to dodge and leap away. It was only his quickness that saved him from the swirling cleaver time and time again as Erik retreated, taking only minor scratches in the process. But it gave him the opportunity to read his opponent and when the heavy broadaxe pulled the Jarl a bit too far around on one massive stroke, Erik was able to score a long gash from shoulder to elbow that, while not life threatening, incapacitated the arm on that side and made the King hold the weapon in one hand more like a sword.

Now Erik found openings and the fight raged on more evenly for a while, back and forth, a flashing blade against the more lethal axe that had to connect only one time with Erik's unprotected body to end it all. The Jarl suffered only minor cuts on the rare occasions the sword pierced his armor, which left only the King's limbs and head vulnerable. Meanwhile Erik, weakened from the loss of blood from deeper wounds, searched urgently for an opening to make a last desperate attack. Garnering all his remaining strength, Erik focused on his opponent's head and drove Magnus away from the cheering crowd toward the tree line on the far side. The furious onslaught left them both breathless a few feet from the woods where the Jarl finally went down to his knees. As Erik swung for the exposed head, Magnus threw some dirt in the boy's eyes, blinding him and causing the blade to miss.

Swiftly taking advantage of his subterfuge, Magnus sprang to his feet and raised his axe to split open Erik's head while he was defenseless, just like he had done to his father. But before it could descend, an earth shattering roar behind the Jarl froze him into inaction as a nine-hundred-pound behemoth of a cave bear streaked from the forest and, rising up on two legs, bit through his mail at the shoulder, completely severing the arm holding the axe, and dragged the wailing King back into the woods. The suddenness of the attack took all by surprise and silenced the crowd. Only Red Beard's dire cries continued appallingly, finally ending in one long drawn-out scream when the dripping fangs in those terrible jaws finally closed on his skull and crushed it like an eggshell. Then there were only the ghastly sounds of the gnashing of teeth, the rending of flesh and the crunching of bones for some time thereafter.

All who saw it swear it was Odin's hand in the form of the revered bear, striking down the evil in their midst and signifying Erik as the new Jarl. But the acute senses of Tarzan knew better, for he had known Ursa was there, having scented it before the fight and, guessing its purpose in remaining in the area, encouraged Erik to maneuver Magnus near the woods in his whispered comment. Understanding the nature of beasts, the sharp vision of the ape-man left him unsurprised that this man-eater only had one eye. The cave bear had continually returned to the scene of its worst pain and took its revenge after waiting patiently for the chance.

Even though the final stroke had not been his, Erik had retribution for his father's murder much like B'yat-zor-hul had to be content with Tarzan casting the deadly blow that avenged his brother, Ry-blat. When he picked up the axe, the hand and arm held on in a grisly death grip, so Erik threw both on top of Wulfstan's body and directed Ulf to place everything in the ore cart for disposal later. No send-off in fire or trip to Valhalla for these two since they had died cowardly, without their weapons in hand, despicable to the end. Then, addressing his people for the first time, the new Jarl's pledge to rule fairly, and restore honor to the throne and peace in the valley brought a thunderous ovation from the assembly, which then surged forth and, lifting Erik to their shoulders, carried him to the King's lodge, where he embraced his beaming mother.

His subjects were ready to have the coronation festival on the spot, but now that the path was clear to the mine, Erik wanted to be off to rescue London so, after binding his injuries during the congratulations and tending to some minor formalities, he left Freyja in charge of making preparations for the next day and worked his way over to Tarzan and B'yat-zor-hul. Neither the ape nor the ape-man enjoyed crowds and they knew what was utmost in the new Jarl's mind, so Erik did not have to ask for their help. After directing Ulf to follow with the ore cart laden with its gruesome remains, they drifted away from the group and then raced for the mine.

Chapter Eighteen

ERIK TO THE RESCUE

With both men hunting to avoid spending time together, their larder was well stocked, not that Madame ever ate much of the highly seasoned creole food, even though the boudin with red beans and rice was actually quite good. It was not an aversion to eating the small game that made up the largest portion of it because the sharp spices overpowered any objectionable tastes; instead, it was the pervading atmosphere of hate that constantly existed in the stifling cabin that ruined her appetite. The animosity between Skinner and Lennie was reaching a peak only exceeded by her loathing for the two men who had robbed her of her only child.

Madame had ceased moaning about her fate and crying for mercy since she received only the icy, cruel stares of born killers in response. That they had not beaten her quiet was due to the fact that they enjoyed her suffering and their power over her misery. When the wolves would howl in the night, Skinner would tell tales of the French werewolf, the Rougarou, who is reputed to be able to read his victim's soul when he drinks their blood and eats their flesh. The mental torture was as much for Lennie as for Madame, and the Cajun delighted in seeing them both squirm. The chilling stories had Lennie biting his fingernails but did not affect Madame as much, because at this point she would welcome the end to this nightmare by even a paranormal means. Far worse for Madame was when she was alone with her guard during the day and had to listen to Skinner describe her daughter's plight in the valley below as a Viking slave or hairy man's possession, both ending in the girl's horrible demise. Equally bad was when the repulsive Lennie would pine over London, talking of their time together like he was her boyfriend, and how he would soon have her again.

Everyone has a mother for better or worse, and some of the worst mass murderers had Mom tattooed on their shoulder or over their heart showing their search for mother love. Skinner hated all women as evidenced by the fact that nowhere in all his tattoos did he waste the space for a mother who did not care. The Cajun was born bad, and Lennie willingly grew into it when taught by the master of deceit, so now both were incapable of an honorable act. Since Skinner had never had any redeeming virtues, his recent tutelage of Lennie had erased what little decency his partner had retained from a misguided childhood. But at least Lennie still understood that he could never have London if he killed her mother, so when Skinner told him to get the horn, Lennie was troubled because he knew that if the drop did not kill her, hanging upside down for a long time surely would. The Cajun had already thought of that though, and planned to blow the horn first, wait until someone showed up and then carefully lower her down. When no one came right after the signal, Skinner said, "We give them one day, den slit her throat and take what we have 'cause the jig is up."

The next day Skinner went to bring in the trap lines to take with them when they left, unknowingly leaving Lennie faced with a dilemma. As he sat on guard, Lennie pondered for the hundredth time whether to risk the Cajun's knife again by going against Skinner, and so great was his fear that he almost gave up his raging desire for London. But deep thinking and planning were beyond Lennie's limited intelligence, so it was no surprise that his obsession with the girl overpowered everything else and he finally determined he must have her now.

Before going down in the crater, he set Madame free and led her to the tunnel through the thorn barrier which was on his way to the upper mine entrance. Was this a sign of goodness, a spark of compassion, or a change of heart? Sadly no. Lennie's heart, like his blackened soul, was so shriveled that there was no room for love and passion, as it was already filled with lust and greed. Madame was merely a diversion to keep Skinner busy while Lennie went through the cave, and he did not care what the Cajun did to her, as long as she led him in the opposite direction and he had no part in it.

Skinner was incensed when he returned and found his plans thwarted, and he immediately followed the two to where they split up at the path through the brambles. What had happened, and why, was evident in the tracks and the Cajun grew even more irate at the stupid Lennie for risking all their gains over a girl, but his devious mind saw a way to turn this to his advantage. Skinner contained his fury long enough to reason that when he left for good, he could always catch the slow-moving woman, lost and alone in the forest with nowhere to go and no one to help her, but now Lennie had presented him with the perfect opportunity to bury everyone else below.

The stupendous force and heat from the crater's formation had also produced its sheer vertical walls, glassy smooth in places with obsidian-like stone, cracked and deeply fissured in others, and honeycombed throughout with natural tunnels extending far into the bedrock, twisting and winding like a maze. The mine was a combination of man-made and natural shafts that led downward to the diamond bearing ore via dark tunnels large enough for a crouching Sasquatch to go, and upward to the surface along a generally torch-lighted, but narrow, bending path full of blind switchbacks, treacherous caverns, and precipitous ledges that a large man would have trouble negotiating. Two such places on the path to the upper surface were called the Squeeze and the Tanngrisnir by the Vikings.

Not too far up from the vaulted rooms where Gorm held London, there was a short length where the walls were so close together that the large Norsemen had to turn sideways to get through, and even then, it was a tight Squeeze, hence the name.

Immediately beyond there the passage opened into a beautiful but dangerous grotto filled with hanging stalactites and protruding stalagmites that had been designated the Tanngrisnir because of the resemblance to interlocking teeth. After that, there were a series of hidden side tunnels that were mostly unexplored to any depth, but the main route ran fairly straight, so by following the torch-smoked ceiling and always going up, eventually the egress on the crater rim was achieved.

When Gorm arrived from the village, he went straight up to the guard that was watching London in her cave room and took over that watch, so the sentry could go below and make sure the remaining Sasquatch were secured before returning with the other keeper to await Magnus and Wulfstan. Gorm wanted to wait to kill the henchmen and Sasquatch until he had superior numbers and was sure he did not need them anymore. That proved to be fortunate when, instead of his confederates, the lookout reported that Erik, Tarzan, and B'yat-zor-hul drew near. As soon as she heard Erik's name, London began calling out for help. Not knowing the results of the challenge for the kingship, Gorm sent the two guards out to delay the trio while he roughly hustled London up the tunnel toward the surface to wait for his Jarl there and apprise Skinner of the trouble.

Erik drew his sword and Tarzan brandished a pike as they closed with the two Norsemen, while the huge Sasquatch, only armed with nature's weapons, trailed closely behind. The skilled hand of the new Jarl made quick work of the first guard, disarming him and shoving him toward the ape and then pushing past to sprint on into the cave entrance, answering London's cries for aid with those of his own of succor. Tarzan battled with the second guard, keeping the sword at bay while searching for an opening to make a fatal thrust with his spear. B'yat-zor-hul leaped upon the other now unarmed Norseman and took all his pent-up retribution for Ry-blat out on the unfortunate Viking by ripping the head from his body and throwing it at the man harassing Tarzan. Sorely pressed by the growling ape-man and thoroughly disconcerted by the roaring ape's action, the remaining guard's eyes grew wide with terror as he bolted around them for the village. But Tarzan was seeking revenge too, for the brutal treatment of his new tribe, so he cast his pike squarely between the shoulder blades of the fleeing Viking, dropping him dead before he hit the ground.

Leaving the unfamiliar weapons behind, Tarzan retrieved the keys from the decapitated Norseman's body and gave them to B'yat-zor-hul and then they raced after Erik into the mine. Once inside, Tarzan lit a torch for the Sasquatch and gave him instructions on where to find the trapped apes and how to free them, since the path up was too small for the giant ape to be of much assistance. Soon, B'yat-zor-hul heard the growls of his fellow clan members to guide him as he descended, while Tarzan listened for the shouts of fighting as he ascended to help Erik.

Gorm had the advantage of knowing the route, but London was doing everything she could to slow him down, sure now that her savior was close behind, so the Viking, also aware of the pursuit, hit her on the head with the butt of his sword and threw the stunned girl over a shoulder, surging ahead again. When London's shouts ceased, Erik feared for the worst and redoubled his efforts to reach her but was hindered by now having to stop and examine every turn off; the result being that Erik did not catch up to them until he came around a last bend in time to see Gorm just ahead, struggling to get himself through the Squeeze while carrying the cumbersome unconscious girl.

Sword extended, Erik slipped easily between the narrow walls as Gorm emerged from the opposite side, and, dropping London, hid beside the exit, sword ready to impale the boy while he was still constrained in the Squeeze. Fortunately, jarred from the fall, London was regaining her senses and called out to Erik, alerting him to the underhanded ploy, and he was able to fend off the cowardly stab while springing into the grotto where the two master swordsmen engaged!

After a blindingly fast first exchange where the blades struck like lightning, Erik gave ground under the larger man's heavy blows. The sword Skinner had tattooed on Gorm's right forearm twisted as the large muscles underneath wielded his heavy weapon in strikes that even shattered the tapered rock formations in an effort to get to the boy. Erik used his superior speed and agility to dodge among the sharp stone teeth and frustrate Gorm while he countered with jabs of his own. The battle ranged over the whole cavern and was fairly even until London, no shrinking violet and now fully recovered, entered the picture and began throwing pebbles at Gorm. She could have escaped on her own or wilted under the strain, but love made her stay and courage made her fight with her hero. While not heavy enough to inflict damage, the projectiles were a constant nuisance, especially when they hit around his head, distracting the Viking, and creating openings that Erik used to his advantage. Together, the victory was in sight and their happiness assured until a huge hand circled London's waist and dragged her away.

The girl shrieked at the unexpected reversal and continued screaming when she saw her captor was the hideous Lennie and he was headed for the far side of the grotto where the exit to the surface awaited. Gorm, relieved of the scourge of constant pebbles, redoubled his efforts attacking Erik, raining thundering blows intended to beat his opponent down, so he could also quickly escape. But it was an inspired Erik that faced him now; his love being borne away by the most repulsive creature he had ever seen, fired him to renew the battle with a sword that fairly flew through the air, creating an impenetrable defense and humming a song of death on offense!

As the screams mixed with the clashing of blades, two new factors injected themselves from opposite ends of the cavern. Delayed from dealing with the guards below, sending B'yatzor-hul to free the Sasquatch, and then finding his way up alone, Tarzan leaped from the Squeeze; instantly taking in the conflict, he knew he could best assist Erik by reclaiming London, so with a terrifying cry he threw himself into a grapple with the giant as the snarling beast in him took over. Lennie sought to retain his hold on the girl and back to the exit while holding

Tarzan off with one hand. The mighty ape-man, who had defeated Kerchak, Terkoz, and recently Zu-yad, was not to be underestimated, so with knotted muscles across his shoulders, he grasped the wrist and throat of his enemy and began to drag both Lennie and his prey back down to the narrow cavern passageway.

The last player entering this tableau was Skinner in the upper tunnel, who was rapidly tying wires around sticks of dynamite and extending fuses along the floor. Still unwilling to relinquish his prize, even while being throttled by Tarzan, Lennie choked out a call for help to the Cajun, knowing he could make short work of the ape-man with his wicked knife. For an answer, Skinner flashed an equally wicked grin and then lit the fuses before sprinting up the tunnel to the surface.

In a dazzling display of sword work, Erik blocked, feinted low, and then reversed his blade across Gorm's neck, leaving the Norseman dead on his feet while his lifeblood fountained from his severed jugular. Joining Tarzan, Erik ripped London free and pushed her into the Squeeze, while Tarzan picked up Lennie and threw him to the ground where a jagged stalagmite tore into his side. As the fuse burned shorter, the ape-man quickly followed Erik and London through the narrow divide and urged them around the bend in the trail to the crater floor. The last thing Tarzan saw out of the corner of his eye was Lennie wedged hopelessly in the constricted space, before the explosion rocked the grotto, bringing down the roof full of teeth and totally sealing the Squeeze and everything above it forever.

Everyone was able to escape the mine in a welter of dust and debris because most of the effects of the blast were contained above the pinched area of the shaft. Reunited at last, Erik pulled London into an embrace which she fought against only long enough to give a sense of decorum before yielding to her man in a passionate kiss. Tarzan was pleased to see B'yat-zor-hul had freed the trapped apes and brought them to the surface where they were blinking from the unaccustomed sunlight. They continued rubbing their eyes in amazement when the tribe historian introduced Tarzan as their new King of the Apes. Everyone was so caught up in the moment that none paused to realize that they were now all permanently trapped in the crater!

Skinner hustled out of the upper tunnel in plenty of time before the detonation; he was quite sure that no one else had escaped, so complete was the destruction from the explosion. He was positively buoyant as he went back to the shack and packed to leave. It took only minutes as there was not much in that squalor to bring: his violin, an axe, a few traps, pieces of rope, and some food and cooking utensils. Then he began to whistle a tune as he dug under the cold ashes in the fire pit, excavating a deep hole from which he pulled a leather bag that clinked when he shook it open and poured into his hand a large pile of uncut diamonds, scintillating in the sun. Replacing them in the bag, he put it in the bottom of his pack and piled the rest of the equipment on top, saving the fiddle until last.

Originally, Skinner had planned to burn the cabin and collapse the tunnel under the briars on Lennie on the way out, but now that everyone was trapped or dead, he decided to leave it as a possible future hideout; so after making sure the long cable by the precipice was securely tied up, he went through the thorn barrier, disguised the entrance and erased his tracks so well that he was not sure even he could find it again. There was one last loose end to tie up and her trail was so easily visible from her blundering through the forest that he casually followed, confident that he could catch Madame before nightfall.

Madame had not been thinking about covering her tracks when she escaped. She did not pause to determine a direction. Procuring food and water would remain an afterthought until hunger and thirst struck later. The only force motivating Madame was the pure, blind terror of a gentle woman exposed to a horror unimaginable in her sheltered life. It propelled her straight into the woods, up and down hills, straight through creeks, stumbling over rocks and fallen logs, at maximum velocity powered by the energy extreme fear can produce until she was deep in the forest, finally exhausted and totally lost.

There was no fight left in her when Skinner caught up in a clearing and, after tying her hands and feet, he set about making camp and cooking dinner while humming a little tune. He shared no food or water or even conversation with her and played his violin to drown out her renewed pleas. She wondered why he did not end it; she begged him to end it, and perhaps that was what saved her for one more day because he seemed to enjoy her anguish. But more likely it was the fact that it was late in the day and he did not feel like digging a hole to put her in after he killed her.

Chapter Nineteen

JUSTICE ABOVE THE CRATER

M r. Fitch was concerned upon discovering Madame missing from the tent because she rarely left and never for any length of time. He called out loudly in all directions, but received only the normal forest sounds in return. Then he searched for a note and, finding none, followed some of her smaller footprints to the edge of the woods, where he lost the trail in the heavily trampled underbrush. That really did not matter because the fact was Mr. Fitch could not tell if the tracks were recently made or from a week ago. He had been close by and had not heard any wild animals and there would have been signs of foul play in that case. Mr. Fitch was ready to light the signal fire and go get help, but now that both women were gone, he was in a difficult personal situation. Should he leave, would he be implicated in their disappearance if anyone even believed his tale at all?

As an honorable English gentleman, self-concern never entered into his decision to go or to stay; they needed help now and any delay to seek aid would be a death sentence. Mr. Fitch clearly saw his duty as more than one of an employee and surely there were heartstrings that tied him to Madame and London so he set about breaking the camp down for supplies he could take with him. The tent gave him a large center pole that he sharpened with the axe into a spear and canvas for a pack to carry a few sundry personal items and what useful camping gear remained. Of food there was none, so without a backward glance, this modern man, armed with primitive weapons, strode into the forest, taking his first steps backward in time to a primordial past in which a man hunted for his woman.

Mr. Fitch had searched around the railroad tracks in ever-increasing circles and knew the area fairly well, so he did not spend a great deal of time going over where he had been before. After a cursory examination, stopping frequently to call out, he pushed into new territory thinking that, like himself, Madame did not plan on coming back. He also needed food, and since he had depleted the local woods with his foraging, he hoped he could find better hunting in a less-travelled place where the game had not been scared away. Mr. Fitch found some late berries that were shriveled on the bush, even too small for the birds, that sufficed for a while and thirst was not a problem as there were plenty of streams to drink from, so he kept his belly filled with water to stave off hunger pains. The larger creeks had fish he could have speared and were crossed by trails at watering holes where a patient hunter might be successful, but Mr. Fitch did not pause. Intent on finding Madame, he trudged on, not realizing the noise he was making in the still of the forest scared away all the small game and would eventually attract larger animals to investigate. Mr. Fitch was an esteemed school teacher with knowledge of many subjects, but unfortunately, how to survive on your own was not taught in any of his classrooms.

As the day drew to a close, he noticed some small caves in a rocky wall that he thought might be good shelter for the night, so he cleaned out some bones and other debris from the largest one and used the piles of leaves and twigs from the back to get a fire going. Mr. Fitch emptied his pack and made a warm bed, with the layers of canvas serving as a ground cover, and settled back in his cozy retreat feeling quite the successful camper. Even though he was hungry and worried about Madame, the strain from the day's labors caused him to fall asleep as soon as the sun set. His fitful slumber was soon interrupted though, as dark forms gathered outside and began to draw closer as the fire burned lower.

The Eastern Canadian wolf is smaller than its cousin, the North-West timber wolf, but can weigh up to ninety pounds. Intermingling with coyotes gave it longer, faster legs more suitable to running down deer and beaver than competing with bear for the larger elk, caribou, and moose. Still retaining the blackish fur on the nape, shoulders, and tail with the grizzled white ends of the gray wolf, it had a cinnamon undercoat and creamy flanks and chest from the coyote. Common to both breeds was nighttime howling to bring the pack together for the hunt, and as the call of the wild grew from the increasing numbers of wolves, Mr. Fitch awoke to find himself trapped by the savage carnivores. Angry at finding the man in their den, the wolves were still wary of the fire and darted in and out, edging nearer each time, testing their courage.

Mr. Fitch immediately shook off the drowsiness and threw the remaining burnable cave detritus on the fire, intuitively knowing that it was the only thing that had saved him from being torn apart while he slept. The flames rose higher, driving the wolves farther away again and giving him a brief reprieve to gather his wits. Why had he not taken the time to lay in a pile of logs for the night? The small twigs and leaves were being swiftly consumed and soon there would be no further deterrent. Mr. Fitch looked frantically around and, seeing the canvas tarp, used the axe to cut and tear sections that could be fed slowly to the blaze.

That bought some more time, but the fast-burning fire was again dying down, so he resorted to throwing rocks and then, as those ran out, his camping gear at the aggressive beasts until he, at last, was down to his spear and axe. One wolf in particular, much larger than the rest, got his head past the side of the fire and snapped viciously as Mr. Fitch pushed it out with the spear point, but quickly the animal was back, and now more wolves approached from the other side of the dying blaze. The man swung from side to side, constantly thrusting to keep them at bay, but there were too many, and he was forced to move to the rear of the cave where the narrowness of the space saved him, since only one beast at a time could get at him.

The din was deafening as the barks and howls echoed in the confines of the cavern, the horde sensing they had their quarry trapped. In the last bit of light from the sputtering flames, Mr. Fitch found a gap in the wall that led deeper into the hillside, and he edged into the shadows, fending off the monstrous leader of the pack. The passage was only wide enough for the two of them to continue to battle, so the man was able to retreat more rapidly, but then the dying embers were accidentally scattered by the raging wolves still outside, and they were plunged into darkness.

Feeling his way with one hand, Mr. Fitch slowly backed up while blindly thrusting with the spear, occasionally gratified to feel the point meet flesh and elicit a yelp of pain. The huge, relentless beast continued after him with the rest of the wolves content to let their alpha dog pursue in the dark, underground, restricted space. The man had only the growling to guide his jabs while the wolf, like a lion facing a tamer's whip in a circus, sought to catch the offending stick in his powerful jaws and tear it away to gain access to the vulnerable man.

Farther into the unknown depths they moved until Mr. Fitch slipped and a foot became wedged between two rocks, halting further retreat. Now the wolf sensed the helplessness of his prey and began lunging with bared fangs to get at the man instead of the spear. Mr. Fitch saw the fierce eyes and rasping teeth coming at him and furiously beat back the charge while searching for the unexpected source of a feeble illumination. Directly above him was a small patch of moonlight filtering through a chimney leading to an opening, common in many earthen caves, where the undermined soil gives way to the rain's erosion. Before another assault could commence, Mr. Fitch ripped his foot free of his shoe, scratched and clawed his way rapidly up the fissure, and used the spear at the top to enlarge the hole wide enough to escape.

Mr. Fitch lay on the grass collecting himself while the wolf howled in vain below. He could thank his years of Spartan living for giving him the thin rangy physique that had enabled him to squeeze through this experience alive. He was badly cut and bruised from the sharp rocks and had lost everything except his spear and the axe he still carried in his belt. The fall night had a cold wind that blew through the tears and rents in his clothes, so he got up and, using his spear as a walking stick, hobbled off to try to find some safer shelter further away from the wolf pack. Walking in one shoe aggravated his limp, so he discarded it, taking yet another step backwards to becoming a primitive man.

The next days were filled with horror for Mr. Fitch. The wolves had his scent and they continued to doggedly pursue him, almost as if the leader of the pack had a score to settle with the man. Once they chased him into a great patch of thorns that allowed him to escape again but left him scratched and shirtless and so turned around that he had no idea of where he was. The nights were no better, spent shivering and sleepless, clutching a tree trunk high above the horrible sounds from the feeding denizens below. However, that did occasionally lead to finding a nest with eggs, and he became an expert on which trees had fruit and nuts so he didn't starve, but Mr. Fitch was left gaunt and haggard in his search for Madame.

It was evening, and the wolves had treed Mr. Fitch after catching his scent where his trail had crossed a creek. The pack was circling, baying and howling in frustration over not being able to reach him, and he was faced with yet another hungry night, awake from the fear of falling. The large male who seemed to have it in for him was closest and presented a perfect target at times. Mr. Fitch recalled his days at university and how he threw the javelin on the track team, but that was for distance and not accuracy, and here he would only get one chance. But there was the meat he craved and possibly an end to the harassment, so he climbed down to a height just above where the wolves could leap and found a sturdy limb that gave an unobstructed view. Bracing himself, with his bare feet gripping the bough and one hand steady on a branch above, he drew back the spear and waited for the huge male to stand sideways.

When the moment came, he knew it and launched the spear with all the strength in his wiry frame. It struck right behind the shoulder and penetrated deep through the ribs and into the heart and lungs, instantly killing the beast. After a moment of indecision, the pack went crazy, pawing and nipping to rouse their fallen leader, and then redoubled their efforts to get at the man. Mr. Fitch, prompted by a primal urge he did not understand, threw back his head and screamed into the wind, announcing the triumph over his arch-enemy. It might be some time before he could descend and claim his kill, but Mr. Fitch's mouth was already watering for the taste of meat and he was thinking of how warm that fur would be once he had properly cleaned it.

Surprisingly, the wolves suddenly wheeled about and bolted away, leaving the way clear for Mr. Fitch. He waited to be sure they were gone and was just about to climb down when he heard the sounds of a violin in the distance. Forgotten was the conquest and the hunger and the cold, for this represented the presence of humans who might aid him in his quest or be another foe to overcome. Either way, he pulled his spear from the carcass and followed the music, because he had questions and he would have his answers now.

Skinner checked on the pot of stew resting in the small fire to see if it was boiling yet, between songs on the violin. Madame lay up against a tree, tied hands and feet, quiet now and resigned to her destiny. The Cajun was fiddling, so no one heard Mr. Fitch approach, and neither recognized the scruffy, half-naked, filthy savage, brandishing a bloody pole, who broke into the clearing. Madame thought this was some new terror to add to her nightmare. Skinner put his instrument down and his long knife slithered from his belt as he hissed sibilantly, "*Sacre bleu!* Another wild man?"

Upon seeing Madame disheveled and tied on the ground, her formerly robust figure now shrunken from a lack of food and deprivation of comforts, Mr. Fitch looked at the Cajun in a red rage and immediately threw his spear, missing badly from his impatience and Skinner's quick roll to the side. Then, drawing his camp axe from his belt, he rushed in, swinging wildly, intent on splitting the much shorter man in half. Skinner's size and speed allowed him to slip unscathed under the taller man's flailing arms while his experience with a knife enabled him to slash Mr. Fitch on the body and across a leg, drawing blood each time.

Madame stared in rapt attention, her bound hands in a position of prayer across her rapidly rising and falling bosom, silently willing the unknown challenger on, inherently knowing she could be no worse off in his hands than in Skinner's. At that moment, her heart raced and her exhaustion was forgotten as the two men armed with primitive weapons faced off for possession of her.

Realizing he faced an unskilled opponent with a sharpened stick that he could play with before killing, Skinner taunted, "Come on beanpole, I cut you down to size!"

Reeling from exhaustion and bleeding badly, Mr. Fitch bent down and advanced more warily, this time using the superior reach of his long arms to try to strike Skinner while staying away from the flashing blade. The Cajun continued to bait the wild man, dodging in after each swing of the axe and inflicting small cuts on the arms, content to wear him down before the kill. It was a deadly dance in the clearing that might have lasted some time had not Madame, finally recognizing Mr. Fitch, called out his name in amazement. When Mr. Fitch glanced to the side in response, Skinner caught the crouched man on the side of the head with a backhand sweep that used the butt of the knife to open a bloody gash, knocking him down and leaving him lying dazed on his back in the dirt.

Enjoying his moment of triumph over a larger man, Skinner stood straddling Mr. Fitch's chest with outstretched arms in a victory pose to make sure Madame was watching before he administered the *coup de grace*, but she had already fainted dead away.

Tarzan was the first of the group to realize there was no way out of the crater now and, typical of any wild animal, he felt that any restriction of his freedom, no matter how large and nice the cage, was intolerable. London also wanted to let her mother know of her safety, but Erik knew of no other way to leave. When Tarzan translated their concerns to B'yat-zor-hul, the ape reminded the ape-man that he had not originally come to the surface by way of the mine when Ry-blat had first been trapped in the pit and inadvertently freed by Tarzan. The Sasquatch had their own way up, used for generations to enable them to spread across North America from the valley.

Since Erik was not about to let London out of his sight again, and the ape-man could travel much faster alone, Tarzan told London he would look for her mother while he was above the crater. Anxious to see if this other trail was still intact after the explosion, Tarzan got directions to the nearby cave and a description of the passageway up and, after tying a couple of torches to his back, swung away into the trees. A rockfall at the base of the crater marked the unattainable entrance, thirty feet up a sheer wall with tiny projections that could only be climbed by a Sasquatch, but this posed no difficulty for the agile ape-man as he clambered up and struck a light to one of the torches.

Perhaps because it started so much higher on the wall, the tunnel was much shorter than the mine shaft had been and the ceilings were high enough for the large apes to pass easily. Tarzan was heartened by a distinct flow of air that caused the torch to flicker on the right passageways and also denoted a still viable opening at the surface. He passed through some beautiful rooms, where raw diamonds and gold shimmered in the torchlight and eventually tied in through a narrow hidden switchback to the same path used by Skinner and the Vikings, well above the blasted area. Making a note of where to turn off on his way back, Tarzan soon found himself emerging under the thorn barrier and was forced to crawl a few feet to get to the upper rim of the crater. He had passed by this same place on his first trip around the crater and never noticed the well-concealed opening. Instead of going back to the overhanging fallen tree that had initially been his path over the brambles and was also sometimes used by the Sasquatch on their forays out, the ape-man headed toward where he expected to have a final accounting with the Cajun.

Familiar with the way now, he approached the pit trap with great anticipation and was delighted to find all his weapons still lying at the bottom. Lowering the same tree trunk in the hole, he retrieved them but not before carefully training all his senses on the surrounding area to be sure he would not be trapped so easily again. Most precious to him was his father's hunting knife, found in a cabin a continent away, but equally important to survival were his spear, rope, and bow and arrows. Thus armed, Tarzan was confident now that none could stand before him, but he was still cautious as he advanced because he was unsure of the whereabouts of Skinner.

First checking the deserted shack, Tarzan was not surprised to find evidence of a swift departure, so he retraced his steps to the tunnel under the circling briar wall and picked up the spoor of a small man entering the forest. Tarzan surmised that the giant, Lennie, had died in the cave-in, but was puzzled by the tracks of a woman visible under Skinner's footprints. The Cajun was obviously following her and since they went in the same direction, the ape-man set off in pursuit.

Mr. Fitch was so disoriented that he had actually been chased into the outside of the thorn barrier the previous day, and when finally treed by the wolves, was in a position located between Tarzan and Skinner's camp. So as the ape-man followed the Cajun, he first came upon a pack of wolves just as an inhuman scream echoed across the forest. When he investigated, the frenzied wolves attacked him like they were specifically looking for a human to kill and Tarzan, unable to swing away through the pine trees, turned to lead them on a long chase until he could find a suitable tree to climb. From there, he calmly shot

MICHAEL A. SANFORD   199

arrows into their ranks until the wolf pack had enough and left for easier prey.

This detour took Tarzan off the trail and delayed the ape-man, but he too had heard the violin, so instead of retracing his steps he went unerringly straight to where the sounds had originated. Hearing the noise of conflict, he crept up to observe from behind some brush just as Skinner laid out a man with a backhand blow and stood with knife bared, glaring at a bound woman across the camp. In the blink of an eye, Tarzan took in the whole scene and faster than that, he reacted. Not taking the time to unhitch his own spear from his back, all in one fluid motion he sprang into the clearing, snatched up the sharpened tent pole laying in front of him and launched it at Skinner. So powerful was the throw that the spear went through the chest of the Cajun and out his back with still enough force remaining to carry the small man up against a tree and pin him there like a mounted butterfly.

Tarzan retreated back behind the brush to watch unseen as the man began to recover and crawled over to the woman, gently stroking her face while holding her hand after cutting her free with Skinner's knife. She stirred and when her eyelids fluttered open she softly whispered, "Oh Ernest, you came for me?"

Mr. Fitch responded, "My lady, may I presume?" She nodded yes and he swept her into his arms. After a long embrace, they parted, as each had many questions for the other and Tarzan, knowing he had their answers, stepped into the clearing. Startled by the silent intruder, Madame gasped and Mr. Fitch grasped the knife, but they were both quickly put at ease by the handsome stranger's manners and demeanor when he addressed them in perfect French saying, "*Madame et Monsieur* I bring you word from London."

So overwhelmed to learn she was alive and well, they broke down in tears and were unable to speak, but when they recovered from the shock, both wanted to leave immediately to join her. Knowing they could never make the arduous journey back at night and seeing their emaciated state, Tarzan insisted they spend the night to recover first and made them split Skinner's delicious boudin, still simmering on the fire, while he disposed of the body.

The ape-man's muscles bulged as he pulled the deeply embedded tent pole from the tree and returned it to Mr. Fitch, commenting on what a fine throw the schoolteacher had made. Mr. Fitch remembered little of the fight after being knocked out and was unsure he deserved any credit, but it was clearly his makeshift spear and the evidence seemed to substantiate it. The clincher came when Madame went on and on about her hero and how she had seen Mr. Fitch vanquish the evil Skinner and save her from certain death. While she recounted the story, each time embellishing the valor of her savior, Tarzan tossed the body over a shoulder and slipped away.

When he reached the cabin on the top of the crater, he took the long cable from the overhanging tree and used some of the length to securely wrap Skinner's body around and about so it would dangle forever unreachable, midway down the wall. Then without any ceremony or words, he kicked the despised form off the precipice, where the birds could feast until only the bones were left as a grim reminder to any who would despoil the beauty of the valley below again.

Returning to the camp, Tarzan found his charges sound asleep, keeping warm in each other's arms. The ape-man rested too, as an animal does, all his senses alert and ready to bound into action at any threat, but the woods were cleaned of the filth that the Cajun had wrought and peace reigned throughout. In the morning, they were all reinvigorated after breakfast and eager to rejoin London, so the happy group set out with Tarzan in the lead followed by Madame and with Mr. Fitch protecting the rear. After passing through the thorn tunnel, they managed to squirm through the briars near the rim to where the ape-man had left the torches to light the way down through the underground shaft of the Sasquatch. Then, Tarzan lowered each of them to the valley floor from the elevated cave entrance with his rope.

Chapter Twenty

CELEBRATIONS AND FAREWELLS

P rimitive societies embrace the wonders of the modern world, often to discover later that they come with a price. There are beneficial medicines that can cure, but also the exposure to new diseases that can decimate a population, improvements in housing and lifestyle at the cost of the destruction of their natural environment, and powerful weapons to protect that give the ability to slaughter faster and in greater numbers. Just as willow bark gave us aspirin, by not realizing they already had all they needed, simple lives were transformed into complex interactions that fail under the influence of greed and corruption. Is modern art, locked away in museums and private collections, more beautiful than the cave drawings of the prehistoric man? Why does every generation reminisce about the good old days and wish for the simpler times of their youth?

Civilization ruins and then destroys whatever it touches. Look no further than hunters wiping out entire species of animals for profit or pleasure and the subjugation and near extermination of native tribal peoples by the European expansion for evidence of this. Is it a surprise then when a modern man yearns for a cabin in the woods or a camp beside a lake, not even understanding that the peaceful security around a fire is satisfying a longing for his primitive roots? But once lost, it cannot be regained in these temporary escapes, so pervasive and overwhelming is civilization's reach that there will be few places of serenity left.

The malign effect of Skinner on the Vikings' simple society worked its way through to the Norsemen's treatment of the primeval clan of the Sasquatch, poisoning both cultures with modern man's greed. But they were lucky this time to get a rare second chance to reclaim what they had, now that the evil was completely purged. B'yat-zor-hul sent the rescued Sasquatch back to the tribe to explain the mystery of the missing apes while he went to wait for the return of Tarzan at the base of the crater near the elevated cave. Erik had Ulf drop the remains of Magnus and Wulfstan down the deepest hole he could find in the bottom of the mine, and he and London found themselves alone at last.

As they walked back to the village, Erik, with the impetuousness of youth, voiced the fear that was uppermost in his mind, "If Tarzan can find a way out, will you go back to your world?"

"There, I have all the modern conveniences while here, I am but a thrall," London responded coyly, and then teased, "You could come with me and leave this savage place behind."

"Here I am a Prince and you are my Princess," he worriedly countered and then dropping to a knee and taking her hand, he gazed up into her eyes and fervently proclaimed, "I would make you my Queen if you would consent to marry me."

"You earned my respect as a thrall, and I gave you my love at Eden Falls, and you fought for my life today," London declared loudly, though there were none to hear, and then she whispered for his ears alone, "Forever, you shall be the Jarl of my heart." No more words were necessary as they sealed their promise with a lingering kiss.

When they entered the village amidst the cheering crowds, Queen Freyja was overjoyed to hear the coronation would be followed by a wedding and snatched London away to the King's lodge to prepare her for the celebrations, banishing Erik back to the men's barracks with a wave of her hand. He had much to do himself to prepare since tomorrow was a Friday, sacred to the Marriage goddess Frigga, and the traditional day for

nuptials. The whole valley emptied into the village, erecting
tents for the week-long celebration, and all pitched in to get
ready for the festivities. Beer was sweetened with honey to make
the bridal-ale that the new couple drank together for four weeks
after the ceremony, hence came the term honey-moon for this
lunar month. A tall bowl with handles on two sides in the shape
of animals, called a kasa, was blessed to become their loving
cup in which this mead was served. A sow was sacrificed in
honor of the Love goddess Freyja and then roasted for the feast.
Torches were set up in the village green with floral decorations
after the two cages were permanently dragged away, recently a
site of so much violence under Magnus but from now on a
place of community celebration.

The next morning saw even more excitement with the safe
arrival of the strange group of Tarzan, B'yat-zor-hul, Mr. Fitch,
and Madame; London and her mother were overjoyed to be
reunited and the Norse people were fascinated by the other
three. Mr. Fitch had barely gotten used to the idea of a new
species of intelligent reasoning apes that had a language Tarzan
could understand, and now he was in an authentic four-hundred-
year-old Viking village speaking in French to its residents. After
cleaning up and borrowing some clothes, he was the center of
attention as the school teacher in him marveled in the opportunity to study living history. The three women excused
themselves to head to the steam baths and get dressed, and
Tarzan and B'yat-zor-hul slipped away for a while, by nature
uncomfortable in the large crowds.

They returned just after mid-day and privately called this
same group together again in the King's lodge to help with the
wedding contract. Norse marriage is governed by strict rules
and is often political in nature with serious presents exchanged
to solidify the holdings and estate of each family. Tarzan placed
a heavy bag in front of Madame, London and Mr. Fitch calling
it the heiman fylgia, representing the bride's part of her father's
estate, and gave a lighter one to Erik and his mother naming
it the mundr, to be used as payment to the bride's family for

the loss of her labor. Understanding what came next, Freyja passed the leather sack over to Madame and Mr. Fitch as the required bride-price and when they opened it they found handfuls of diamonds. In turn, they gave their weighty bag to the Queen wherein she discovered a huge amount of gold and silver as the dowry from the bride's family; she promptly accepted the contract, saying that she would see this made into a crown for London.

Madame and Mr. Fitch caught Tarzan alone afterward and asked about the ritual, saying they could never accept or hope to repay such generosity. Tarzan explained he had found the diamonds in Skinner's pack and the gold and silver at Gorm's cave in the mine and considered it spoils of war to be given to those who suffered the most. They protested and tried to get him to at least take a share, but the ape-man declined; having already given away his title and estate in England to the man Jane was duty bound to marry, what meaning could any fortune hold for him?

Late in the afternoon, everything was ready. Mr. Fitch looked the proper Viking in a tunic and sandals, as he went to join London in the bride's tent. The baths had erased the previous weeks' trials from Madame, elegant now in an embroidered blue dress with silver accents, as she stood next to Freyja. The Queen was striking in a red gown over a purple shift with a matching sash as she took her place in the center of the gathering with Annulf's golden crown in her hands. Tarzan and B'yat-zor-hul were on her other side each holding some items, and all were under tall arches made of pine boughs covered with blossoms. Erik entered first, walking up a torch-lit corridor formed by his people, majestically handsome in a royal purple shirt and leggings set off by a black leather vest, belt and boots.

Peeking out of a gaily decorated tent, London watched the simple coronation take place as Erik knelt before his mother and the Queen loudly proclaimed to all, "By right of birth and trial by combat, I crown you, Jarl Erik, from this day forth, lord over all the realm!" The crowd broke into wild applause and long cheers that finally died down as everyone turned to the tent for the main event.

Two guards pulled aside the colorful flaps and London stepped out, pausing for a minute before proceeding, to give the audience time to hush after they sighed and murmured at her beauty. Her gown was purest white covered with new silver freshwater pearls beaded in patterns all about the neck and bodice. In the dwindling sunlight and flickering torches, she sparkled like she was on fire. An heirloom bridal crown of delicate silver filigree, festooned with sprigs of liriope, topped her head. Like the dress, it was last worn by Freyja when she married Annulf. In keeping with the customs for single girls, her long blonde hair flowed freely down her shoulders, for the last time unbound before she would use pins and cloth to hold it up when married. London's face was radiant from the baths with only a line of kohl on the eyelashes and a little rouge for the lips and cheeks adding to her beauty.

Flashing a brilliant smile, she slowly walked down the flower-strewn aisle, with Mr. Fitch as an escort, her fragrance of scented oils joining the aroma of the fresh-cut blossoms and pine.

Music accompanied London until she reached Erik and took his hands as they gazed into each other's eyes. Then Tarzan gave them the items he had been safekeeping, Annulf's sword and two simple gold rings. Using the handle of the sword to exchange the bands signified their commitment to protect one another. Then holding the sword's hilt together, they invoked the goddess Var to witness their vows as they pledged their troth, also making the time-honored Christian promises, binding a divine covenant from this day forth. After the final kiss, a tumult rose from the spectators as they surged forward, everyone offering congratulations and best wishes to the new couple.

The commons was filled with raucous games until well after dark, with Tarzan winning a few contests and even Mr. Fitch joining in for the spear throwing. The ape-man enjoyed the competitive festivities, since this time he was not about to be butchered or burned alive as the main event, but neither Englishman could convince the Norsemen that the British Isles was anything more than a conquered port for Viking longships in the North Atlantic. B'yat-zor-hul was the favorite of all the children in the wrestling events, where he fought many eager Vikings, as hairy as the ape and often smelling worse. The timid Sasquatch also enjoyed the bouts after Tarzan explained to him that it was not to the death and only minor biting was allowed. Then the bridal party and most of the villagers adjourned to the grand lodge for the feast while the rest of the crowd carried on the festivities outside with plenty of food and ale for all. While waiting for the bridal couple, Tarzan noticed that all the apples in a large decorative centerpiece disappeared, cores and all, and suspiciously questioned B'yat-zor-hul, who was standing nearby. With a lowered head and raised eyes, the remorseful ape said he thought it was his place setting since he did not eat meat.

Erik carried London over the high threshold as it was considered a bad omen if the bride tripped when entering, and then he thrust his sword deeply into the main log holding up the roof. The depth of the scar left on the trunk of this supporting pillar foretold of luck for a new family. Toasts and salutations were traded by all, with Mr. Fitch, very deep in his pints by now, going on in a speech about the new bride's name, Queen London Gunderson Wildefarer, being more than a mouthful. Then, inside and out, there was dancing and contests, with music and games. The skalds circulated, trading ribald insults and telling lying stories of great exaggeration, to all who would listen. This went on throughout the night and would continue for the next week.

At one point, Erik motioned Tarzan and B'yat-zor-hul to stand next to him for his first proclamation as Jarl. His words were carried through the crowd as he called out, "Honor shall be restored to the throne." After the applause died down, Erik announced, "A permanent friendship from this day on will exist between the hairy men of the forest and the Norse people and the deep woods will forever be the exclusive domain of the Sasquatch, never to be disturbed by man," thus giving the apes the privacy they desired while still remaining open to interaction at the times of their choosing.

Tarzan translated for B'yat-zor-hul and then taking Skinner's horn from the ape held it high and declared, "This horn once sounded meaning death for my tribe. As King of the Apes, I pledge that if you blow this three times, the apes will come as brothers in the valley and we promise no harm shall ever come to any human from us," as he passed the instrument to Erik.

Toward daybreak the royal couple sought to escape, so they changed back into more practical clothes and, after promising to return in a week, Erik took his hunting gear and a bundle of supplies from the Queen mother, and they made their way out of the lodge to find all the guests had taken positions along the road for as far as they could see, holding torches to light a path. Amid the shouting well-wishers, the new King and Queen raced to the secure privacy of Eden Falls.

Soon after Tarzan and B'yat-zor-hul left for the Sasquatch camp and by ones and twos, the party retired to sleep. Before the celebrations continued later in the evening, the dowager Queen tasked all the skilled craftsmen with building a new Jarl's lodge and all its furnishings, to be done by week's end for the royal couple's return. With so many eager hands working, the undertaking was easily accomplished as the mission turned into part of the gala affair. Madame became fast friends with Freyja and Mr. Fitch reveled in his unbridled time among the Vikings.

Tarzan roamed with his tribe in peaceful contentment for a week. The same reason he could not remain forever with his tribe in Africa was also true here. Even though the Sasquatch possessed a higher intelligence, the ape-man needed more to challenge him. There was yet much of the world to explore outside the crater and more battles to be won; without the chance of dying, Tarzan was not truly living, merely existing.

The ape-man had the solitary nature of the ape, but reveled in a man's desire for conquest, so he brought his tribe together and announced that he was leaving and declared B'yat-zor-hul as King in his place. The simple apes barely noticed the change except for B'yat-zor-hul, who was despondent at losing his friend. As they moved their open hands from the heart for the last time, Tarzan told him they should both remember their time together when the Dum Dum was celebrated under the full moon. Soon after this, Tarzan saw B'yat-zor-hul's spirits improve when Koho-lul began combing his fur and batting her eyes at him while her mother, Litu-lus, looked on approvingly. Thinking the worst problems we have are often the ones we wish upon ourselves, Tarzan swung away into the trees, leaving the new King to fend for himself in the politics of love.

Erik and London had returned and were in their new home by the time Tarzan stopped at the Viking village on his way out of the crater. He stayed for a couple days enjoying the company of the rough, primitive men in the convivial atmosphere that now pervaded the gregarious people. When he got ready to leave, the time for good-byes was also a time of decisions since only five people knew the way out and it could only be easily reached by Tarzan or a Sasquatch. Jarl Erik decided he would not disclose the location or permit ladders to be built to the high cave entrance after seeing the effects of civilization on his valley, and he wisely realized the Norse would never fit into modern society. Once subject to wanderlust, Erik Wildefarer had found his Princess and knew the modern world had nothing more to offer.

London had made her choice to stay with the swordsman who had fought for her and won her heart. The spoiled, head-strong girl was gone, left behind with the harrowing memories of all she had been through. Now, she planned on being a teacher to her people, instructing them in only the best of human progress, enlightening them in culture and the arts as they were ready for it and bringing them along slowly to the modern times.

Madame had launched this venture with the crazy idea of marrying her daughter into the nobility to be accepted in modern society. Ironically, she had been so successful in her quest that London was now a Queen, but the ordeal had also changed Madame in ways that even she did not yet fully understand. Rather than continue to live through her child, she too had a man who had fought for her, and now wanted her to share a life together with him, so for the first time in a long time, she began to see possibilities for herself in the future. But Madame and Mr. Fitch had both lived too long in civilization to give it up, and as much as they enjoyed the journey to the past, they realized their future was in modern times, so with assurances they could return each year to visit, they prepared to go with Tarzan.

At the base of the crater wall, final farewells were exchanged amid tears of sadness in parting and smiles at the promised reunion. It was agreed that Erik would call B'yat-zor-hul with the horn on the summer solstice every year and together they would meet Mr. Fitch and Madame by the railroad and bring them back for a vacation in the valley. Tarzan ascended the wall and used his rope to bring Madame and Mr. Fitch up, and with a last wave goodbye, they entered the tunnel to the surface.

Tarzan led them through Skinner's passageway under the thorn barrier and made sure the outside hidden entrance to the crater was secure. On the way through the forest, Tarzan suddenly drew his knife and motioned for silence when he heard a large animal moving in the woods. Mr. Fitch stood ready to defend Madame with his spear while the ape-man scouted ahead. The smell of a single horse and man told Tarzan what he would find long before he got there, so he was not surprised to see an officer of the Dominion Mounted Police dressed in his high-collared red serge tunic over steel gray breeches, wearing black riding boots sporting nickel spurs on his feet and the characteristic flat-brimmed, brown Stetson hat on his head.

The Mountie smiled broadly when he saw the ape-man, saying, "I am Constable Claude D'Arnot. I became worried and just started looking for you after getting the note to meet you for some hunting and camping from your chauffeur some time ago."

"Well met, *monsieur*," replied Tarzan, "Your brother Paul said I could rely on you, but I need assistance first for two who I found lost in the forest."

Once they were all together, Tarzan was delighted to find the chauffeur and his touring car had stayed nearby after leading the Mountie to the area, and they were able to engage his services to drive Madame and Mr. Fitch back to civilization. The Constable noticed the strange clothing the couple wore and that Mr. Fitch was insistent upon taking his tent pole with him while Madame carried their only bag. They lavished such profound thanks and were so heartfelt in their good-byes to Tarzan that Claude asked later in camp what had happened to them in the deep woods.

The ape-man simply answered, "They found their way."

THE END

Epilogue

I f the reader made it this far and enjoyed the tale, here is where they can find some odds and ends wrapped up to prolong the experience, much like some fine cognac after a gourmet dinner. However, if they did not like it, there is probably no amount of alcohol that will save it at this stage. There was no further word of those who remained behind since the crater remains undiscovered to this day. The others never spoke of their ordeal so, except for Tarzan who had many more well-documented adventures, there is little to add to their stories.

Tarzan explored the Canadian wilderness with Claude D'Arnot as he moved east toward the coast, inexorably drawn to the ship that would take him back to his native Africa. Almost twenty, the ape-man had already seen much of the world considering the late age at which he started traveling, but his youthful thirst for adventure drove him to continue to seek excitement and thrills in each new day regardless of the risks and danger. Tarzan will return because only in the unknown depths of the Dark Continent can those perils be found.

Despite frequent sightings of the Sasquatch in North America, little evidence of their passing has ever been found and none have ever been captured, showing they continue to keep to their reclusive ways and have private haunts, like the crater, that man has yet to discover. Notable too is the fact that the apes keep their pledge to never harm mankind, but this leads to no interaction at all which is unfortunate, since much could be learned from them if civilization did not destroy them in the process. B'yat-zor-hul also remembered his promise to Erik and yearly answered the horn to help the Jarl and his guests in and out of the now peaceful valley.

Madame married Mr. Fitch soon after their return to New York and, financed by some of the proceeds from her bag, they had a wedding for the ages. While teaching at the university, Mr. Fitch became widely recognized as a leading scholar of Norse studies. They lived for years in a fashionable mansion in a tony district and took an extended holiday in the middle of every summer, but never to the Hamptons where the upper crust vacationed. They always went north by train and never spoke of their destination when the other elites carried on about their privileged summer adventures on the seashores. Rumor had it that they were seen exiting the train by some weather-worn cross made from railroad ties in the middle of the wilderness, so primitive an area that Mr. Fitch needed a walking stick to get around, but this was impossible to believe given their present dignified circumstances. These breaks got longer and longer and then one summer they did not return at all.

Lord Bridgestone was brought to justice when complaints from a wealthy traveler were registered with the railroad about his treatment of London and, although he avoided incarceration, he suffered a far worse punishment to his pride when he was dismissed from the board and had to return to England financially ruined and in disgrace. Skinner's bones may have rotted and fallen from the cable by now, but the legend of the Dog Man persists in the North Woods. But surely these are only tales to frighten children into good behavior.

It is curious to observe that in the early 1900's, an Ezra Fitch purchased a controlling interest in a sporting goods store owned by David Abercrombie in New York City and subsequently became a very successful retailer of apparel, but as far as is known he had no relationship to the Ernest Fitch of this story. Equally interesting is the 2006 opening of the Victor Diamond Mine in Ontario, but here again, there could be no correlation between it and the Viking mine, could there?

Now the story is told and I miss the nightly escape into the realm of adventure. It came to me in tantalizing tidbits and was recorded in segments, and, as I arranged them in sequence, possibly some were lost or misunderstood in the transition. I cannot verify it is all true, but it is the truth as it was revealed to me by someone guiding my hand from above.

Acknowledgements

As a first-time author, I want to thank all the people at ERB, Inc., who had a part in publishing Tarzan on the Precipice. Jim Sullos was especially instructive in shepherding me through the process. Will Meugniot has my highest regards for bringing my characters to life on his cover and frontispiece. George McWhorter, longtime curator of the University of Louisville Burroughs' collection, issued a challenge to the Burroughs Bibliophiles for a new author to continue the series and this novel is my answer.

My son Darek, as the first reader, had great insights and always provided just the right words of encouragement. My daughter, Devon, was creatively inspiring and lifts my spirit with her music. My wife, Sharon, is forever my model for London and still as beautiful today as when I met her beside our own limpid pool. My sister, Laurie, was there for me without fail in the endless job of editor and enlisted her husband, Dave, for his technical expertise and their children, Michael and Jennie, for the youth perspective. My mom, Joan, gave me the confidence to undertake this challenge by believing in me throughout my life. My only regret is my dad, Robert, is not here to share in all this but we are all sure he is smoking a cigar in celebration.

ABOUT THE AUTHOR

L ike his literary hero, Edgar Rice Burroughs, Dr. Michael Sanford was born in south Chicago. By high school, he was living in Kentucky. Completing his education at Vanderbilt University and the UK School of Dentistry, Dr. Sanford returned to the bluegrass state, where Michael and wife Sharon raised two children, Darek and Devon. The retired couple now divide their time between Kentucky and Florida, where Michael enjoys playing the piano, working on art projects and where he penned his first Tarzan novel. A lifelong Burroughs fan, he welcomes other enthusiasts to contact him at drmichaelsanford@gmail.com.

TARZAN ®

Return to Pal~ul~don

"This first authorized Tarzan novel from the sure hand of pulpmeister Will Murray does a fantastic job of capturing the true spirit of Tarzan, not a grunting monosyllabic cartoonish strongman, but an evolved, brilliant, man of honor equally at home as Lord Greystoke and as the savage *Tarzan the Terrible*."

—*Paul Bishop*

$24.95 softcover
$39.95 hardcover
$5.99 ebook

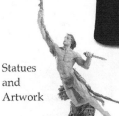